The sight of her stopped him in his tracks

She huddled against the far wall, hands behind her. Her hair was a short, soft halo around her pale, thin face, and for a moment Tag wanted nothing more than to mourn the loss of her long, blond ponytail. He took another step in her direction and saw her flinch.

He had frightened her, and that angered him all over again. "After all these years, I think you owe me an explanation, Susan."

She only stared at him, her stormy eyes growing bigger as she seemed to sag against the wall for support.

"I'm not going away, Susan. Not until I understand. I need a few anwers. Don't you think I deserve that much? You promised to wait, Susan." He heard the pleading in his voice and was powerless to stop it. "Why, Susan? Why didn't you wait?"

Her legs seemed to tremble. Maybe this was just as hard for her as it was for him. Maybe—

She shook her head. Her whole face was tense with effort. "Who? Who...are...you?"

Dear Reader,

My heart has never left Sweetbranch, Alabama, I guess.

Sweetbranch, the setting for my 1993 Superromance *Late Bloomer,* is a composite of a number of small Southern towns that I knew as I was growing up in Alabama. When I close my eyes and think about the diner and the beauty shop and the men in overalls walking the sidewalks of Main Street, I feel myself going home to the places of my childhood.

So when I thought of doing a trilogy about homecomings, there could be only one place for me to take my characters home—to Sweetbranch.

In my 3 Weddings & A Secret trilogy, you'll find out what's happened to Rose and Ben since the final pages of *Late Bloomer.* Plus, you'll meet four other very special couples who find the kind of love that says we're truly home. In *Double Wedding Ring, Addy's Angels* and *Queen of the Dixie Drive-In,* you'll experience first loves, lost loves, and even the kind of love that can endure seven problem children—and if that's not love, I don't know what is.

I truly hope you enjoy your visit to Sweetbranch as much as I have.

Wishing you love,

Peg Sutherland

Peg Sutherland
DOUBLE WEDDING RING

Harlequin Books

TORONTO • NEW YORK • LONDON
AMSTERDAM • PARIS • SYDNEY • HAMBURG
STOCKHOLM • ATHENS • TOKYO • MILAN
MADRID • WARSAW • BUDAPEST • AUCKLAND

Special thanks to Lauren Stayer in the Multi-Skills
Training Center at Central Piedmont Community
College; and to Rose Harris and Jacqueline Mruk at the
Charlotte Institute of Rehabilitation.

ISBN 0-373-70673-1

DOUBLE WEDDING RING

ABOUT THE AUTHOR

Peg Sutherland, who now lives in North Carolina with her husband, Mike, is originally from Alabama. She grew up in a series of towns she has transformed into the fictitious setting of Sweetbranch, Alabama, where her riveting trilogy takes place. Peg knows each character, each building, each house intimately, since for her, like the protagonists, visiting Sweetbranch is like coming home.

Peg, a critically acclaimed author, has created perhaps her strongest body of work here. The trilogy begins with *Double Wedding Ring*, which is followed by *Addy's Angels* in January and *Queen of the Dixie Drive-In* in February. Don't miss them!

Books by Peg Sutherland

HARLEQUIN SUPERROMANCE
398—BEHIND EVERY CLOUD
428—ALONG FOR THE RIDE
473—ABRACADABRA
525—RENEGADE
553—LATE BLOOMER
580—SIMPLY IRRESISTIBLE
599—PIRATE MOON
620—SAFEKEEPING
630—THE GOOD FATHER

HARLEQUIN TEMPTATION
414—TALLAHASSEE LASSIE

PROLOGUE

August 1995

SUSAN REACHED FOR the corner of the faded quilt at the same instant her daughter reached for the opposite corner.

"I'll get this, sugar," Susan said, the response automatic and protective. "You grab the basket."

Malorie gave Susan the funny smile, the one that said mothers are an everlasting mystery, and dropped the corner of the quilt. Susan finished folding the familiar patchwork, telling herself that any comfort she imagined in the soft fabric was merely the fancy of a desperate woman.

The remains of their picnic gathered up, the two women linked arms and passed beneath the canopy of giant oaks. The campus was small, old-fashioned. The traditional brick buildings said your sons and daughters would be safe and nurtured and lovingly force-fed the values of a simpler, saner era. Having grown up in a time that had rejected all those traditional values, Susan was now just the right age to want her daughter to be blanketed in them.

"You sure you're not going to be lonely?" Malorie asked as they reached the dilapidated blue station wagon in visitor parking. At least, it *had* been blue once upon a time; after twelve years, it was hard to tell. The vehicle, which leaned to one side where the shocks had finally given up the ghost, looked out of place amid the shiny, sedate sedans rimming the U-shaped drive in front of the college.

Susan hoped Malorie wouldn't decide she was as out of place here as the old family wagon.

Smiling her best smile, the one that had seen her through the past year, she said, "Now, Mal, you know I'm going to be way too busy for tomfool stuff like being lonely."

"I know what you *say*."

Malorie set the picnic basket on the front seat, atop the worn quilt Susan had placed so carefully on the passenger side. They faced each other over the door frame, elbows propped identically on the rust-pocked car roof. A stray blond curl danced along the side of Malorie's slim, freckled face, and Susan checked the urge to tuck the hair away, behind her daughter's ear. At twenty-one, Mal no longer needed that kind of mothering.

"You know I've got a pile of work screaming for attention," Susan said instead. "And you know I've been away from it too long. I'm as eager to get on with things as you are."

As Mal closed the passenger door, Susan hoped that was true, for both of them. She knew she had no choice but to let Malorie go, to let her daughter make her own way.

Susan had firsthand experience at being the object of someone else's controlling tendencies. So she smiled breezily and pretended she didn't worry for a minute about her baby's belated flight from the nest. Buddy would have made it easier. The old Buddy, not the hollowed-out shell with the empty eyes she and Malorie had nursed, babied and protected for two years. But the old Buddy, who'd had enough confidence and bravado for all three of them beneath his mechanic's overalls.

But Buddy was gone now. Susan still felt guilty for considering it a blessing; wondered if she would have felt that way had things been different during their twenty-plus years together.

At any rate, that left only Susan to give Malorie a boost, to press gently for her daughter to get on with her life. Both of them had been carrying around this emotional umbilical cord for way too long now.

Okay, Buddy. Today I'm cutting the cord. The way you told me to a long time back.

She was confident that somewhere, in a place where he was no longer sick, Buddy saw and was glad.

Mal stepped back from the hug and clasped her hands tightly in front of her, looking uncertainly at the ground. "You tell...tell Cody I said bye. Tell him...I'll think about him every single day."

Susan could still hear the tantrum the sturdy little two-year-old had pitched when they left him with old Mrs. Harkins next door that morning. No little brother had ever been as fiercely loyal as Cody Hovis. "He'll do fine, you know."

Mal's smile had a tight look to it, a look that said she wasn't going to give in to all the feelings spinning around inside her. Leaving Cody might be the hardest part for Malorie, Susan thought, but the only thing to do now was move on. That's what Buddy would have said. And he would have been right.

They walked around to the driver's side. Knowing they both needed to end on a smile, Susan said, "Now, sugar, I want your solemn promise to call me every single day."

Malorie laughed. "And twice on Sunday."

She opened the car door, which groaned in protest.

Susan didn't dally, but she did watch in her rear-view mirror until she couldn't spot the slight figure in slip dress and T-shirt amid the trees and cars and red brick buildings. It bothered her that Malorie watched for that long, too. In a way Susan was grateful her daughter's scholarship had come from a college three hundred miles from home. Queens College in Charlotte was just the right distance from Susan's little seamstress shop in the garage behind their house in Atlanta.

Susan needed that distance, too, so she could find the energy and the time for being a mother to a two-year-old and for getting back to work. Working at home had been tough while Buddy was sick. Picking up that needle or plopping down at her old Singer hadn't distracted her the way it once had. Just keeping up with the costumes for Lolly's dance studio had been next to impossible.

Business was off. If she was going to survive—if she was going to make enough to keep herself and Cody going—she had plenty to concentrate on this fall without worrying about Mal.

"What we've got here is a new beginning," she said into the silence as she pointed the wagon onto Interstate 85. At forty-four, she wasn't exactly crazy about the idea of a new beginning. But there it was. Once again, God hadn't seen fit to ask her whether or not she liked things fine just the way they were.

The drive from Charlotte to Atlanta called for a headache powder, the way it always did. Trucks clogged the interstate all the way to Greenville, South Carolina. Each time a semi whizzed past, Susan felt knocked around in her old wagon. She was darned tired of being knocked around.

Still, Susan wasn't prepared when one mud-encrusted tractor-trailer passed her, then pulled back into her lane a few yards too soon. Even as she saw what was happening, she expected a last-minute miracle. The crunch of metal took her by surprise. No time for fear, even, as her car lurched to one side and swerved into another car coming down the on-ramp. More tortured metal. The steering wheel slipped from her hands. The world became flashes of light and sound that she couldn't name.

The car stopped rolling. Susan heard nothing. Saw nothing. Felt nothing. She only knew. Knew that it was too late, forever and ever too late. *Tag.* If only... *Tag.*

She knew nothing more until she heard the rescue workers speaking to her. Gibberish. Words that were scrambled in her brain. Still, nothing moved, nothing *felt.* Except her fingers. Clutched around the corner of the quilt.

Tag. He was all she could remember. *Tag.*

TAG HUTCHINS LINED UP the eighth long-neck beer bottle in a Miss Goody Two Shoes straight line with the first seven. Least, he thought there were seven. He supposed he could be seeing double.

"Yer sorry ass is drunk, Eugene," he mumbled, wondering if there was another beer in the refrigerator. And if he could manage to make it over there to find out. "Guess you're a Junior, after all."

"Aw, hell, Tag, I ain't drunk," he replied, for there was no one else to talk to him in the narrow, dingy trailer he called home, sweet home. "I'm jus' drinkin'."

That struck him as mighty funny, so he laughed and lurched into a standing position. The room whirled around him, leaving him to wonder if somebody had hitched up this rolling tin can he lived in and taken it for a spin. Tag's laughter died quickly.

"Daddy, how the hell'd you manage to do this ever' blessed night of your life?" he mumbled, for he'd swear and be damned his old man must be close by.

Tag remembered now why he'd never taken another drink after that first rip-roaring drunk back in 1975. One bottle of beer, it appeared, turned into another. And another and another. Tag had seen that routine before. He might be Eugene Junior, but hell if he planned to turn into a carbon copy of Eugene Senior.

Right this minute, he couldn't even remember what had made him pick up that first bottle tonight.

"Musta been a damn fine reason," he told himself as he loosened his grip on the metal counter and started for the other side of the trailer. Only four feet long, the path to the refrigerator was treacherous, land-mined with uneven linoleum and a bump in the floor that looked like an upside-down iron skillet, maybe the one he'd used to fix his supper. He stubbed his toe, stumbled against the counter, and ultimately found himself in front of the refrigerator. Grateful that reprieve was near at hand, Tag managed to get his fist around the door handle and yank.

The refrigerator bulb flickered on and off. But light or dark, bleary-eyed or not, Tag could see well enough to discern the ugly truth. The icebox was empty.

"Aw, hell."

He sank to the floor.

Sitting there on the cold, sticky floor, that was when he noticed it. Living in this traveling hellhole for two years, he'd never noticed the pattern in the linoleum. The interlocking circles. In pink and green.

Like the quilt.

The pattern of circles had a name, but he couldn't pull his thoughts together enough right now to think of it. He could only remember the way she'd worked on it those last two years in Sweetbranch. Sitting curled up on the porch swing, with a sea of rose and green and white spread out across her lap. Her long, slim fingers working the needle, in and out, in and out.

For her hope chest, she'd said the first time he asked. Almost defiantly, as if she expected him to make fun, the way he'd made fun all those years before when she'd been his best friend's kid sister.

But that summer, 1960-something, he'd looked up and realized she wasn't a kid anymore.

Tag stared at the interlocking circles on his filthy floor and thought if he didn't have one more beer, just enough to usher in oblivion, he wouldn't be able to stand it.

Why didn't she wait?

Then, eight bottles of beer or not, everything came rushing back. Vietnam. The homecoming that must have been God's idea of a bad joke. Rehab. Staring at the little aluminum-sided house in the middle of a block of matching houses, knowing she was inside.

Why the hell didn't she wait, the way she'd said she would?

No more beer. Only bad memories. Tag stared across the ten-by-ten room—small enough that he could see the whole thing even when he was seeing double—and saw the torn screen window over the sofa that made into a bed, when he bothered to fold it out. Through the window, he could hear the roar of the bikes. Round and round on the track.

He pulled himself up, inch by head-spinning inch, until he hung over the counter. Where the hell was his helmet? He was supposed to race tonight. If he could find that helmet . . .

If only she'd waited . . .

He steadied himself along the counter, moving slowly toward the door. No helmet. Hell, no need. Hadn't his nephew told him long since that he must have nine lives? About what you'd expect from an old tomcat.

Tag tried to remember how many lives he'd used up, but he kept losing count somewhere between the bullring in Tijuana and that dirt track outside Wedowee, Alabama. Or was it Wetumpka? Hell, he must have at least one good life left. And if he could just manage to kick start his bike, point it into the wind, then he wouldn't need another long neck bottle. He could find the oblivion he craved in the wind, in the night, in the speed.

He made it to the door, got his hand on the knob. It rattled, fell off in his hand. He made a sound, something between a sob and a chuckle. As the doorknob dropped, he stumbled and crashed heavily against the door. It gave way under his weight and he felt the cool night air on his face.

He fell through the door and down the stairs, thinking of Susan. All the rest, in between Susan and now, he could forget. He could pretend she'd waited, after all.

He slashed his forehead on the bottom of the rickety metal stairs as he hit bottom.

In the darkness, Susan was waiting.

CHAPTER ONE

Sweetbranch, Alabama
November 1995

SUSAN COULDN'T REMEMBER a single blessed thing the young woman was telling her she ought to remember.

Not "young woman." Malorie. Her daughter.

Susan resisted the temptation to look at the young woman in the driver's seat. But earlier that morning, when she had looked at her, then looked immediately in the hospital mirror, Susan had known it must be true. Their hair was the same color, although Susan couldn't remember what to call that color. They both had those funny little spots sprinkled across their noses.

"Those are freckles, Mother," Malorie had said the day Susan had asked, the same day she'd been frightened of the way the red cubes called Jell-O had jiggled when she touched them with the knife. Spoon.

Then Malorie had looked away, shielded her eyes. It hadn't taken long for Susan to learn to recognize that look. To give it a name, even. Pity. The young woman with hair the color of sunshine reflected through a jar of honey felt sorry for Susan.

That ticked Susan off. If anybody was going to feel sorry for her, she'd do that little job herself. And she hadn't slipped that far yet.

Why, Susan wondered, could she remember a jar of honey sitting on a table—a chipped, green-and-white Formica table with matching vinyl chairs—and not remember the imp-faced young woman everyone told her she had given birth to? Right now, she wasn't even sure what that meant. Giving birth. What was it like? Had it been fun? How did it happen? Could she do it again so she could remember it on this side of her life?

Susan didn't look at Malorie. She looked out the car window at the things Malorie said she should know all about and tried not to wonder where all those memories had disappeared to. She was glad to be out of the hospital. Three months, they told her, although that was another notion that didn't mean much to her right now. All the same, after two months of green walls— Malorie had told her that color, after Susan said she hated it—and long, echoing corridors and red-and-green food that gave her the heebie-jeebies when it moved, Susan discovered she liked the outdoors very much.

Sweetbranch, the sign beside the covered bridge had said. Malorie had pronounced it for her. Most of the alphabet had come back to Susan, although she still found it hard to make the sounds out loud herself. Mostly, they came out slurred, funny-sounding. Like a drunk, Malorie had said, giggling as she went on to explain the concept.

"Tell you what," Malorie had said to her last night at the hospital, "I'll give you a demonstration. Your first night at home, I'll tie one on for you."

Susan wondered where you tied it—around the neck? around the waist? around a wrist?—and looked forward to seeing one. She gobbled up each new experience. And most of it, she discovered, stuck. She was relearning things at a remarkable pace, the rehab therapist had said.

It was only her yesterdays that wouldn't return to her, didn't stick even when Malorie explained them to her.

The place called Sweetbranch didn't look much like the place called Atlanta, where the hospital lived. Huge ribbons of concrete didn't twist and wind through Sweetbranch, providing parking places for thousands of cars and trucks and vans. The big trucks made Susan nervous.

Tall trees the colors of fire spread every which way in Sweetbranch. The houses sat far apart, separated by green carpet that was nothing like the sickly hospital green.

"I might take a liking to green, after all," she said, forgetting that it was easier all the way round when she didn't speak.

"What, Mother? Are you all right?"

Susan heard the alarm in the young woman's voice and sighed. "Green. It's pretty."

"Oh. Yes."

But Susan heard the uncertainty in Malorie's voice and wondered if she had made herself understood. Would she ever be able to speak clearly again?

"There's where you went to church when you were a girl, Mother."

Eagerly, Susan followed the direction of Malorie's gesture. The brick building with the center spire seemed vaguely familiar. "Reckon I should've gone more often?"

Again, that funny look from Malorie. Her therapist had liked it when Susan made little jokes. Malorie took it all way too seriously.

"And there's the high school. You were on the debating team, if you can believe that."

Susan looked again, this time at a two-story brick building. Home of the Bobcats, read a brick-framed sign between the street and the gravel drive. The squat, square building stirred more vague feelings in her, feelings of anticipation, feelings that something good was about to happen. She smiled.

Malorie must have seen the smile. "Do you remember Sweetbranch High, Mother?"

"Maybe." Susan could tell, although Malorie went to great pains to hide it, that every missing memory, every forgotten skill, was like a personal loss to her daughter.

"That's good. Dr. Kerr said being back on familiar territory like this could be very good for your memory retrieval."

Susan remembered that, and took it as a good sign. "Yeah. Maybe someday I'll be normal again." She laughed, despite the frown her daughter shot in her direction. "Shoot, maybe someday I'll even know what normal means."

"Mo-ther!"

Susan smiled at the admonition. She didn't know if she'd always been the type to try to do things against the grain, but she was discovering she liked it now.

"This is Main Street coming up," Malorie said.

Having heard the expectation in Malorie's voice, Susan sat forward in her seat. She didn't want to miss Main Street, and the chance for more memory retrieval.

The two lanes of traffic along Main Street crept between rows of adjoining brick buildings. Susan's heart leaped at the familiar sights, until she remembered that they had passed by similar Main Streets in other small towns all along the way from Atlanta. As in those other small towns, the brick buildings housed a dress shop and a bookstore and a drugstore and a post office and various other offices. Signs read The Picture Perfect and Holy Spirits Tavern and *Sweetbranch Weekly Gazetteer.* People here didn't bustle around the way they did in Atlanta. These folks seemed to have more time as they made their way along the sidewalks, stopping to talk, laughing over something in the bins at the hardware store, calling out to people passing slowly in their pickup trucks.

Susan didn't recognize any of them. She didn't recognize anything.

Except for Hutchins' Lawn & Garden.

The sign made her heart skip again, and when it resumed its regular beat, it had sped up.

Hutchins' Lawn & Garden was on the northeast end of Main Street. The wooden sign had been hand-painted years ago and needed freshening. The building took up almost half a block with its big plate-glass windows, framed by faded and tattered green-and-white awnings. Right now the windows were bare, but Susan was almost certain that once upon a time, in the spring, those windows had been decked out with hanging baskets of lacy Boston ferns and blood-red geraniums. The wooden bins built out onto the sidewalk in front of the windows now were filled with dusty, ungainly bags of weed and feed. But Susan could see as clearly as the freckles on Malorie's nose a time when those bins had held tulip and gladiola and iris bulbs, each bin labeled with a colored picture of the bulbs in full, glorious bloom.

"Let's go there," she said.

"What, Mother?"

Susan pointed. "There. Go there."

Malorie smiled and patted her hand in a way that made Susan want to jerk away. She knew what that pat meant. Her daughter thought she was addlebrained.

Well, could be she was.

"Would you like to shop around, Mother? We'll do that soon. Just as soon as you're ready to get out. But right now, Grandmother's waiting. Aren't you excited about seeing Grandmother?"

"No."

Malorie looked at her and smiled, but the smile was strained. That was one good thing about being injured. Susan could say whatever the heck was on her mind and get away with it. The thought made her smile; *her* smile wasn't strained at all.

"What about Cody, then? Cody can't wait to see you. He's missed you something fierce."

Susan remembered the sturdy-legged little boy. Malorie had brought him to the hospital twice. With his little round chest and his toddler's swagger, he looked ready to pick a fight with the world. But his smile was as sunny and uncomplicated as Malorie's. He troubled her, too, although in a different way than Susan's grandmother troubled her.

"I'm not much of a mother anymore," she said.

"Now, Mother. That's no way to talk."

"You may have to be the mother for a while," she said. "For me and Cody."

Malorie was silent and Susan wondered if her words had been too slurred. The trip had worn her out, and when she got tired, her speech got worse.

"Well, I know Cody and Grandmother are both excited about seeing you," Malorie said at last. "And we're almost there. Just two more blocks."

Susan remembered blocks from the rehab hospital, painted all colors with the letters of the alphabet on them. She wasn't sure what that had to do with finishing the drive to Grandmother's house, but she was growing too tired to ask. All she knew was what she had admitted to Malorie, that she wasn't looking forward to seeing the woman Malorie called Grandmother.

Grandmother was Susan's mother. She knew that much because her therapist had explained it to her after Grandmother's first visit. Rather, the first visit Susan could remember. Grandmother's name was Betsy Foster, and Susan still remembered the first words she'd heard her speak at the rehab hospital.

"Oh, Susan, what have you done to yourself now? This would break your father's heart if he were still alive to see you like this."

Susan hadn't known how she looked at that point. After hearing Grandmother's reaction, it had been a long time before she'd been willing to glance at herself in the mirror. Once she finally had the courage to look, she realized she had nothing to compare with her present image. The thin, pasty-white woman with the shaved head and the limp left arm and leg looked no worse to her than anybody else she saw at the rehab hospital every day. And the woman who had been Susan Foster Hovis before the accident no longer existed in her mind. Still, she felt a little queasy whenever Grandmother showed up, because she sensed the disapproval.

And now, she and Malorie were coming to live with Grandmother. Malorie said they had no choice right now, nowhere else to go. That they should be grateful there was somewhere she could get better, that there was someone to help her.

She kept the sign that said Hutchins' Lawn & Garden framed in the side-view mirror until the van turned the corner and all she could see was the high fence around the back of the building. She wanted to go down Main Street one more time so she could memorize the sign. But Susan knew that was the kind of thing that made Malorie worry her mother would never again be right, no matter how much memory she retrieved.

As it turned out, the sign stayed in her head all the way to Grandmother's house, anyway.

Susan liked the street. Mimosa Lane, the sign read. Trees lined the sides, dressed for autumn in reds and golds and oranges, making Susan smile. The houses made her smile, too, houses with gables and front porches and crisp green shutters fanning out from tall, wide windows. The houses looked friendly. Maybe living on Mimosa Lane wouldn't be such a bad thing, after all.

Malorie stopped the van in front of the friendliest of the houses on Mimosa. White, with a second story and a peaked roof and a wooden wheelchair ramp off the screened side porch. A willow tree weeped in the front yard and stirred in Susan a desire to sweep beneath it, dancing from bough to bough, fluttering the fall of leaves with her outstretched arms. The desire was strong, almost a physical ache.

Before Malorie could get around to the passenger side of the van, the front door of the house opened. Leading the way was Cody, laughing, barreling full

speed toward the new van, which Malorie said a
trucking company had bought for them. Settlement,
Malorie called it. Behind the little boy, a tall, stocky
man with sandy hair more than half filled with white
came out behind a tall, gaunt woman whose back
would never have bent enough to allow her to sweep
beneath the boughs of the willow in her own front
yard. Susan saw that and understood it, even if lots of
other things flickered just beyond her grasp these days.

Susan retreated into the shell her injuries allowed her
to create. The same way she had retreated to her
wheelchair when she left rehab, so no one could see
how she walked, staggering and shaking, unsteady on
her feet. Susan didn't want to see disapproval on the
face of her mother and she didn't want to see pity in the
eyes of the other person, whom she couldn't remember right now. She didn't want to hear the clank and
rattle of the wheelchair Malorie was dragging out of the
back of the van right now. She wanted this to be over.
She wanted, maybe, to be back at the hospital, where
at least everyone laughed *with* her when she called an
apple a pencil. She didn't want to be here. If her brain
had to be bruised, she wanted to go back to the hospital, where everybody else was bruised and incomplete,
too.

It didn't work that way. The man with the sandy-
white hair opened the car door.

"How's my little sis? You better not have put on any
weight eating all that hospital food."

Then he lifted her, groaning in an exaggerated way
that was supposed to make them all laugh. Susan let
them all laugh. She let him place her gently in the
wheelchair. She listened to Betsy Grandmother Mom
Foster greet her and pretended she didn't hear. She was

being mean. Hateful. She knew it. But right now, she needed her shell. *Please, God, just for right now. Just for these few minutes when I don't want anyone to see or hear how broken I am.*

"Mommy! Mommy!"

The little boy stood in front of her, his blue eyes bright with delight. The stripes on his T-shirt matched his eyes. He flung himself into the chair, into her arms, filling her lap.

"Now, Cody, you be careful," admonished Grandmother. "Susan does not need you crawling all over her like that."

So Susan put her good arm around the hard little body and pulled him close. Cody put his arms around her neck. "I love you, Mommy. Me ride? Me push?"

"Yes," she said, hoping that was enough response to his exuberance for the moment.

The man who called her "sis" pushed the chair around the front of the van. That was when Susan saw the house directly across the street, over the sunny fuzz of Cody's hair. The house was brick, one story, set back in a wilderness of overgrown azaleas and rhododendron. A broad porch stretched clear across the front, but it had no rockers, no swing, no invitations to sit a spell. Chimneys rose on either end of the house.

"Tag," she whispered, her brain grasping frantically at the memories stirred by the forlorn-looking house.

"What, Mother?" Malorie bent over her, but Susan shook her head. Her daughter straightened and spoke to the others. "You wouldn't believe how fast she's learning to read again. Don't worry, Mother, I've got your books and everything else in the back of the van. You'll be settled in no time."

Susan had no side-view mirror on her chair to keep the house in sight, so she closed her eyes and tried to carry it with her all the way into Grandmother's house. Like the big green-and-white sign on Main Street, the house touched some part of her that nothing else had touched since the accident. She closed her eyes and tried to remember what the sign, what the house, might mean. What Tag might mean.

Light shimmered in that part of her memory, but it was too weak yet to fight back the darkness.

As DUSK CREPT into Sweetbranch, Tag Hutchins stared out the living room window. It had become his daily penance. His own Southern Baptist, guilt-and-hellfire version of a dozen Hail Marys.

Waking up with a hangover and a stitched-up head two months ago had scared the bejesus out of him. Scared him so bad he'd gone on the run but good. Eight states in six weeks. Racing so hard and fast and dirty he'd won twelve second places, two thirds, a disputed first place and a dislocated shoulder. Of course, the dislocation actually came after the race, during the fight over the dispute, but that *did* make it race-related.

Then the past caught up with him again, only this time he couldn't run. Here he was, smack-dab in the one place he considered his own personal hell on earth. Sweetbranch. So about this time of day, he would stand at the window and stare at her house, forcing himself to live out the old memories, looking each old bitterness square in the face. Daring each memory, each resentment, to drive him back to a long-neck beer bottle.

"Have you decided about the store?"

His nephew's voice drew Tag away from the window. He let the heavy green curtain drop and limped across the room. His bad knee was worse since the fall down his trailer steps. "Yeah. I'll keep it open."

Sam raised an eyebrow as he jabbed the dying coals in the fireplace. "You?"

"Yes, me. Why the hell not me?"

Sam Roberts was one of the few people who didn't flinch when Tag Hutchins growled. Somewhere during his twenty-seven years, Sam had lost both his awe and his fear of the gravelly voiced uncle with the messy reputation.

"Because you always hated the place," Sam snapped back.

Tag picked a medium-sized log from the haphazard pile he'd brought in earlier in the week and tossed it onto the ash-covered grate. Sparks crackled and flew.

"It makes money," Tag countered.

"Barely."

"Mama had no business managing the damn thing all by herself. I'll get it back in the black."

The accusations in Tag's head seemed to spill out into the silence. His mother had had no choice but to manage the place herself after his father died. Even if they'd known at which dirt track in which two-bit town in Alabama or Mississippi or Georgia to find him, Tag would have had ten good reasons why he needed to run this race or that one before pointing his rolling tin can toward Sweetbranch. Eula Hutchins had been on her own after the liquor finally did in Eugene Senior.

"I know," he finally said, facing the fireplace so he didn't have to face Sam. "Her son didn't do her a damn bit of good while she was alive. What makes me think my help is wanted now?"

Sam didn't rise to the bait; his voice stayed level, calm, rational. That ability to stay cool might be the only thing Tag didn't like about his only living relative. "It's yours now. You can do what you want with it. Sell it if you want to."

Tag had thought of that. He'd sat on the bench at the park and stared across the green at the old brick building where he'd spent way too much of his growing up years to suit him. He'd tried to picture the sign coming down. Being replaced with something cutesy and creative made up by some former debutante yuppie Junior Leaguer from Birmingham with romantic notions of small-town living. Bootsie's Garden Boutique. There would be no more fifty-pound bags of manure against the back wall. No more posthole diggers. No more contracts for bush-hogging family garden plots come spring.

And no more Hutchinses in Sweetbranch, Alabama.

Everything his old man and his mama had worked for all those years would be erased, dead and gone. Even Sam, his brother's only son, had another man's last name now.

If Tag let the old store go, he would have his wish. He really wouldn't belong anywhere at all.

"What is it, Sam? Afraid an old vagrant like me can't keep the place going?"

"You're not a vagrant. Old, maybe. But not a vagrant."

Tag shot Sam a cynical look. His nephew had been sitting there when Tag awoke two months ago, his head pounding so hard he was certain his skull would explode. Sam had taken him home from the hospital, back to a trailer reeking of stale beer. Sam had propped him up on the side of the couch where the springs weren't broken and stared at him long and hard.

"Tag, what do you plan to do with your life now?"

"Have a beer," Tag had rasped, although for the life of him he couldn't quite imagine being able to move his head enough to swallow.

"That's not funny."

"Maybe I wasn't trying to be funny."

"Have you been drinking long, Tag?"

"Hell, no. Last night. That's all."

"What started you off?"

"I don't know." But he did know, now. Now, in the cold light of day, he could remember. Too clearly. A birthday not his own. A birthday he wanted to curse and couldn't quite. And it was easy, once again, to appreciate the lure of oblivion that alcohol promised.

He wondered, fleetingly, what his old man had sought oblivion from. Chastised himself for never caring enough to find out while his father was alive.

"You know the risk," Sam had continued. "You're that much like Grandpa. One is too many and a hundred isn't enough."

"You're a smart-ass."

"I know. It's the family plague," Sam had countered, unperturbed. "Tag, if you're going to start drinking, you might as well go out there and get on that bike of yours and sail over a cliff somewhere. Do it fast. It'll be a lot less painful for all of us."

All of us being Sam and Tag's mother, for nobody else who gave a rat's ass had been left. Still, Tag saw the wisdom in Sam's words. And without the murkiness that came with a six-pack, crashing and burning on his motorcycle had little appeal. Neither did going the way his old man had.

Tag hadn't had another drop since. He'd even called his mama regularly, which was how he'd known when she had the stroke. Sometimes, especially since he'd had to drag himself back to Sweetbranch to watch his mama die, he could taste a cold one going down, could feel the damp tickle of a head of foam on his mustache. Sometimes he felt like a forty-six-year-old grizzly with a thorn in his paw. Acted like it, too.

"I know I can sell the store," he said now. "And I know I've never run a business in my life. But I can do the bush-hogging and the deliveries. I've still got a strong back, you know. But even I'm responsible enough to figure out I'm not ready to get the store back on its feet. I'm gonna hire somebody."

"Who?"

"Hell, I don't know," he snapped. "I put some posters out today, around town. I'll advertise in the paper. Somebody'll turn up."

"What about the house?"

Tag's head was beginning to pound. "Hell, I don't know about the friggin' house, either. She's been dead a week, for chrissake. Cut me some slack."

Sam propped the black iron poker against the stone fireplace and stood. It always surprised Tag that Sam looked him eye-to-eye. He remembered Sam as a skinny, gap-toothed five-year old. When had he gotten to be a good-looking man on a six-foot-two frame?

"Sorry, Tag."

"Nah." Tag clapped Sam on the shoulder briefly. "I'm the one who's sorry. I'm sore as an old wet hen these days."

"Let me know how I can help, okay?"

"I will."

Sam stopped at the door. "Mother said to tell you . . . she hoped you'd understand if she didn't come by."

Tag had seen Emily at the funeral, with her husband and their two teenaged kids. "Sure. Yeah. You tell her I said she looks great, okay?"

Tag hadn't expected his sister-in-law to pay a friendly visit. For all he knew, she was still pissed at the way he ran out after he was back on his feet. With Tag's brother dead in Vietnam and a little boy to raise, Emily had seemed to think it wasn't too much to expect Tag to hang around, be a role model for her fatherless son.

All Tag knew was, Emily would've probably ended up a lot more pissed off if he *had* stayed around to be a role model. Tag Hutchins was nobody's hero. Especially not some impressionable little kid's.

He looked at Sam. The boy had done just fine without him. Real fine, in fact. "You think I can do it? The store, I mean."

Once the question was out, Tag realized Sam's opinion was important to him.

"I know you can."

Tag wondered, as Sam closed the door behind him, how long he could manage to feed off his nephew's belief in him.

Dusk was thick now. The house was growing dark. But Tag didn't turn on any lights yet. He stood in the halo from the fire, which was once again dying, and stared at the front window. Finally he gave in.

The new van was still parked out front. But one thing had changed, one thing was different from all the other times he'd stared out this window since coming home to Sweetbranch a few weeks ago.

There was a light in the corner front bedroom upstairs. Susan's window.

CHAPTER TWO

April 1967

"SO WHAT ARE YOU gonna do in June?"

With high school graduation six weeks away, Tag still didn't have the answer to the question everybody was asking. His mama. His old man, especially when he was tanked. Now even Crash Foster.

"I don't know, man. Do you?"

Tag and Crash lay in a circle of grass enclosed by Tag's mama's pink-and-white azaleas and stared up at the stars.

"We could join up."

Tag didn't have to think twice about that. He'd been Elliott's shadow all his life. He didn't want to follow his brother into the army, too.

"And end up in Vietnam?"

Crash tossed a stick into the air and caught it on the way down. "Where is Vietnam, anyway?"

"If you hadn't been such a slack-ass in school, you'd know where the heck Vietnam is."

"Okay. I'm a slack-ass. So where is it?"

"Indochina."

"Oh." They sat in the dark for five minutes, listening to the season's first crickets. "Where's that?"

"Look it up." Tag figured he was under no obligation to reveal—even to his best friend—that he knew too much about this tiny spot that was beginning to create such a big stink.

"It wouldn't be bad if we could go together," Crash said.

Tag wasn't so sure. Six months after he'd shipped out, Elliott didn't write much, and when he did, his letters sounded funny. Spooky funny, that is. Tag had been reading about Vietnam in the Birmingham paper whenever he could sneak away from the store and get to the library without anybody noticing. From what he was reading, Tag wasn't so sure he wanted to end up rotting in the jungle in a place called Vietnam.

"I think I'll save my money," he said. "Buy me a car."

He didn't mention the things he thought about doing with the car. Driving to Hollywood and learning to be a stuntman for the movies. Or driving over to Hueytown, Alabama, to see about working on the pit crew for a stock car driver. The way Tag figured it, he had lots of options.

"Save what money?" Crash said.

"I'll get a job."

"You've *got* a job. And your old man doesn't pay you diddly."

"A *real* job." Tag hated working for his old man. Hated Hutchins' Lawn & Garden. He figured lawns and gardens were fine for women, but men had other business. "Construction, maybe."

"If you don't want to join up, maybe you ought to go to college. Before the draft gets you."

Tag rolled over on his belly. He wasn't about to tell Steve Foster—known as Crash because he'd managed to do exactly that to three cars within one month of getting his driver's license—that college was the one thing he *really* wanted to do. He gazed across the street at Crash's house, a big white two-story with a weeping willow in the front yard. Crash's old man had the Cadillac dealership for the whole county, which made him practically a millionaire compared to storekeepers like Tag's old man. Tag wondered if he had the brains to get as rich as old man Foster, then figured it didn't matter, anyway. Tag Hutchins wasn't going to college and get all brainy. No prayer of that.

"Who needs college?" he replied to Crash's question. "Say, what's that?"

"What?"

Propped on his elbows in the cool, dew-damp grass, Tag pointed to a front window upstairs at Crash's house. A light was on, and the ends of filmy yellow curtains drifted out the open window. Inside, someone moved back and forth across the room, all graceful arms and legs. The backdrop for the movement was some kind of classical sounding music, which also floated out the open window.

"Oh, that. That's Susie."

"What's she doing?"

"Dancing."

The fluid movements of the slender body that was framed only fleetingly by the open window looked nothing like the Jerk or the Swim or the Monkey. This looked like his mama's gladiolas swaying in a summer breeze.

"Susie? No kidding?"

"Yeah. What a dope, huh? She does that every night. Mom yells at her, but Susie doesn't pay any attention. Every night, she practices those dumb dances. Then she comes out on the porch and works on this blanket she's making."

Tag had known Crash's little sister practically all his life. He couldn't remember when the skinny, freckle-faced girl with the long blond ponytail hadn't been a pest, spoiling things, tattling on them. But this person floating back and forth in front of the upstairs window bore no resemblance to that gawky, goofy kid. This person moved like a cloud. This person wasn't skinny; she was slender and perfect.

This couldn't be Susan Foster. This person in the window was a...a...a girl. And he meant that only in the best possible way.

Tag sat up. His mouth felt dry and his chest felt big and empty, the way he felt when he got the wind knocked out of him on the football field.

"Let's go over to your house," he said.

"Nah. That's a drag. Besides, I told you, Susie'll be down soon and she'll mess up everything. Let's go into town, see who's at the Dairie Dreme."

Almost a week passed before Tag found a way to get over to Crash's house without Crash figuring out what was going on. He and Crash'd had plans to double-date with Debbie Compton and Alta Fay Wills that Friday night, but Tag backed out at the last minute. Alta Fay was knock-kneed, anyway, and he'd only agreed because Crash said Debbie wouldn't go out with him alone the first time. Buddies came through for buddies.

This time, though, Tag figured Crash was on his own.

Almost every night after seeing her that first time, Tag had figured out a way to be sitting in his mama's garden about the time Susan Foster went upstairs to practice. He watched her and thought about god-desses in the mythology junk he'd managed to tick off

Old Lady Strawbridge by not reading. Some nights, Susie wore her hair loose, and it hung way past her shoulders, down her back, like a cloak of butter-colored dandelion fuzz. He wondered what it would be like to hold a fistful of that hair in his hand and blow it, watch it float away, feel the weightlessness of it.

He knew he was getting mush-headed over a girl, because his grandpa had warned him this day would come. He'd never believed it before. Not that he hadn't felt an itch that needed scratching real bad sometimes, but feeling that kind of itch was a whole lot different from this. Grandpa was right. This was mush-headed.

The hardest part was acting like nothing was different during the day at school. Because the worst thing that could happen would be for Crash to find out that his best friend since the first grade had a crush on his kid sister. Crash clearly had not matured enough to recognize that his kid sister had been transformed into a goddess.

So Tag kept away from her at school and resorted to spying on her at night from the protective darkness of his mama's circle of azaleas, which would soon curl up and turn brown. Seemed like a waste to Tag, tending them and fretting over them and babying them all year long, like his mama did, for a few short weeks of color every spring. But for this short week, the delicate blossoms seemed somehow tied to Tag's discovery of this delicate creature who now lived in the body of a one-time pesky kid. All of it—flowers, music, stars, girl with the cloud of butter-colored hair—were some form of magic, and he walked into the spell willingly, eagerly.

He discovered Crash was right. After she danced, she came outside, onto the screened-in side porch, and curled up on the porch swing. She set the swing in motion with one bare toe, then set to work.

Tag made up his mind he would talk to her, that he would make her realize that if she could overcome her years as pesky Susie that he, too, could be transformed. He hoped that didn't mean he would have to start letting people call him Eugene Junior. But if it did, so be it.

This night, with Crash safely at the movies with Debbie Compton, Tag made his move.

She sat there, just the way she always did, only this time she was closer. He came around from the back of the house, knowing he didn't have the guts to march right up the front walk with her looking at him, all curious. So he was at the back edge of the porch before she realized he was there.

"You scared me, Tag Hutchins. What are you up to, sneaking around like that?"

He realized her voice was different, too. Not a whiny little girl's voice anymore. Soft, almost shy-sounding.

"I'm not sneaking around. I just saw you sitting here and thought I'd say hi."

She stopped her work and looked down on him. She had pulled her hair back into a ponytail, even though almost nobody wore ponytails anymore. But it looked right on her. And it made her big, dark eyes easier to see.

"Steve's not here."

"I know."

She looked at him another moment, then lowered her eyes to the big sea of material in her lap. "I thought you were doubling?"

"I don't like Alta Fay."

She didn't answer. He didn't know what he'd expected. Had he thought she would ask him who he did like? Tell him she was glad he wasn't squandering his attention on somebody like Alta Fay? It sank in that if he wanted this encounter to turn into something like a conversation, it was up to him to get it rolling.

He walked up the five steps and opened the screen door without being invited, the way he would have if it had been Crash in the swing, even though he suspected the rules he knew didn't apply to this strange new situation. He sat on the concrete floor, his back against one of the porch rails, facing her. He was close enough to touch her bare foot. Her ankle was narrow, all bone and pale skin. Her toes were long. He'd never before in his whole life realized that toes could be pretty, but it struck him that hers were. Her toenails were painted a pale, shimmery pink.

"What are you working on?"

"Nothing you'd be interested in."

"Tell me."

"Just a quilt."

Tag wasn't sure how a quilt was different from a blanket, but he sure wasn't about to ask. "Is it hard?"

She looked at him without raising her head from her task. He saw that she worked with a needle and thread, and that her fingers were as long and graceful and pretty as her toes.

"It's tedious," she said.

"Why do you do it?"

"Because when I finish it will be a work of art. And..."

"And what?"

"That's all."

"What are you going to do with it?"

"Put it in my hope chest." She raised her chin, daring him to poke fun at her, the way he'd poked fun at her as long as he could remember.

He couldn't see any way to poke fun at her anymore. All he could see when she mentioned a hope chest was this picture of her in his mind's eye, dressed up in white the way Emily had been when she and Elliott got married. There was old Susie, dressed in white lace and dancing in front of a cedar chest.

"Oh." He had to draw a deep breath, because somehow he couldn't quite get his lungs full. "I didn't know you were talented until I saw you dancing in your window."

"You watched me?"

Tag knew right away from the tone of her voice that he'd said the wrong thing. "I can see you. From the house."

Her mouth looked tight and displeased. It called to mind the contrast from moments before, when her mouth had looked soft. He knew then that he wanted to kiss her.

Gee willikers, what was he going to do about that? Wanting to kiss Crash Foster's kid sister. Crash would never let him live it down. Or else Crash would kill him, because nobody wanted one of his horny pals messing around with their kid sister, even if their kid sister had always been a pest.

"You look..." Tag swallowed hard, but his mouth remained dust-dry. "You look real beautiful when you dance."

She let go of her needle and stared at him. "If you're trying to josh me, Tag Hutchins, I'll—"

"No! I'm not. I swear it."

"Did Steve put you up to this?"

"No!"

She started back on her needlework, but her pursed lips told him he'd made a real mess out of this.

"You won't tell him, will you?"

She frowned. "Tell him what?"

"That I...came over tonight. That I said you look...beautiful."

"Now, why would I tell him that?"

She smiled a little then, and her lips grew soft once more. And Tag thought if he didn't touch some small part of her soon, he might just die from lack of...whatever it was she had that he needed.

"How long are you going to work on that thing tonight?" he asked.

"Oh, I don't know. Usually I work on it till bedtime."

"Suppose you might want to quit early tonight?"

"What for?"

"We could take a walk."

"To the Dairie Dreme?"

Tag almost said yes, then he remembered that Crash and Debbie and everybody else getting out of the seven o'clock movie would be crowding into the parking lot at the Dairie Dreme before long. Including everybody who knew he'd bailed out on his date with Alta Fay tonight.

"How about down by the creek? It wouldn't be so crowded. We could talk."

"Down by the creek?" Once again, her voice rose an octave in that tone that signaled he'd said the wrong thing. "Alone? At night?"

"It's not scary. Crash and—" Then it hit him. What she really meant. "Oh. I didn't mean anything by it."

"You didn't?"

He looked up then, and saw the strangest look on her face. Sort of expectant, sort of teasing. He felt himself stirring and felt the least bit ashamed. "Well, maybe I did mean a little something by it."

She laughed at that, and her laugh was as light as her hair when it floated on the spring breeze while she danced. Tag thought his heart might thump its way right out of his chest.

"My mother would never let me walk down to the creek alone with you at this hour, Tag," she said softly. "I'd have to sneak out to do that."

"I don't mind sneaking out," he said, hazarding an uncertain smile.

She smiled that unfathomable smile again. "Neither do I."

He waited on the edge of her lot, sitting under the big oak tree, on the side away from the house, just the way she'd told him to. But he couldn't keep himself from peering around the big old trunk right at ten to see if she was coming. What she was doing was climbing right out her bedroom window onto the waiting limb of the apple tree. He grinned as she shinnied down, thinking he'd never seen anything half so mesmerizing as a goddess who shinnied down apple trees.

"What are you grinning at?" she asked when she reached him. She looked down at him, hands on her hips.

"You. Climbing out the window."

"I may be a girl but I'm not a sissy."

He took the hand she offered and leaped to his feet. He didn't let go of her hand all the way to the creek. The difference between her hand and his was the difference between his mama's everyday plates and the Sunday-best china with the roses twined around the rim. His hand was thick and ordinary and maybe a little rough; hers was fine and smooth and delicate.

"Why do you do all that dancing?" He marveled that he'd never noticed the way the moonlight glittered on the surface of Willow Creek.

"That's what I'm going to be when I grow up." She looked at him expectantly.

"A dancer?" The notion intrigued him. All the girls he'd dated talked about being clerks for the county or maybe moving to Birmingham for secretarial school or going away to college to make a teacher.

"What's wrong with that?"

"Nothing. It's just... I never knew anybody who wanted to be a dancer before." More than anything, he admired her courage in admitting she wanted to be different from all the everyday folks in Sweetbranch. It made him a little ashamed that he'd never been that brave himself.

"If *everybody* wanted to do it, it would hardly be worth doing, now, would it?" she asked with a certainty that amazed him.

"Crash said your mother doesn't want you dancing."

She frowned. "Mother thinks it's a disgrace if you don't want to be just exactly like everybody else."

Everything she said came as a revelation, an epiphany, to Tag. How could it be that here was someone who didn't desperately want to be like everyone else? He'd spent his whole life wishing to be normal, wishing to be regular, wishing for nothing more than to be one of the guys, plain and simple.

"Why would you want to be different?"

"Why would you want to be the same?" she asked fervently. "Don't you have things inside you that are dying to get out, things you never heard anybody around here talking about, things that make you wonder how the rest of the world got dull as dishwater?''

And Tag thought of his crazy dream. The one about going to college and learning how to help people who couldn't figure out all the confusing things in their heads. He thought about being someplace where people wouldn't notice if he slipped up and used big words or wanted to talk about ideas instead of what kind of defense the Tide would be using come fall.

"Yeah," he said. "Sometimes I do. I just never knew anybody else did."

"Maybe they don't," she whispered. "Maybe we're the only ones."

That was when he kissed Crash Foster's kid sister, his lips touching hers ever so slightly, his big ugly knuckles against her heart-shaped face, leaning over carefully so as not to touch her anywhere else. Her mouth was as soft and sweet as he had imagined it to be. But one thing was different. It wasn't cool the way he'd figured a goddess who danced in the spring breeze would be.

Her mouth was warm. He breathed in that warmth, drank it right from her. It spread all the way through him, filling him up with something golden.

By the time he walked her back to her house and stood at the foot of the apple tree while she climbed back up to her bedroom window, Tag Hutchins had discovered the wonder of being in love with the most perfect creature in the world.

CHAPTER THREE

MALORIE RATTLED THE FRONT door of the unkempt-looking storefront on Main Street, then cupped her hands around her eyes to look through the grimy glass. The place certainly *needed* a manager.

At her grandmother's suggestion, Malorie was looking for a job. It had not been a subtle suggestion. Betsy Foster was not a woman who minced words.

"I understand you want to be here with your mother while she recuperates," her grandmother had said the day before, after her uncle had returned home. "But we have a physical therapist coming every day starting tomorrow. Fixing Susan is not your job."

"But there's Cody..."

"I'll be here all day myself, like always. I dare say I'll have a better idea how to handle him than you."

Malorie had flinched at the harsh judgment and all it implied.

"Besides, you're twenty-one, Malorie. High time you got on with your life."

Malorie had known better than to explain to her grandmother that, as tragic as her mother's accident had been, Malorie accepted it as another excuse for avoiding exactly that—getting on with her life. Nothing would make Malorie happier than escaping into a life made up of two-year-old Cody and a mother who needed her again.

She was worried, too, that her grandmother hadn't paid attention when the people in rehab had talked to her about working with Susan. Had she really listened when they'd talked about Susan's mood swings, about how easily distracted she was now, about the myriad ways the accident had left her impaired and in need of patience and understanding?

Malorie had watched her grandmother closely since they had arrived and was convinced that Betsy Foster could undo in a few weeks all the progress Susan had made.

Betsy insisted on bombarding Susan with information—where she had stored towels and soap and a supply of kitchen utensils at a level Susan could reach, for example—although she'd been told lots of details all at once might make it difficult for Susan to process the information. She also insisted on doing every little thing for her daughter, despite the fact she had been encouraged to allow Susan the independence to do things for herself, even if she was slow, even if she didn't get things quite right.

"Well, that's ridiculous," Betsy had said when Malorie followed her into the kitchen to remind her that Susan should be allowed to pour her own glass of juice. "Then who'll clean up the mess she makes, that's what I'd like to know?"

Malorie sighed. Her concerns about Betsy Foster aside, here she stood on the sidewalk in front of Hutchins' Lawn & Garden, wondering if whoever had taped up the hand-lettered Store Manager Wanted sign had changed his or her mind.

These days, Main Street bustled. Over the past few years, Sweetbranch had perked up economically, and its resurgence was reflected in the bright new awnings

on storefronts such as The Picture Perfect beauty sa-
lon and the window box of mums adorning the front
of the Sweet Boutique. Sweetbranch had become a
different town in the years since the paper plant
opened. Compared to the rest of the shops on Main
Street, however, Hutchins' Lawn & Garden looked
forlorn and abandoned. Malorie saw no lights inside
the store, no indication of any activity.

She was about to walk away—her mother's therapist would make his first visit soon and she planned to
be there, even if Grandmother didn't think she was
needed—when she heard the metallic thunk of a dead
bolt being thrown. She looked up just as a glowering
face appeared in the partly open doorway. Instinc-
tively she stepped back.

"We're closed," the man said in a voice that could
only be described as a growl, both in tone and timbre.
A perfect match for the expression on his face.

"Yes. I see." He moved to close the door, and Malorie remembered her purpose. "I'm here about the
job."

He didn't follow her gesture when she pointed at the
sign to the left of the double plate-glass door. He stared
at her, his eyes dark beneath the shadow of low, heavy
brows. He was all darkness, it seemed to Malorie, from
the hair that nearly touched his shoulders to the brush
of a mustache and his sun-bronzed skin. Even his
T-shirt was black. The whole package made her heart
thump. Nothing about the man—including his de-
pressing store—fit with the rest of this sunny, cheerful
town.

"You know how to run a store? This isn't just a
clerking job."

Malorie had no illusions that running the cash register at a fast-food restaurant during those awful months her dad was sick actually qualified her for anything. But the challenge in his voice made her unwilling to admit that, at twenty-one, she had absolutely no marketable skills and little if any practical experience.

"I can do it," she said.

Her heart sank as he stepped back, opened the door wider and gestured her in.

BUMP FINLEY SAT on the vinyl-covered stool at the counter of the Around the Clock Diner, keeping one eye on his mug of coffee and another on his great-nephew. The coffee pretty much stayed put. Three-year-old Jake was another matter. Once, when no one was looking, he had emptied a pepper shaker into a pot of coffee Mellie had left sitting unattended on a table. Nobody much had minded except that old geezer Luther Eggleston, who'd discovered Jake's experiment with his first swallow.

"You're grinning like you know something you can't wait to pass on, Bump," Mellie said, leaning one ample hip against the counter and taking a sip of her own mug of coffee.

"Naw," Bump said. "I was countin' on you folks for something worth tellin'."

At midmorning and midafternoon, The Clock was the place to congregate for most of the old-timers in Sweetbranch. Rose, Bump's niece, swore her beauty shop was the only place in town where gossip passed muster. At The Picture Perfect, Rose said, gossip was either deemed fit to pass along or died a fast death amid the fumes of permanent wave solution and copious amounts of hair spray.

Rose was Jake's mother and Bump pretty much let her run the show back at the house. But when it came to swapping tales, Bump had his own sources.

Mellie exchanged a glance with Hec Griffin, whose Adam's apple more than made up for his lack of a chin. Hec was the mayor *and* the funeral director in town, so Bump set great store by Hec's view of the world.

"Susan Foster's back in town," Hec said.

Bump raised an eyebrow over that one. "Thought she dang near died in that wreck a few months back."

"All we really know is what we heard from Betsy," Mellie reminded him.

Bump grunted. "And Lord knows it's been harder on her than on anybody."

They all chuckled, although after all this time Bump still felt a twinge of guilt for speaking ill of Betsy.

"Saw the girl on my way over here," Hec continued. "Knocking on the door of the Lawn & Garden."

Mellie took a new paper place mat over to the table where Jake sat coloring the one she'd given him when they came in. "Tag still in town?"

"Yep."

"Looking like the very devil, I'd say." Bump reached for the pot to warm up his coffee. "Seen him at his mama's funeral. Been up a lot of hours if you ask me."

"Nobody asked you, Bump Finley," Mellie said. "Rough as a cob, I'll grant you, but there's something about him . . ."

"Womenfolk! Rose said the same thing."

"I say they'll get back together now they're here in the same town." Mellie was a big one for predictions.

"Not if Betsy has anything to say about it," Bump reminded her.

"She's not exactly the sentimental sort, is she."

Hec threw his dollar bill on the counter and stood. "Still, might be interesting to have a few fireworks in town this fall. Either of you seen the girl, Susan's daughter?"

Bump and Mellie shook their heads.

"Spittin' image of Susan." He called back over his shoulder as he opened the door. "Hope Tag Hutchins still has a strong heart."

SUSAN SAT IN HER CHAIR on the side porch. She shivered slightly but didn't have the ambition to tackle the task of pulling up the ugly orange afghan her mother had tucked around her legs. She had started the job with her one good arm. The afghan had slid farther in the direction of her knees.

She liked the side porch. It was the only place she felt she could breathe in this house where they said she'd grown up. From here she could see the edge of the woods, the fluttering willow tree as it lost its leaves, and neighbors moving up and down the street.

The door back into the house opened directly into her bedroom. Not really her bedroom. She'd overheard her mother and understood right off that the house had been turned upside down to make room for Susan and her wheelchair.

"I've had to turn the family room into her bedroom, of course," Betsy Foster had said to someone on the phone the very night Susan had arrived. "Malorie is sleeping in Susan's old room, which is fine. But I've had to send the piano home with Steve. And the dining room furniture, too, because of this therapy she'll be doing. Seems ridiculous to me. She can't even walk! At any rate, I expect she'll be falling and I don't want her hurting anything. And I'm glad for Steve to have the furniture, of course. Still..."

There was a pause. Still, the silence said, Betsy Foster didn't mind one whit making all the sacrifices she was having to make. As long as it was known around town that she was making those sacrifices.

"Oh, no," Betsy continued. "I don't think you'd want to do that yet. I don't really think she'll want anyone to see her for quite a while."

When she heard that, Susan had also understood that she ought to feel ashamed of her present condition. She remembered she ought to feel grateful that her mother was even willing to take her in.

She thought it must be part of her illness that she didn't feel grateful. Why should she feel grateful for being a burden?

So Susan sneaked off to this screened side porch whenever possible, a place where she could pretend she had nothing to be ashamed of.

"Mommy?"

She turned toward the high-pitched voice, thinking she would have to force a smile for Cody. But, as always, his bright eyes made it easy to return his mischievous smile.

"Me can push?"

She leaned closer and lowered her voice to a conspiratorial whisper. "Not now. I'm hiding."

Although she wouldn't have thought it possible, the round-cheeked face grew even brighter. "Awright! Me, too?"

"Sure. You, too."

Cody clambered into her lap, which sent the slip-sliding afghan all the way to the floor. No matter. With Cody in her lap, the world already seemed warmer.

"Whatcha hidin' fwom?"

"A new doctor. He's coming today."

Didn't she wish hiding was possible! Right now, she would have given anything to sit out here in the fall sunshine long enough to avoid this first meeting with her new physical therapist. She wanted to get well. Had given her therapy everything she had back in Atlanta. But she had trusted her therapist. They understood each other. Yolanda knew how tough it was for Susan to remember little things, such as whether or not she had already shifted the weight from one leg to the other so she could take the next step. Yolanda didn't frown no matter how many times Susan couldn't get her left hand up to grab the foam ball when it was thrown in her direction. Even when Susan slurred her words or slumped in her chair or couldn't get a spoonful of soup from her bowl to her mouth, even at times like that, Yolanda had respected her.

Susan feared discovering that a new therapist wouldn't respect her. Or worse, that a new therapist would decide she had made all the progress she was ever going to make. That particular fear grew stronger daily.

"Him have a needle?" Cody squirmed around to aim a solemnly sympathetic look in her direction.

"Ooh, I hope not."

Cody nodded. "Me'll pertect you, Mommy."

"Thanks, pal."

Then Cody launched into a vivid retelling of his most recent experience with doctors and needles, while Susan reminded herself of the incredible joy of being able

to feel the breeze, see the bright colors of the falling
leaves and the dazzling autumn sky. While Cody chat-
tered, she pretended this accident she couldn't even remember had never happened. She was whole again. In
a few moments, she would get up and go to Lolly's
dance studio. She remembered Lolly because the
woman had visited her at the rehab hospital plenty of
times during her two months there. So Susan could
imagine talking to Lolly about the costumes she wanted
made for the next recital. And when Lolly left and the
studio was empty, Susan might stay behind for a while.
Might just punch the buttons on Lolly's fancy sound
system. The music would begin and Susan would rise
on her toes and leap into the air and settle back to the
ground with a sweep of her arms. She would dance.

She felt the thrill of the movement, as real as the
wiggly little body in her lap at this very moment.

"Me wants a party, Mommy."

"A party?"

"Mallie said so, for my birfday?"

She remembered a party then. A party on the lawn
right outside this very porch. A metal card table had
been set up and covered with a yellow-and-white paper tablecloth. Her mother—much younger then, with
a softness about her angles that made her less forbid-
ding than she was today—brought out a white cake
decorated with yellow roses. Nine yellow candles
burned on the cake and everyone cheered when a
gawky, freckle-faced girl with a wispy blond ponytail
blew them out. Susan knew she had been the girl, and
she could almost grab hold of the feeling of being
there, blowing out the candles, hearing the cheers.

In a sudden flood of memory, she could also picture
that same girl sitting on this porch with her best friend

Rose Finley and cutting paper dolls out of discarded Sears Roebuck catalogs. She remembered a man they all called Pops teaching that little girl—taller and even gawkier, now—to pitch, catch and bat before softball season. She remembered a basket of fabric and the tedious work of cutting that fabric into tiny, uniform pieces. She remembered—

Him again! The image shot through her, a jolt that left her heart thumping. She saw his face all the time. Lean and dark, sometimes teasing, sometimes brooding. And sometimes, ah, sometimes, tender. Eyes dark. Hair dark, flopping onto his forehead and covering the tops of his ears in a way that made her mother purse her lips tightly.

There he was again, sitting at her feet on this very porch, telling her things.... She tried so hard to remember what things. But all she could remember was the way those things had made her feel.

And a name. Without thinking, she breathed the name aloud, as if she might beckon him from the past.

"Tag."

TAG FIGURED HE MUST be crazy, because he gave the girl the job even though he knew who she must be.

He watched in fascination, barely listening as Malorie Hovis told him about her experience. Afterward, he couldn't have repeated a word of it. And it didn't matter. He hired her for one reason. He hired her because of the cloud of soft, honey-colored waves that floated around her face and nestled around her shoulders. He hired her for her pixie nose and the golden freckles that dusted it. He hired her for her half-shy eyes the color of the sky right before a storm, not quite blue, not quite gray.

He hired her because she had to be Susan's daughter.

"Really?" she said, her impish face brightening in delight when he asked if she could start the next day. "Just like that? You're sure?"

She sounded so much like Susan he wanted to laugh. Or cry.

"I said it, didn't I?" He questioned his sanity with every word that brought him closer to the thing that still had the power to bring him to his knees—his memories of Susan. "You're not hard of hearing, are you?"

She laughed in the face of his grumpiness. The same way Sam always did.

"Well, gee!" She stood and whirled around, her knee-length skirt swirling. The way Susan's long skirts had swirled when she danced, once upon a time. "This is really exciting! And... and I promise you won't be disappointed. I won't let you down."

Her promise brought a flash of bittersweet memory. Tag reminded himself that the last he'd known of Susan was her broken promises.

"Fine," he said, and tried once again to let go of the thing inside him that still hurt, that still felt betrayed.

He walked her to the door. Her eyes kept sweeping the high-ceilinged barn of a room, gauging its possibilities, he supposed. It seemed such a familiar mannerism; reminded him of the enthusiasm and excitement with which Susan had always viewed the world's possibilities. Even the possibilities in a skinny kid with oversize hands and feet who thought he could do something with his life besides follow in his old man's footsteps.

He'd damned sure been right about that.

It was when Malorie Hovis turned back to him once more, from the street, and said to him with such breathless innocence, "Thanks again. So much!" that he lost his resolve.

"You're Susan's girl, aren't you?"

A startled look crossed her face. "Susan? Yes. I am. Did you know Mother? From before, I mean?"

"Pretty well. She . . . she never mentioned me? Tag Hutchins?"

He waited with a hitch in his pulse. Surely he had been important enough to her to mention to a daughter. Surely . . .

When Malorie frowned and shook her head, Tag felt as if Susan had abandoned him all over again.

CHAPTER FOUR

SAM HATED SEEING the ones who had lost their fight. His Uncle Tag had been like that at first, long before Sam was old enough to understand what it did to a man to accept the fact that his legs or arms no longer responded when his brain gave the order to move.

Now Sam always knew his first battle—long before he could begin to tackle weak muscles or haywire coordination—was to help them rediscover their spirit. Without it, he knew, his task as physical therapist was a hopeless one.

This new one was one of those.

"We have to make an agreement before we get started," he said, squatting in front of her wheelchair to bring his eyes to a level with hers. Hers were haunted, fearful, with emptiness flirting around the edges. "Understand?"

She looked at him hesitantly, then shook her head. He smiled, to reassure her. He'd seen Susan Hovis's chart, knew her history. Knew her age, even, although it was hard to believe this woman with the elfin face and the wispy body was forty-four. The baby-fuzz hair that was just getting long enough to brush her ears made her look like a pixie; her softly freckled cheeks were smooth; the long-boned hands resting in her lap, elegant. He would have guessed her to be closer to his age than his uncle's. Which just went to prove Tag's derisive boast that he'd been ridden hard and put up wet too many times to have aged well.

If Tag was weathered leather, Sam's new patient was lambswool soft.

He took one of her hands—her good right hand—in his and squeezed it gently. "I'm Sam. Do you mind if I call you Susan?"

She hesitated, then gave a tentative shake of her head.

"Good. Now, we've got a lot of hard work ahead of us, Susan. Hard for me. But especially hard for you. Understand?"

She nodded.

Sam tried to keep his sigh inaudible. "I wish you'd answer me, Susan. Speak to me. Could you do that?"

Her eyes slipped away, focused on her lap.

"I ask because I want to know that you'll make this commitment, too. I can't do it alone. You're going to have to do most of the work. I need to know you're with me, Susan."

He stopped, waiting for her response. She continued staring at her lap. He felt the fingers of the hand he held twitch, a sign of nervousness, of agitation. That was good. That meant she understood. But he wanted more. So he continued waiting.

According to her records from the rehab institute in Atlanta, Susan Hovis had made more progress than she was exhibiting today. Her speech was still slurred and ataxia still made her wobbly on her feet, according to her records. But in the few days since leaving rehab, she had apparently retreated to a wheelchair and clamped her jaws tightly shut.

Having spoken with her primary caregiver, Betsy Foster, Sam wasn't surprised at the change in Susan.

Family reaction and cooperation could be a significant component in any patient's speedy recovery. And Betsy Foster struck him as a critical and contrary partner in the process. Or course, Sam had heard those things about her as he grew up, had seen signs of them occasionally at church. But his interview with her last week, before Susan arrived, had been his only firsthand encounter with Betsy Foster.

He had explained the techniques he would use in Susan's therapy, how he would initially focus on everyday tasks like dressing or feeding her young son or learning to bend over and retrieve things off the floor without falling. He had shown her some of the special adaptive equipment Susan could use to do little everyday tasks for herself, such as cutting her own food despite her weak grip. They would spend hour-long sessions each day on such simple tasks as learning to balance on one leg or to squat while holding on to the kitchen counter. He explained that Susan's love of dance could even be used to encourage her recovery.

A sharp furrow had appeared on Betsy Foster's high, wide forehead. "Dance? What a lot of nonsense! She can't even walk straight."

"With practice, she can learn to," Sam had said pointedly. "Look how far she's come already."

No matter how encouraging Sam had tried to be, Betsy's negativity pervaded everything she said. And apparently none of what Sam had said sank in. He'd noticed right away when he arrived this afternoon that, despite his instructions to leave the house just as it was, she had cleared the dining room of furniture and informed him to limit his work with Susan to that one room.

Her mother's outlook had apparently already begun to do its work on Susan. Sam hated having to fight his way through that, as well as through Susan's physical limitations.

"How about it, Susan. Are you with me?"

Finally, she looked up and nodded. He shook his head and shrugged, turning the tables on her. A frown flickered across her forehead. She pulled her hand out of his. Good. A sign of her willingness to fight. She was put out with him and not afraid to let him know it.

"Okay!" Her impatient exclamation was barely slurred. Apparently Susan Hovis's pride was intact. Also good. Pride could be a strong motivator.

"Okay what?" he persisted.

She grunted out a sound that he thought might have been a laugh, but before he could decide, a youthful voice sounded behind him.

"Mother, you won't believe what— Oh!"

Sam registered the relief and the welcome on Susan's face. Without standing, Sam pivoted, staying on Susan's level.

The woman who had entered was a softer, rounder, perkier incarnation of Sam's new patient. The daughter, he assumed. She brought a glow with her into the room, and suddenly Sam discovered he had few reservations about the prognosis for Susan Hovis. Once, he was certain, she had been just like this delightful package of energy and excitement. And she could be again. *Would* be again. He knew it, with the instincts that had come from working intensely with impaired patients.

"Sam Roberts," he said, extending his hand but staying at Susan's eye level. "You must be the sister."

Well, he wasn't above using a little of the old Hutchins charm to win a new patient's confidence.

The young woman laughed, shyness settling around her smile. "I'm Malorie. The *daughter*. I'm sorry to interrupt."

"That's okay. Susan and I were just getting to know each other. But I'll bet she'd like to hear your news. Wouldn't you, Susan?"

He looked at her, challenging her with his eyes.

She nodded, almost smiled.

"What was that you said, Susan?" he goaded.

Now his new patient's smile was more pronounced. "Yes. We'd like."

He felt triumph.

Malorie squatted, too. Her skirt settled softly over her knees and Sam tried to pretend he hadn't noticed the sprinkling of ginger-colored freckles on those knees. But when he raised his gaze, he found himself swept up in the girlish glitter of her blue-gray eyes. "I got a job, Mother. I'm going to be managing a store in town. Isn't that exciting? Imagine, *me*, managing a store."

Sam almost lost his balance, for he knew of exactly one store in the whole of Sweetbranch that needed a manager. And he couldn't quite imagine his crusty old uncle holding up against the youthful effervescence of Malorie Hovis. He grinned at the prospect. *Do the old coot good.*

"Good," Susan said, and Sam's heart turned over with the understanding of how much more must be in her heart, feelings she couldn't yet label, couldn't begin to express.

He was going to help open her up again. He knew that now. He was going to give her back to her daughter, give her daughter back to her.

And along the way, who knows, maybe Malorie Hovis could remind Tag that he, too, had been young once. This could be a win-win situation for everybody. He glanced again at Malorie as she chatted and wrapped a strand of hair around a long, lithe finger.

Everybody, he thought. Maybe even him.

MALORIE SAT CROSS-LEGGED in the grass and watched Cody's gleeful attempts to keep up with the other children. She'd brought him out both to keep him from getting underfoot while her mother worked with the therapist and to get away from the disapprovingly watchful eye of her grandmother. As soon as they hit the yard, a small but vocal horde of children had descended from across the street, bringing a rubber ball, a bicycle with training wheels and a bubble-making machine.

Malorie was relishing every moment she spent with Cody, although she felt she had to sneak around to do it. She'd missed so much of the boy's first two years. As soon as he'd been born, she was whisked off to stay for the next six months with her grandparents. *It will be better that way,* she remembered her grandmother saying, in that sharp, certain way she had, as if all the answers had been personally delivered from God straight to her ear. *Give everyone a chance to adjust.*

Everyone except me, Malorie thought.

But maybe that wasn't true, either. Maybe she *had* adjusted. Maybe it was only her mother's injury following so closely on the heels of her father's death that had Malorie feeling as if her emotions were up for grabs. As if her life might suddenly spurt free of the tight hold she had on it and scatter, like debris in the wind. What would happen, for example, if her mother didn't make a full recovery, was never again well enough to take care of Cody herself?

Traitorous, Malorie's heart gave a leap of excitement at the thought.

She laughed, suddenly, despite her somber thoughts, as Cody waved to her from his precarious perch on a dent-and-scratch bicycle. His stubby legs were too short to reach the pedals, but two of the little girls from across the street stood on either side of him, holding him securely, giving him a ride. His white-blond hair waved like dandelion fuzz in the breeze and his dimpled smile was bright as the sun.

"Your little brother's lucky to have you."

The deep voice behind her startled Malorie. She jerked her head around to see Sam Roberts standing between her and the house, his hands shoved deep into the pockets of his white slacks. His burnished-gold forearms contrasted darkly with the pristine uniform.

"How did it go?"

She caught his momentary hesitation.

"Pretty well."

"Not as well as you'd like," Malorie said. "She's depressed."

"She's angry." Sam dropped to the ground beside her. "You would be, too. Acquired brain injury is hard, because she remembers that she wasn't always like this. She *knows* she isn't what the rest of the world calls normal."

Malorie winced, felt the now-familiar tug of guilt and pain. "You should have seen her dance."

"Do you dance?"

She frowned at the personal question. "I'm not a talented person."

He looked inclined to disagree, but he didn't speak again right away. "Addy's kids seem to be enjoying your little brother."

"Addy?" She should have known who lived across the street, she realized. But she hadn't been into neighborliness when she stayed with her grandmother two years ago. She'd been into isolating.

"From across the street." He gestured toward a neat yellow frame house. "Addy Mayfield. Aren't these hers?"

"All of them?"

He laughed, a sound that was soft and deep and made Malorie want to laugh with him. She didn't. It didn't seem like a good idea, letting herself get close to people. Not right now, with so much else to worry about.

"Addy's the soft touch of Sweetbranch. None of them are really hers. Except for the little girl in the red corduroy overalls, and she's adopted. The rest are foster kids, of a sort. Abandoned. Neglected. Orphaned. That kind of thing."

A sharp feeling penetrated Malorie's heart. The laughter of the children playing in her grandmother's yard suddenly took on deeper poignance. "How sad."

"They seem happy enough," Sam pointed out. "Addy's special."

Malorie wondered at the love it took to embrace a child who wasn't your own, when so many birth parents couldn't do the same.

"I was thinking," Sam said. "Maybe Addy could help Susan."

"How?"

"Addy sews. Sells some of her stuff, actually, at a gift shop out on the highway. Maybe she could work with Susan."

A flutter of hope rose to the surface of Malorie's heart. "You think Mother can sew again?"

"Maybe. Trying will be good for her. And if she succeeds, that will be even better."

"But she already has reading and writing to work on, plus her therapy with you. Isn't that enough?"

He shook his head. Malorie felt a surge of confidence in the set of his jaw. Thank goodness for someone who was sure of himself. "The less time your mother has to sit around feeling useless, the better. You didn't like it, did you?"

Another flash of uneasiness. What did he know? "What do you mean?"

"Going out and getting a job while she recuperates. We all want to be productive, involved in things."

Malorie felt it wise not to disagree this once. She really wasn't ready to tell her mother's physical therapist that she would like nothing better than to climb the stairs to her mother's old bedroom and close the door on the rest of the world.

"What were you doing before Susan's accident?"

Irritation with his curiosity overcame her. She would have served up a rude reply to his nosy question, but she had been raised not to cause ripples. "College."

"Why don't you go back? Susan has her mother. No reason to disrupt your life any more than it has been already."

"I want to be here," she said tightly.

"What are you studying?"

She absolutely refused to tell him she hadn't had enough of a start on college to know what she planned to study. Instead, she stood. "I'd better take Cody in for his nap."

"Let him play awhile longer," he said, also standing. "He's having fun."

"He needs a nap." He took a step when she did, and she began to worry that she wasn't going to be able to get away from him.

"Lucky for him his sister is so much older. He needs a little more mothering than Susan can give right now."

"I don't mother him." Horrified, Malorie realized she had snapped at him. Uncertain what to do in the wake of her unacceptable behavior, she marched across the yard toward the children, aware that Sam was right behind her.

Before he could speak again, however, a thunderous roar filled the air. Frightened, Malorie turned to the street in time to see a sleek black motorcycle pull up at the curb. Leaving the engine idling, the rider yanked off his helmet, revealing a head of long, salt-and-pepper waves.

Her new boss. Had he come to fire her already? Had he suddenly figured out she didn't know a thing about running his store?

"Sam, you already telling tales to my new manager?"

Sam laughed and walked to the street, clapped Tag Hutchins on the arm. "Figured somebody ought to warn her off."

Malorie saw the resemblance then. Although Sam was sandy-haired and Tag as dark as the devil, they had the same prominent noses, rangy, muscular builds, and square jaws that spoke of hardheadedness. But while Sam looked loose and easy, Tag looked tough and prickly.

"Sam here's my nephew, Miss Hovis, and likely to say most anything to a pretty girl," Tag said, his voice gruff despite the teasing words. "I wouldn't believe much of what he says if I were you. 'Specially anything he says about his old uncle."

Malorie smiled, uncertain how to take the interplay between the two. She trusted the fondness she saw in Sam's face more than she did the crustiness in Tag's words. "I'll remember that."

"How'd you manage to be so quick on the draw making the acquaintance of the first pretty girl to come to town in twenty years?" Tag asked, combing his fingers through unruly hair.

"Her mother is one of my new clients," Sam said. "You might remember her, Tag. Susan Hovis. Used to be Susan Foster."

CHAPTER FIVE

READING AND WRITING were the things Susan had enjoyed most at the rehab institute in Atlanta.

With Betsy as her new tutor, she knew right away that was about to change. It was morning, the time everyone had agreed Betsy would tutor Susan in reading and writing. But Betsy quickly grew impatient.

"You mean to tell me you're still *printing?*" Betsy had snapped. "You'll never make progress at this rate. It's time you started working on cursive writing."

Susan was positive someone at the hospital had said cursive was not good, especially around children and the members of the clergy who came for daily visits. But she didn't say so to her mother, because Betsy's mood was sour enough without any help from her daughter.

"Okay, dammit," she had muttered, determined to use cursives if her mother wanted her to. Who knows, maybe it would help.

Susan had also tried to mimic the pencil strokes her mother showed her, but the results were disastrous, and soon Betsy had stormed away from the desk in Susan's room.

"Hopeless!" she had exclaimed. "Why are we putting ourselves through this!"

So the reading and writing lesson was short this morning. After watching Betsy grab her gardening hat and the key to her garden shed from the hook beside the back door, Susan decided she would work on her physical therapy, instead. With her mother out of the house, she wouldn't mind doing some of the exercises her new physical therapist had showed her the day before. There would be no one to remind her how silly and inept she must look.

She rolled into the hallway and paused, realizing she couldn't quite remember which direction to turn for the dining room. But Susan was learning not to panic when she couldn't remember the simple things that others took for granted. She knew if she sat here for a moment, she would think of what to do next.

Before she could think, however, a bell jangled in her ear. Startled, she turned toward the sound and saw the telephone on the highly polished library table. She stared at it for a moment. If she answered it, would the person on the other end be able to understand her? Would she say the wrong thing?

Swallowing against the sudden dryness in her throat and mouth, she reached for the phone with her good right arm.

Triumphant, she held it to her ear and even remembered what to say. "Hello."

The sound of the word made her smile. She had done it.

"Susan? Oh, Susan, that *is* you, isn't it?"

The happiness in the lilting drawl on the other end of the telephone line deepened Susan's smile. "Yes. Who are you?"

"This is Rose, Susan. Rose Finley." A laugh. "Well, Rose McKenzie now. You know, it's been almost four years and I still have trouble remembering that sometimes."

The woman's friendly laugh made Susan feel at ease, and she said, "I have trouble remembering some, too."

Rose's answering laughter made Susan feel they had shared a joke. She couldn't really remember Rose, except in the childhood memories that were beginning to surface. But she had mentioned her at dinner the night before, and Malorie had told her about the woman who had been Susan's best friend since childhood. Susan had been in Rose's wedding four years ago, Malorie had said, and had been named godmother to Rose and Ben's first child, a little boy named Jake.

"Gosh, Susan, it's so good to hear your voice," Rose said.

"I like it, too. Hearing yours, I mean."

"Can I come visit soon? This afternoon, maybe?"

A cloud descended over the sunniness Rose's call had brought. Susan remembered what her mother had said, remembered that she should be ashamed for anyone to see her right now.

"Not...not today. Soon. I can tell you when later."

They talked for a few more minutes, Susan pleasantly surprised that her speech was coming so easily. Then Cody toddled up and began trying to scramble into her lap. The distraction made it hard for Susan to concentrate on what Rose was saying. She said goodbye to her old friend, promising to call, although she couldn't imagine how long it would be before she felt brave enough to let outsiders see what she had become.

She tugged Cody into her lap and once again faced the dilemma of finding the dining room.

"Which way?" she asked Cody, who now snuggled in her lap. And she followed the direction of his pudgy finger, figuring he had at least as good a chance as she did of knowing where they ought to be going.

Cody turned out to be a master of navigation, and within minutes they were crossing the threshold into the room where Susan's first therapy session had taken place the afternoon before. For an hour, the physical therapist had made her practice standing, moving her feet a little closer together all the time. The young man had been right: it was hard work. Just balancing, after so many days of relying on her chair, had been exhausting and sometimes humiliating. Susan tended to shy away from that kind of hurt. But he was a nice young man and she liked the lines of his face.

Today when he came, she would concentrate very hard and perhaps she would be able to remember his name.

For now, Susan wanted to try some of the exercises he had shown her the afternoon before. She would be alone—Malorie was off at work, at her new job. Susan smiled, remembering how pretty her daughter had looked in her soft, gauzy dress, printed with tiny pink flowers. Looking so grown up and at the same time so much a little girl, at least in Susan's mind. She wondered if regular mothers thought their grown children still looked like babies, or if that was one more bit of warped thinking that came with her accident.

"But that's what *I* thought, anyway," she said to Cody, who was just about the only person she didn't mind hearing her clumsy speech. After all, Cody's diction needed some work, too. "Didn't you? Pretty and young?"

Cody looked up, his round face eager and his blue eyes wide. A milky crust from his morning cereal clung to the side of his pouty pink mouth, making Susan smile. Was she supposed to wipe his face, the way they had reminded her to wipe her own back at the hospital? Or was he supposed to do that for himself? Never mind, it looked baby sweet and she decided to leave it.

"Okay, down." She urged Cody to hop out of her lap as she rolled her chair up to the pull bar that had been attached along one wall just over the chair rail.

The little boy looked up, smiling even as he issued an adamant reply. "Not down. More ride."

"Not more ride," Susan insisted. "Down."

For the next five minutes, Susan wondered if everyone had as much trouble negotiating with two-year-olds. At least other people had two good arms to lift the boy and put him wherever they wanted him. Susan had to appeal to his cooperative nature, which apparently was not well developed.

She felt tired by the time she had given him two trips around the perimeter of the dining room. But Cody had also grown tired of riding and cheerfully scrambled down. He toddled over to his pile of coloring books in the corner of the room and Susan once again rolled to the pull bar.

"Tired," she said with a sigh. But she remembered the stern look her therapist at the hospital had always given her when she tried that excuse. Mimicking Yolanda's standard retort, she said, "Tired don't win no races."

With her good right fist tightly in place and her less effective left elbow hooked over the bar, Susan pulled, using her good right leg for further leverage. Remembering the games she and Yolanda had played in the early days when any movement seemed agonizing, she pictured a determined lion in her mind and let out a long, low growl as she slowly rose to her feet.

She stood, gripping the bar, leaning one hip against it, but standing nonetheless. An instant of exhilaration flooded through her and she heard a baby-sized cheer from the corner of the room. Pressing her lips together to keep them from trembling, she looked over her shoulder.

Cody sat, a coloring book spread open across his lap, and clapped his hands together. "Yeah, Mommy! Good girl, Mommy!"

For a moment, Susan thought she might have to sit again to allow the tears that had risen in her eyes to subside. But she blinked them back, managed a thanks that might have been intelligible only to a two-year-old, and focused her attention on her left leg.

"Okay, move!"

Before she got her toes three inches off the ground, some kind of bell rang. This one was different from the bell that had rung earlier, when Rose called. Susan froze, struggled to interpret the sound. Squeezing her eyes together, she tried to force her brain to come up with an explanation, with a course of action. But when the noise came again, she still had no answer.

"Mommy, door. Me get door?"

Susan let out a frustrated sigh. The doorbell. Of course. Someone was at the door. But what in heaven's name could she do about it?

FED UP WITH ACTING civilized, Tag pounded on the door. *Somebody's home and they can damn well answer.*

He'd steamed over it all night. Actually, he'd steamed for a while, then started to stew over it, and finally, about daybreak, he'd erupted into a full-blown boil.

Imagine, Susan was right across the street and couldn't be bothered to call. As if nothing had ever happened between them. As if she didn't owe him…something. An apology. An explanation. Some damn thing.

When his insistent pounding on the door raised no more response than ringing the bell, Tag decided they must've seen him coming. Must have it in their heads to freeze him out. The way they'd been freezing him out for the past twenty-odd years.

Screw that.

Barely making an effort to check his pent-up rage, Tag shoved the big, pristine-white front door open, barely noticing that it slammed with a thump against the coat tree as he stormed into the entrance hall.

"Susan!"

Silence.

"Come down here right now!"

He looked up the curving flight of stairs toward her room, but before he could make up his mind what to do, he heard a noise from the dining room. He looked down the hall and saw a flash of movement as someone ducked back inside the door.

He was in the dining room in six quick strides, not even pausing to notice anything about the house or the rooms he hadn't set foot in in more than a quarter century.

"Susan, dammit, I—"

The sight of her stopped him in his tracks, stole the words and the breath right out of him.

She huddled against the far wall, hands behind her. Her hair was a short, soft halo around her pale, thin face, and for a moment Tag wanted nothing more than to mourn the loss of her long, blond ponytail. Ah,

Lord, how many times had he remembered the feel of that soft stream of hair sifting through his fingers? He took another step in her direction and saw her flinch.

He had frightened her, and that angered him all over again. "After all these years, I think you owe me an explanation, Susan."

She only stared at him, her stormy eyes growing bigger as she seemed to sag against the wall for support.

"Don't you think I deserve that, Susan? *I* waited. Why the hell couldn't *you?*"

She shook her head haltingly.

"I'm not going away, Susan. Not until I understand. I've spent half my life trying to explain it away. Now I want a few answers. Don't you think I deserve that much?"

He noticed her legs seemed to tremble and he had an instant of sympathy for her. Maybe this was just as hard for her as it was for him. Maybe she, too, had her moments of regret. Maybe—

"Who—?" Her voice, always soft, was something more now. Weak.

"You promised to wait, Susan." He heard the pleading in his voice and was powerless to stop it. "Why, Susan? Why didn't you wait?"

She shook her head again. Her whole face was tense with effort. "Who? Who...are...you?"

For a moment, he entertained the notion she was trying to hurt him more, was saying this insane thing purely to cause him more pain. Then everything sank in. The confusion on her face. The limp left arm that had fallen away from the metal bar that lined the wall she leaned against. The wheelchair nearby. And, finally, the long, pink scar inching along her right temple, across her forehead, disappearing into the soft, short growth of new hair.

The ground shifted, buckling beneath Tag's feet. He staggered back, touched the door frame for support.

"Susan?"

Further awareness slapped him in the face. The spacious dining room, empty save for this woman and her wheelchair, a floor mat for exercise, and a variety of foam balls in different sizes. The kinds of things his nephew used with patients in rehabilitation. And hiding behind the wheelchair, peering out at Tag, a little boy in diapers.

Of course, Sam had said she was his patient. But he hadn't imagined, somehow, that it was serious. Not his Susan.

Tag looked back at the woman who had haunted every memory for so long and was stricken with a bitter knowledge. The Susan he had longed for, hated, come to confront, that Susan no longer existed.

He turned and ran out of the house, back to the motorcycle at the curb.

He couldn't ride fast enough to leave behind the memory of her pale, thin face and those wide, confused eyes. Eyes that had no idea who he was.

OPERATING ON GUT-LEVEL instinct she didn't understand, Susan lunged after the fleeing man. But the message didn't reach her left leg and it refused to budge. With a small cry, she landed in a heap on the floor.

Over the sound of Cody's wails, she cried out to the man. She couldn't understand the bereft feeling filling her heart as the roar of an engine met her feeble call. She sat on the floor, unable to decide what to do, unable to make sense out of what had just transpired, unable to dispel the sense of doom in her heart and head.

She automatically opened her arms to the crying little boy who sought her comfort, although she was too disoriented for a moment to remember why he called her mommy. But she held him, anyway, certain she could have no comfort for him when she so plainly had none for herself.

The only thing clear in her mind was the raging darkness in the eyes of the man.

She had wanted so desperately to help him, to tell him what he wanted to know. But his sudden appearance, his vague familiarity, had created a jumble of thoughts and sensations in her. Joy and excitement and pain had whirled through her. Nothing was clear to her, while he stood there shouting at her, except the small, still voice that said if she could reach him, if he held her in his arms, everything would be all right again.

But he was gone and nothing was all right.

Susan wished she could cry, the way Cody was, with relish and abandon.

"Oh, for heaven's sake! I just knew something like this would happen!"

Betsy's sharp voice broke through Susan's misery. She looked up, feeling inexplicably guilty.

"Didn't I always tell you, Susan Marie Foster, that young man is trouble?"

Betsy snatched Cody out of Susan's arms, set him on his feet and looked him in his watery eyes. "Nothing to cry about, little man. Susan is just fine and so are you. No thanks to Tag Hutchins."

Betsy bent down to help Susan back into her chair.

"Tag?" Susan asked, remembering the word that had come into her mind so many times since returning to Sweetbranch.

"Tag Hutchins is nothing but trouble. Never has been anything but trouble. He's not to come into this house again. Is that clear? I won't have him disrupting things."

Susan was breathless now, both from the excitement and the struggle to return safely to her chair. But she had to know. "Who is Tag?"

Betsy looked down at Susan, her square hands on her square hips, her lips drawn into that thin, unyielding line that made Susan wish Yolanda was around to help her pop a wheelie in her wheelchair.

"Tag Hutchins is nobody you need to concern yourself with. If you don't remember, so much the better." Betsy marched around to the back of Susan's chair and pushed her toward her bedroom. "Now, why don't you have a nice rest. Working so hard at all this therapy business isn't good for you. Rest is what you need."

"Have to work," Susan insisted as her mother prepared to close the door to her room and leave her alone once again.

"What you have to do is accept reality, Susan. You'll never be the way you were before. Get used to it."

The words chilled Susan to the bone. Before the door closed, she called out, "Quilt."

Betsy sighed heavily. "What now?"

"Quilt. I want my quilt."

Betsy pointed at the bed. "There's a quilt on your bed."

"No! *My* quilt."

"That's the only quilt you've got, young lady. Now, calm down and rest yourself for a while."

The door slammed shut. Susan felt tears at the back of her eyes again and gave one of her wheels a spin, sending her chair whirling in a circle. She spotted the quilt folded at the foot of her bed, a blue and green Log Cabin she had made for her parents' thirtieth wedding anniversary. But it was not the quilt she wanted. In that incomplete part of her mind that was memory, she could see the one she wanted, a quilt of interlocking circles made up in the colors of pink-and-white azaleas she had seen somewhere.

Susan closed her eyes tightly shut and tried to hold the image in her mind. If she only had that quilt, everything would be better. If she couldn't be held in the man's arms, the quilt would help. She just knew it would.

TAG HIT THE BRAKE, spinning his rear tire and spitting out a shower of gravel. His bike stopped a half foot shy of the rear bumper of Sam's van. As Tag yanked off his helmet and hung it from a handlebar, Sam appeared at the garage door of his house.

"That was almost a grand entrance," Sam said, wiping flour-dusted hands on his jeans.

"I'll do better next time."

Tag pretended not to notice Sam's heightened interest once he heard the tone of his uncle's voice. He knew how he sounded, because he knew how he felt. But he wasn't in the mood to talk about it. Or hear one of Sam's lectures, either.

Then what the hell are you doing here?

"I'm hungry," he growled. "When's supper?"

Sam's response was half grunt, half chuckle. "Just finished rolling out the biscuits. I'll get a juice glass. You can cut."

If anybody else had expected Tag to cut biscuit dough and lay it out in a baking pan, he would have bellyached clear to Sunday and back. But he could see that Sam had his hands full with the mashed potatoes—no dehydrated flakes, just potatoes and butter and milk—and the gravy he was stirring in the pan where he'd just fried the chicken. Besides, Sam made damn fine biscuits. If Tag could get in on a couple this easily, he was game.

"You must've known I was coming," Tag said later as they filled their plates and sat at the antique oak table in the middle of his nephew's eat-in kitchen. "All my favorites."

Sam cocked an eyebrow at him. "I had a hunch."

They exchanged a look.

"I saw you leaving the Foster house today. You looked . . . like you might want to talk."

Tag did want to talk, and he didn't. What could he say to his nephew that would explain the demons that drove him? Instead, he forced himself to concentrate on the satisfying crunch of the fried chicken, the buttery richness of the potatoes. By taking solace in the food, he might be able to put today out of his mind—for now. But today no amount of speed, no amount of wind in his hair, had been enough to rid him of his anger, his bitterness, his images of Susan. The feelings had all but eaten him alive.

And the most intense, most frightening feeling of all was the one that kept insisting his life could at last be made whole if he could once again hold her in his arms.

How long had he fought to accept the fact that would never happen? And how quickly had he abandoned his resignation when he saw her? More important, how long would it take him to resign himself to the inevitable again, now that he knew the truth?

The woman he'd never stopped loving didn't even know him.

Would she ever? The question had haunted him all day. He needed the answer, and he feared it.

"You should have talked to me before you went over there," Sam said.

"Lots of 'shoulds' on the road to hell, Sam."

"What's the story, Tag?"

Tag placed his fork on the edge of his plate, all the fight draining out of him. "It's an old one. We were kids. Thought we were in love. That's about it."

Said like that, Tag thought, it didn't sound so bad. Maybe, now that he'd seen her, this old obsession would start to heal.

Then the sweet softness of her voice, speaking to him out of some darkness where he couldn't go in to save her, washed over him again. And he doubted he would ever heal.

"And?" Sam prompted him.

"And nothing. I told you. That's it. End of story."

Sam looked at him skeptically and Tag rewarded his nephew with a stony glare.

"I thought we could...catch up." He shrugged. "Guess not."

"She didn't know you?"

Tag shook his head.

"It'll come back to her, Tag. Things are coming back every day."

Tag almost wished he hadn't heard that. What he didn't want, didn't need, was a reason to hope.

"Tell me what happened," he said at last, almost against his will.

Sam said things Tag understood only well enough to know that he hadn't really wanted to hear them. Acquired brain injury. Some permanent damage. Recovery slow and difficult. Some motor impairment. Some speech impairment. Behavioral changes. Memories wiped out. Like starting over, an infant trapped in a grown-up body.

"Damn it, Sam." He clenched his fists between his knees and looked up at his nephew. "Can she...will she..."

"Every case is different, Tag. I've seen some miraculous recoveries."

Tag latched on to that one word. Miraculous. He'd never had much faith in miracles. Didn't know how to start at this late date, either.

Sam's soothing professional delivery was designed to inspire such faith, Tag knew, so he took little comfort as his nephew continued.

"How much recovery she achieves depends on how severe the damage. And how determined Susan is."

Without realizing it, Tag smiled. "That's one thing on her side, then."

"I thought so," Sam said, smiling back.

"I...should I stay away?"

Sam considered the question and Tag waited, uncertain what answer he wanted to hear. "Hard to say," Sam said at last. "If seeing you is going to upset her the way it did today..."

On the ride home from Sam's house in the country, Tag had plenty of time to think. He realized he'd forgotten to ask his nephew about the cozy picture he'd made with Malorie Hovis the afternoon before. But he quickly forgot that again, lost it in the memory of the Susan he had met that morning.

This was worse torment, even, than thinking of her all those years with another man.

CHAPTER SIX

WITH A SHARP BUT undefinable longing as her constant companion, Susan settled into a routine.

Mornings were the low point of the day. After Susan stubbornly struggled through the laborious process of bathing and dressing on her own, Betsy came in at ten. Stern and unencouraging, Betsy waited to pounce on the slightest mistake while Susan read from a Little Golden Book or practiced printing. Her letters were wobbly and her reading halting, so Betsy had ample opportunity to pounce.

"I can't imagine why you put yourself through this," Betsy said at least once every morning.

Susan couldn't, either, to be perfectly frank. She only knew that both of them were usually out of sorts by the time their hour was over. Even Cody, playing in the corner, had usually resorted to whining and throwing his plastic race cars by the time he'd listened to enough of Betsy's fussing.

Once Susan tried to ask her mother about the angry man who had come to the house. Over and over again, he came into her head, giving her no peace. She wondered why he was angry. Where he had come from. What she might have known of him in her other life.

But all she could manage to ask was, "Why are you mad at the man?"

Watching her mother's reaction, Susan grew anxious. Betsy grew very still and very quiet, and gradually every tiny bit of expression drained out of her pale blue eyes. When Susan at last became convinced there was no soul left in her mother's body, Betsy said, "What man?"

And then Susan was truly afraid. For hours she'd worried she had invented the man in her mind and made him so real she believed in her own fabrication. And if that were so, how sick did that make her? It wasn't until the middle of the night, when the light from the moon filtered through the bare trees and the lacy curtains played on the far wall of her room, that Susan realized the truth.

The only way Betsy could control the man was to pretend he wasn't real.

Susan couldn't have said why she was so certain of the truth of that, but deep in her heart she knew it was so. And it made her less afraid of her own fuzzy memories of the man.

She didn't mention the man again, and as the days passed, Betsy grew more agreeable in the mornings. Still, she seemed to think her daughter's reading and writing were a waste of time. Susan told herself sometimes that was only Betsy's way of denying another reality. Maybe Betsy liked controlling her daughter, too.

Early afternoons were better than mornings. Addy came three afternoons a week, right after lunch, a basket of fabric scraps and yarn needles and scissors tucked under her arm.

"Got your sewing hat on, Susie-Q?" the neighbor from across the street always asked, pulling a wicker chair up close to Susan's wheelchair.

Susan didn't quite know what the question, or the funny name, meant. But Addy asked it with such infectious enthusiasm that Susan never failed to answer with a nod and a big smile of her own.

Sam had asked Addy Mayfield to come. The first day she came, she brought a big tote bag full of pillows and place mats and even stuffed dolls decked out to look like angels. She made them all and sold them at a gift shop on the highway, she said as she settled into a chair on the side porch.

"It'll help me if you keep me company while I work," Addy had said that first day. "I understand you did a lot of sewing before your accident. Maybe you'd like to start up again. How'd you like to cut out some patterns for me?"

Susan had looked down at her thin hands, especially the left one, which still didn't like to cooperate most of the time. Right now she was wearing the ugly brace Sam said would keep her weaker arm from curling in, growing even more useless. Then she looked up into Addy's warm brown eyes and all she could say was yes. This was was all Sam's doing, she knew, a way to improve her fine motor skills. But she found she liked both the company and the work. While Susan plodded along with her swatches of fabric and her clumsily wielded scissors, trying to recapture gestures that had once been second nature, Addy clipped and stitched and chatted.

"How many?" Susan asked, incredulous, as Addy talked about her children and gathered a row of ivory-colored lace to create a halo for the angel she had appliquéd onto a pretty pink apron.

Addy eased the lace along her gathering thread. "Five. Two boys, three girls."

With her soft, cinnamon-brown ponytail and petite build, Addy looked very little older than Malorie. The mystery of motherhood grew deeper for Susan as she contemplated Addy and her five children. "And a husband, too?"

Addy laughed. "Definitely a husband, too. The *best* husband, in fact."

Susan smiled back at her new friend. She liked hearing that Addy had the best husband, because she already liked the bubbly woman. "All of them look like you?"

Addy's smile dimmed, but only slightly. "No. None of them look like me. They're only foster children, really. Except for one. She's adopted."

Susan frowned. "Foster children?"

Addy paused. "My foster children, they. . . they really belong to someone else. I just take care of them until their real parents can take care of them again."

Susan could see that something about her explanation made Addy sad. "Like Cody. Maybe you should have Cody for a while."

Addy leaned over to help Susan repin a pattern that had come loose. "Cody has plenty of love right here with you and Malorie. And his grandmother."

Susan watched and listened as Addy reminded her again how to push a pin through to secure the pattern to the fabric. Handling the tiny pins was hard work for her clumsy fingers, but not as hard as remembering what she was supposed to be doing.

When she grew weary of the task, she placed everything flat on her lap and said, "Tell me again about the best husband."

By the end of the first week, Susan could cut fabric in a fairly straight line and she knew the names of each of Addy's five children by heart.

Sometimes she rested after Addy left. Sometimes she did the exercises Sam wanted her to do—the bridge to raise her bottom off the floor and the straight leg lifts.

Late afternoons were Sam's time. Susan both dreaded the physical therapy and welcomed it greedily. Some days he had her practice changing Cody's clothes or tying his shoes. She worked in the kitchen, opening soup cans or buttering bread or pouring from a pitcher. Some days she spent the entire hour trying to balance on one leg or the other. Once he tried to coax her into one of her dance steps, but she refused.

Always, her body shook and trembled and perspired. The sessions were sometimes painful and always frustrating, reminding Susan as they did of her body's betrayal. Each muscle, it seemed, carried the memory of a leap, a turn, a dancer's move, for she had danced for her own pleasure since childhood. But her injured brain would no longer process the memory in those muscles.

Susan couldn't dance. She could barely walk.

Without Sam's confidence in her, that realization would have been too bitter for Susan to confront each and every afternoon.

During her forth session, she was standing on her right foot, with the left propped in her chair, trying to catch a large foam ball when he threw it. The trick was to do all those things at once without landing on her backside.

"Can I ever dance again?" she grunted out, breaking her concentration and almost losing her balance.

"Whenever you're ready," he said.

Susan stared at him.

"You're the key, Susan. You can't do any of this until you're ready."

"*I'm* ready," she insisted, stubbornly. "*Legs* aren't ready."

"They won't be, either," Sam said, dropping the ball and walking over to steady her as she placed her left foot back on the floor. "Not as long as you spend so much time in this wheelchair."

She glared at him as she settled back into the seat of the chair. How could he possibly understand how excruciating it was to know that walking from one end of the room to the other—an action the rest of the world took for granted and accomplished in a matter of seconds—might take five minutes. And might land her in an undignified heap in the middle of the carpet, at that.

"You don't understand," she accused him.

"*I* understand. *You* don't understand. You have to be willing to fail before you'll make any real progress."

Susan wanted to shout at him that she understood all about failure, that she felt it acutely each time she hoisted herself awkwardly over the edge of the tub for a bath, each time she couldn't manage to lift her own son into her lap. But she couldn't dredge up the right words from the ruins of her brain.

That made her all the more angry.

"Why don't I take the chair away, Susan? You'll progress so much—"

"No!" She started wheeling herself out of the room. "No, no, no!"

But no matter how many tantrums she threw, Sam was always back the next day. He was as stern as Betsy, but he added smiles and encouragement. And that made it possible for Susan to keep going.

Often Sam stayed on after the sessions were over, braving Betsy's brittle reception to sit on the screened side porch outside Susan's bedroom and enjoy the late afternoon sunshine. At least, that's what Susan thought he was there to enjoy. After the third time, however, she realized that what Sam really waited around for was Malorie.

Malorie always showed up about twenty minutes after the end of Susan's sessions with Sam. She glowed, it seemed to Susan. And as soon as Sam saw her, he instantly grew more charming.

"How are you getting along with Mr. Hutchins?" he asked, and they exchanged a look that Susan thought spoke of some shared secret.

"He's a very interesting man," Malorie said, a little dimple sneaking up at the corner of her mouth. "If you like rough edges."

"And do you?"

Malorie's cheeks grew pink. "I can take them or leave them, actually."

"Can you?" He smiled and looked at Malorie as if he didn't quite believe her. "You're sure about that? The Hutchins charm is pretty potent."

Releasing her long hair from the messy knot that had kept it out of the way all day, Malorie ruffled her honey-colored curls to loosen them. The act gave Susan a bittersweet memory of trying to tame and smooth those waves with rubber bands and hair barrettes in years long gone.

Then Malorie raised her chin and directed her most impudent smile at Sam Roberts. "Are you assuming you've inherited some of that potent charm? Or is it just the rough edges you share?''

He smiled back and stretched his long legs out in front of him, taking up the width of the side porch. ''I never thought of it.''

Malorie laughed at that, and Susan couldn't help herself. She laughed, too, although she wasn't quite sure why.

''What commendable humility, Mr. Roberts.''

Then Malorie flipped her shoes off and ran out into the yard in her bare feet. She grabbed Cody up from his solitary game of racing plastic trucks and gave him a big hug. Sam seemed content to watch the two play together for the next half hour. It was only when Betsy came out with her prim reminder that supper would be on the table in fifteen minutes that Sam finally left for the day.

Susan watched as he walked out through the side yard, where he paused to speak to Malorie. She backed away a step as they spoke, but stared after him as he walked to his van.

Watching them stirred up that unidentifiable longing in Susan once again. She remembered... but she couldn't name what it was she remembered.

The next day, Sam brought the puppy.

''For Cody,'' he said, letting the short-legged, round-bellied, sand-colored pup loose on the dining room floor. With a delighted squeal, Cody dropped to the floor beside the puppy. ''No boy ought to be without a four-legged best friend.''

The afternoon's physical therapy consisted primarily of playing with Cody and his new best friend, who was instantly christened Butch. The only one not thrilled with the new addition to the family was Betsy

Foster, who immediately recited ground rules governing puppy ownership. Rules that no one but Betsy even listened to.

When Malorie arrived after work, she acted even more delighted than Cody. Once again kicking her shoes off, she got down on the floor with Cody and Butch, squealing as Cody held her face so Butch could deliver a puppy kiss.

"You look like a woman who's never been kissed before," Sam said, sitting on the floor and rolling Butch around with one of his broad hands.

Again, Susan noticed, her daughter grew pink in the cheeks. "Not by a puppy."

"No?" Sam looked at Susan, a stern frown on his face. "Do you mean to tell me your daughter never had a puppy? Not in her entire life? Shame on you, Susan."

"I want a puppy kiss," Susan replied.

And Sam delivered Butch into Susan's lap, helped her hold the wiggling, tail-wagging puppy up to her face. Susan laughed when Butch obliged with a warm, wet slurp under her chin.

The three of them watched and laughed while Cody and Butch played. Betsy, after her initial tight-lipped reaction, stayed away from the noisy fun. The only thing they heard from her for the rest of the afternoon was the staccato rap of a butcher knife on the chopping block in the kitchen.

To Susan, her mother's work had an angry, lonely sound to it.

When Sam offered to take Malorie to the grocery store for puppy food and chew toys and other essentials of puppy parenthood, Malorie rose from the floor and shook her head.

"No need," she said, smoothing her skirt as if she'd just remembered to act grown-up. "I'll go after supper."

"I'd like to take you," Sam persisted.

"You've done enough. Thank you."

"It wasn't much. I like your baby brother."

Malorie, already standing primly straight-backed, seemed to grow stiffer yet.

"Come on," Sam persisted. "We'll have fun. I'll show you the twenty-seven varieties of dipping snuff in little tin cans on aisle nine. Bet they don't have *that* in Atlanta."

Malorie ducked her head and dimpled. Susan thought she would agree then, because he'd made her smile. But when Malorie looked up, she'd managed to bury her smile again. "I don't think so, Sam."

After supper, when Cody was in bed and Butch banished to the garden shed on Betsy's orders, Malorie sat beside Susan's bed and read to her from the morning paper. Susan tried to listen to news of a business in Muscle Shoals adopting a poverty-stricken neighborhood, offering job training and moral support and donations for day-care and rec centers and refurbished bikes. But she was more interested in understanding the interplay she saw each day between her physical therapist and her daughter.

"You should like Sam," she said at last, knowing her comment wasn't subtle but no longer certain how to initiate the polite little subterfuges she knew most people employed.

"I like Sam," Malorie said, rattling the paper.

"No. *Really* like him."

"Mo-ther. Don't be silly."

"*You* don't be silly. He likes you. I can tell."

"He's your therapist, Mother. And I'm not interested in a romance."

Susan smiled. "Did you ever have a romance before?"

Malorie frowned and gave the paper another noisy shake. "Do you want to hear the rest of this story or not?"

"Not."

"Fine. Then you can go to sleep."

"Not sleepy. I want to know why you don't like Sam."

"I do like Sam, Mother. I—" Malorie folded the paper and set it aside, then leaned over and clicked off the bedside lamp. She stood in the moonlight and looked down at Susan. In the silvery darkness, Susan thought she looked barely older than Cody, her forehead puckered in a frown, her lips settled into a full pout. "I do not need a boyfriend. Not now."

Susan watched as her daughter walked toward the door. "Because of me?"

Malorie looked over her shoulder and spoke softly. "No, Mother. Not because of you. Because of me."

MALORIE TOOK THE STAIRS slowly, knowing it was too early to sleep. But the only alternative to retiring to her room was keeping her grandmother company. So she called out a soft good-night to Betsy and climbed the stairs.

She stopped on the way to her room and eased open the door to the room where Cody slept.

The full moon made the night-light unnecessary. Cody lay on his back, arms flung wide, legs tangled in the sheet. He had already kicked the blanket to the floor. She tiptoed in, indulging herself for a moment as she tucked the covers around him neatly once again. His body was sturdy and warm and his hand involuntarily groped toward her as she touched him. Just as involuntarily, she pulled away before the sleeping toddler could grab her.

She hurried on to her room, as if she could walk out on her thoughts of Cody and Sam and the confusing set of lies that were— now that her mother no longer shouldered part of the burden—hers alone to bear.

TAG FELT HIMSELF pulled into the sparkling enthusiasm in Malorie's soft blue-gray eyes.

"So I think," she was concluding, "that if we offer a landscaping service, instead of just selling the plants and shrubs and shovels people need to do it themselves, you'd not only have a new source of income, but you'd sell more of your original product line as well."

She sat back then, quite pleased with herself to judge from the small, expectant smile on her face. Just looking at her like that, the way Tag did a dozen times a day, was both a torment and a joy.

"Source of income?" Tag repeated. "Original product line? Hell, Mal, this isn't Atlanta. This is Sweetbranch. People fertilize their own azaleas and yank their own weeds. Sweetbranch doesn't need—or want—landscaping. We've got yards and vegetable gardens, not landscapes."

He noted that her self-satisfied smile did not dissolve into shrinking uncertainty at his gruff tone.

"Excuse me, Mr. Hutchins, but you haven't been around Sweetbranch in a long time and—"

"Oh, and you're the long-time local expert, I guess."

"And I believe you aren't in touch with what has happened here in recent years. Sweetbranch has changed, Mr. Hutchins."

"Changed? Sweetbranch? That'll be the day, Miss Hovis."

"If you'll look around, you'll see that Sweetbranch is thriving, Mr. Hutchins. Thanks to Ben McKenzie's paper plant, there are plenty of jobs. Did you know that last year alone twenty-five new families moved to Sweetbranch because of job opportunities?"

Now she definitely looked pleased with herself.

"Who told you that?"

She pointed her pencil at him. "It was in last week's edition of the *Sweetbranch Weekly Gazetteer*, Mr. Hutchins. We have a tavern now in the abandoned church on Main Street. The story said business was up in all the old businesses along Main Street, from The Picture Perfect to The Clock, sometimes as much as ten percent over last year alone. If you're smart, Mr. Hutchins, you'll pay attention to me, since I obviously have my eyes open."

"And I don't, is that what you're saying?"

Her only response was to give her chin a perky little lift and walk away. "I have a customer, Mr. Hutchins, if you'll excuse me."

Hellfire and damnation, but she's the spittin' image of Susan.

Oh, not so much in her looks, although they had plenty of similarities. Malorie was a honey blonde, with thick, bouncy waves, where Susan's hair was soft and fine and pale as corn silk. Malorie's skin was honey-gold, too, with a fine bloom in her cheeks, where Susan had always been as pale as a porcelain doll. Malorie was tall and softly muscular, where Susan had been fine-limbed. But as far as piss-and-vinegar, they were damn sure cut from the same cloth.

Everything about this musty old store brought out the fire in Malorie's eyes. She saw the possibilities and they revved her up, just the way possibilities had always revved up Susan. For Susan, the world had always been a magic music box, playing a new tune each time she opened it.

Tag hadn't remembered feeling that way himself in a long time. Malorie reminded him that, once, he had.

He'd tried staying away from the store, but each time he saw Malorie, the pull grew stronger. He loved the reminders, and he hated them.

Some days being around Malorie was the only way he kept himself from obsessing over Susan and the fact that she sat in a wheelchair just a few blocks from here, needing help. Some days he wanted to offer that help, needed to offer it with a longing so intense he felt the hurt in the tips of his fingers.

Other days it was all he could do not to listen to that mean streak in him that had been his only defense against pain these past twenty years. The part of him that kept telling him Susan deserved a little pain, too, for not keeping her promise.

But not too much pain.

CHAPTER SEVEN

1969

TAG WONDERED HOW HIS brother had popped the question.

For once he would've been glad to follow in Elliott's footsteps. But Elliott wasn't around to ask. Wouldn't be around to ask, ever again.

The ground beside Willow Creek was damp and the fallen limb where Tag rested his head didn't make much of a pillow. He already felt the cool dampness seeping into his jeans and through the back of his clean T-shirt. It would be hours before Susan finished her shift at the Dairee Dreme and joined him. By then, Tag knew, he would be uncomfortable and lonely and bordering on grouchy.

He also knew that as soon as he saw Susan's cheery face peering around one of the pine trees, as soon as he heard her expectant voice calling his name as she approached the creek bank, all that would disappear.

In the meantime, damp ground and all, this was a better place to be than home.

Here, at least, he could pretend that the days of magic that had started in the summer of 1967 would go on forever. Here, at least, he could forget about the letter to Eugene Hutchins, Jr., lying on his dresser. *Greetings, my ass.* He might even be able to forget about the headstone in the graveyard down by the church, where Elliott's name was etched onto a small, white stone. He wouldn't have to think about the new baby boy, Sammy, who would never know what kind of daddy Elliott would have made.

All those things were still too strange and too overwhelming for Tag to feel them yet.

Tag closed his eyes against the memories swimming in his head. He'd hoped being outside, in the place where he'd spent so much of the past two years with Susan, would make the time he had to kill pass more quickly. Being at home had been no damn good. He'd showered after work, then sat in his room staring at the letter on his dresser, staring at the baseball glove he'd brought in from Elliott's room after... after. Staring at the small, fuzzy ring box and wondering why it had taken him all this time to realize how much easier life could be when you had a big brother.

Too late to be realizing that.

Tag thought he might freak out sitting up in his room all alone. But the rest of the house was off limits, because his old man had been sitting downstairs making friends with a bottle of whiskey and his mama had run out to church to lose herself in her charity work.

That left Tag with plenty of time to worry over the dreams that were about to be blown to pieces.

He lay on the creek bank, hands clasped behind his head, and tried not to think of that first summer with Susan. The very best days of his life. But trying not to remember those days, and all the others that came after, was as futile as trying not to touch her lips with his when she was nearby. As futile as trying not to want to do what their own good sense—and fear of the consequences—told them not to do.

Memories of that first summer called him like a dream, promising him sweetness and joy.

Crash's teasing hadn't meant much, after all. Tag had spent every moment she would give him with Susan. Not that she gave him enough moments to suit him. She wouldn't give up her dancing time and she wouldn't give up her reading and she wouldn't give up the hours she spent hunched over that darned Double Wedding Ring quilt for her hope chest.

Just finding out the name of the thing had given him the heebie-jeebies.

"Never mind what it's called, Eugene Hutchins," she had said with that almost haughty lift of her chin. "This quilt is none of your concern."

"Sure it is, Susie," he said, marveling at the endless rows of tiny, even stitches she made. He was certain that no other girl in all of Sweetbranch High had such long, elegant fingers, capable of such sure and nimble movement. Tag told himself he was a low-life swine to watch her fingers work the needle and wish they were moving as surely and nimbly over other territory. But the thoughts crept in, nonetheless, and Tag vowed to feel the guilt later. "Susie, I want to know everything about you. I want us to do everything together."

A funny, uncertain look wrinkled her forehead. "Well, *I* don't want it to be like that, Tag. I've seen other kids date like that and they end up hating each other."

Tag had frowned, too, because he couldn't imagine another way to be except one hundred percent wrapped up in Susan. "Then what *do* you want us to be?"

"I want you to be with me because you *want* to and not because you *need* to."

"Aw, Susie, you're making everything too complicated. Just tell me what you call the quilt. I really want to know."

So she told him, and he discovered he really didn't want to know as much as he'd thought.

Still, Tag had sat at her feet on the side porch of her big two-story house on Mimosa Lane and talked with Susan for hours while she pushed her needle in and out, in and out.

They talked about Vietnam, which few other kids were doing then.

"Are you scared about it?" she asked him, a question that would have been off limits with the guys.

Tag thought he probably wasn't supposed to answer with complete honesty in front of a girl he wanted to impress. But something about Susan left room for nothing *but* honesty.

"Yeah. I guess I'm just chicken, but I don't want to go over there. I don't want to think about shooting people. Or..."

"That's not chicken," she said, pausing long enough to put her fingers on his shoulder.

Her tiniest touch zapped him like a high-voltage shock. Tag told himself he was a real sicko, feeling that way about a sweet girl like Susan. A perfect, innocent girl like Susan. Sometimes he wished her kisses weren't quite so warm. Sometimes he wished her small, high breasts weren't quite so soft against his chest. That his hardness didn't find such a friendly haven in the V of her thighs when they stood by Willow Creek and kissed.

Sick, Hutchins. Sick and pathetic.

He told himself those feelings were for other kinds of girls. But they were so strong with Susan. And they didn't *feel* wrong. No, they felt way too right.

She argued with him when he told her, after the fireworks on the Fourth of July that first summer, that he'd decided not to leave for college in September.

"Tag, that's crazy! Why would you even say that?"

"I've got a new job, Susie. A better job, on a construction crew."

"Is that what you want?"

She'd sounded so dismayed at the thought that Tag had a moment of doubt about his decision.

"I want to be with you."

She shook her head, her stubbornness all rolled up into one big frown. "That's wrong, Tag. You can't do that. You've got to do what's right for you and—"

"What's right for me is staying here and saving my money. I'll start college when you do. You'll see."

Still she looked uncertain, and he pulled her into his arms. Just having her there, all soft and warm against his chest, confirmed that he'd made the right decision, no matter how much Susie protested. "It's perfect, don't you see? We can be together and I can save up. And then..."

He stopped, because he wasn't ready to tell her what kept coming into the back of his mind. He wasn't sure he was ready to say the words out loud. But he kept thinking about other kids who got married and went off to college together. Two can live as cheaply as one, they said.

But saying so out loud might scare off Susan. After all, she was only sixteen.

Heck, saying it out loud might scare *him*.

"But can't you see, Tag, that's not right. For you to put things on hold like that, just for me."

"Not for you. For me. For us."

He kissed her then, careful to keep his hands at her waist and out of trouble.

But when summer ended, a lot of people got bent out of shape when Tag didn't pack up and leave Sweetbranch. Tag's old man, for one, who found a lot of excuses to drink over the fact that his boy gave up a shot at college ball and wouldn't help out in the family business, either. Crash Foster, for another, who had only applied at the junior college in Birmingham because he thought Tag was going to be there, too.

"Holy moley, Tag, this just isn't right! Friends are supposed to stick together. And here you are ditching me for a *girl.* " Crash almost ran down a mailbox on the corner of Mimosa Lane, he was so upset. As it was, the mailbox took a swipe along the passenger side of the car, but it hardly mattered, the old Studebaker was already so battered. "Not just a girl. Cripes, Tag, my *sister!* You're crossing me up for my *sister!* "

Tag couldn't manage much beyond a guilty shrug. Crash was right, and he knew it. But Tag was in love and he didn't know how to fight it. Didn't even *want* to fight it.

But the person most bent out of shape when Tag's change of plans came out in the open was Susan's mother.

Betsy Foster marched across the street and demanded a summit with Tag's mom and dad, which ended abruptly when Eugene Senior smashed a half-empty bottle of whiskey against the fireplace. Betsy Foster then talked to the minister, who preached the following Sunday on the evils of the flesh. Finally, in desperation, she wielded the secret weapon every young couple dreaded most.

"Young man, I forbid you to see my daughter again," she said, her presence on her front porch so formidable that Tag forgot, for a moment, that she was neither as tall nor as broad as he was. "I have all the respect in the world for your mother, Eugene. But you are your father's son, and I won't have you ruining Susan's life."

"But that's not fair. I'm not—"

"You are wasting your breath, Eugene. And my time. Susan is underage. I think you'd best keep that in mind."

For the first two months of the school year, Susan was so intimidated by her mother's implied threat that she refused to see Tag. For two months, Tag couldn't remember ever being so miserable in his life—not even the summer he was fifteen and he'd done it for the first time with Lida Cooper and she told him she was late. Heck, he hadn't even known what that meant until Crash told him. Then he'd had to spend the next three weeks having nightmares about marrying Lida Cooper and having a little baby with a bleached-blond beehive.

No, that was nothing compared to those two months without Susan.

He went to the homecoming football game in November, knowing he would see her and not sure which would be worse, going and having to pretend he didn't want to hold her and kiss her and talk to her, or staying home alone and thinking about her, wondering if she went alone, wondering what she would wear for the homecoming dance that followed the game.

He was almost sorry he decided to go.

Susan sat smack on the fifty-yard line, in the middle of a bunch of squealing, silly high school juniors on row three in the old stone bleachers out back of the school. Tag watched her from the tenth row near the end zone, which was as high as the bleachers went, and as far away from her as he could sit without going to the visitors' side of the field, which would have set everybody in Sweetbranch to talking. She wore a bright red coat with a black, furry collar, because it was a cool night. Her hair was all done up in little curls on top of her head, with a big red satin bow in back. She looked so sweet and pretty, Tag thought he might start tearing the bleachers apart with his bare hands if he had to look at her much longer.

Then, at halftime, she went out onto the field with the three other girls who were nominated for homecoming queen. She left her coat in the stands and went down on the arm of weasely Edwin Plankton with his glasses and those stringy Beatles bangs. Her dress was creamy white and fit snugly across her small, high breasts, and Tag ached with the memory of those breasts against his chest. She wore a corsage with red ribbons to match the bow in her hair, and when she was crowned homecoming queen, Tag knew everybody could see that Susan Marie Foster was the most beautiful girl at Sweetbranch High—and too good for the likes of Eugene Hutchins Junior.

She spotted him that night when she was going back to her seat after halftime ceremonies, and froze right in the middle of effusive congratulations from Rose Finley, her auburn-haired best friend who had been her only real competition for the homecoming queen crown. Susan's eyes locked with Tag's, and he saw that she was still as miserable as he was.

Knowing it gave him no peace.

In fact, he thought as he pulled his old Ford into his driveway later that night, it might have been easier to put her out of his mind if he'd been able to tell himself that Susan was okay, that she'd forgotten him, that she was now in love with that creepy Edwin Plankton. But he'd seen the misery and longing in her eyes, and he couldn't stand knowing it perfectly matched the misery and longing he'd been living with for two interminable months.

As he killed the engine, Tag toyed with the idea that he might have to leave Sweetbranch.

Clutching the steering wheel in a death grip, Tag was consumed with wondering how far he would have to go to leave Susan behind. So consumed was he that he didn't realize he was no longer alone until he heard the passenger-side door shut. He jumped, startled. Was even more startled when he looked over to see Susan sitting beside him, the black, furry collar of her coat snugged against her chin.

"Susan..."

"I can't do it anymore, Tag."

Her presence stunned him. "But Susan..."

"Just kiss me before I absolutely die from missing you, Tag Hutchins."

And because flying would have been easier than saying no, he did kiss her, with the taste of sweet fruit punch on her soft lips and the tickle of her collar on his chin.

In an instant, he grew painfully hard, and dangerous thoughts possessed him. Knowing he risked going too far, he tried to keep the kiss gentle. But Susan teased against his lips with the tip of her tongue and all the good sense in the world couldn't have kept him from opening his lips and meeting her tongue with his.

"I love you, Tag," she whispered. "Nobody's going to keep us apart."

The words were oil on the fire inside him. He pulled her tightly against him, aching to feel her soft curves and grateful when she let her coat fall open. The pin from her corsage jabbed him in the chest, but he barely noticed, he was so enthralled in the pleasure of feeling her against him once again.

"I love you, Susie. I've been crazy from missing you."

He didn't know exactly how it happened, but as they kissed and murmured, he gradually realized that his hand was grazing the top of her thigh, above her stocking, exploring the forbidden territory of garters and silken flesh. Susan sighed and he felt heat against his fingers. Susan whimpered and thrust the heat against his palm. Tag followed instinct and found the damp softness of her. He explored, the pressure building within him. She cried out then, softly in the darkness, and Tag felt himself gripped in shuddering release.

Instantly humiliated and frightened beyond words, Tag drew his hand away from her dangerous heat. She murmured an incoherent protest, reached for his hand. But Tag took her by the shoulders and pulled her firmly away from his chest.

"Susan, we can't do this. Don't you see? This isn't right."

In the darkness, he saw her lower lip tremble. "You're afraid of what my mother will do, aren't you?"

"No. Listen to me, Susan. I'm afraid of what *we'll* do."

"I'm not." Her chin went up defiantly, one of the many Susan-gestures that he loved.

"You're barely sixteen. I don't want us to spoil it by...making a mistake. I want it to be perfect."

She crossed her hands across her chest and glared out the front windshield. "And when will I be old enough for it to be perfect, Eugene?"

"When you're old enough to marry me, that's when."

Her shoulders lost their stiffness and her chin came down a notch. Slowly she turned to look at him again. "You mean that?"

"I mean it."

Susan's mother fought them all the way, of course, but Tag also wouldn't agree to sneaking around, either. By the end of Susan's junior year, Betsy Foster had just about given up her ranting and raving, probably because everybody in Sweetbranch had gotten so tired of it nobody listened any longer.

Tag worked construction every day, enjoying the hard labor, barely noticing as his eighteen-year-old chest broadened and hardened. He learned that a lot of the men he worked with were like his father, too ready to drink when their fears threatened to confront them. And he made up his mind not to be like that, ever. He worked hard and saved his money and stayed out of his father's way. What money he didn't save he gave to his mother. And what time he wasn't working, he spent with Susan.

He taught her to drive his noisy old Ford with its crotchety stick shift, laughing with her the first four times she rolled all the way back down the hill at the stop sign on Cottonwood Way.

They visited Crash at his first apartment in Birmingham, after he flunked out of junior college and started working for the electronics nut who kept saying computers were the future.

They celebrated her seventeenth birthday, and his nineteenth. They visited the hospital when Tag became an uncle, both feeling funny over such grown-up stuff. Feeling funnier yet when they both looked at the tiny, red-faced baby in the crib and glanced at each other, each realizing the other had been entertaining possibilities.

They fished in Willow Creek on Saturdays with old Bump Finley, who had turned up, as Tag's mama put it, like a bad penny, to move in with his brother's family around the corner on Dixie Belle Lane. He'd left town decades ago in a fit of temper, folks said, and now he was back, having lost his job and his retirement benefits in another fit of temper. But Tag and Susan learned to love the cantankerous old man, who sometimes gave a reluctant chuckle as the young couple splashed and cavorted in the creek Bump vowed was sacred ground, set aside for fishermen only.

Susan taught Tag to dance—real one-two-three slow dancing—in her family dining room the weekend her parents went to New Orleans for a Shriners' convention. He stepped all over her feet, and she laughed as delightedly as if he was Fred Astaire.

The weekend they brought Elliott's remains home from Vietnam she also held his hand, squeezing it tight every time he thought he was going to lose his cool in public.

And he watched her make steady progress on the Double Wedding Ring quilt while they daydreamed about the future. They talked with delight about how poor they would be. About how hard they would work. About how wonderful it would be in that little married students' apartment off campus with nothing but hand-me-down furniture and their quilt to keep them warm.

And they waited and hungered and sometimes got carried away by the desire that grew stronger every day. But never too carried away.

Now, as Tag lay on the ground and watched darkness settle over Sweetbranch, he wondered how much longer he would have to wait. How many more years it would be before their dreams would start coming true.

He heard the crackling of a footstep in the woods and looked up in time to watch her slip between the trees. She was smiling expectantly, her hands behind her back.

"I thought you'd never get here," he said.

"I stopped by the house. I have a surprise."

She swept her arms around in front of her and the quilt came tumbling open, falling in a rose-and-green-and-white sweep to the moss-covered ground. She smiled at him over the edge she still held in her arms. "I finished. It's ready now and it won't be long until—"

Her happy smile, her hopeful words, brought every fear in Tag's heart bubbling to the surface. He turned away, dropped his head into the hands that rested on his knees.

"Tag, what's wrong?"

And she was beside him, her arm around his shoulders. Just her nearness eased some of his fear.

"I've been drafted."

"Drafted? But—" She sank onto her knees. He looked into her confused eyes, watched as realization slowly crept into their smoky gray depths. "Drafted?"

He nodded. "I've got two weeks."

They were silent, communicating their misery and fear with their eyes.

"Will you...will they...you won't have to go to...?"

"There's only one reason they draft anybody, Susan. Everybody's going to Vietnam."

"Oh, Tag!"

She threw her arms around him, and they held each other for a long time, until darkness was all around them. Moonlight sparkling off the creek was their only light.

Tag drew strength from holding her. Enough strength, at last, to draw the little fuzzy box out of his jeans and place it in her hands. She hesitated, then opened it. The tiny chip of a diamond barely twinkled in the moonlight.

"Oh, Tag! It's beautiful!"

"I wanted...hoped you would want to...make it official before I go."

Her bright smile returned. "Oh, yes! How soon can we do it, Tag? While you're in boot camp, I'll get us a little apartment and before you go, we can be together every single minute and—"

He chuckled at her typically Susan, full-steam-ahead solution to every problem. "Whoa, now. I just meant we'll be engaged. That way it'll be official that we're going to get married as soon as I get home."

She closed the ring box with a snap. "Engaged? Tag Hutchins, I don't want to be *engaged*. I want to be *married.* If you're going off God knows where, I want to be your wife!"

The strength of that devotion, Tag knew, was all he would need to see him through whatever lay ahead. He smiled.

"Susan, you're seventeen. You have another month of high school. Your mother would—"

"My mother can eat gravel in her grits for all I care! I'm not letting you go off without marrying you first. And that's that!"

He took her in his arms, but she held herself rigid. "It's not the right thing to do. Don't you see that, Susan?"

"How could it possibly be the wrong thing for us to get married?" she wailed.

"Because you're too young. Because I won't leave you here trying to act like a grown-up married woman all by yourself. Because I want it to be *right* when we do it."

"It would be right, Tag. It couldn't be anything but right. Why can't you see that?"

And she kissed him then, fiercely, as if she could make him see just how wrong he was. Her lips were hard and insistent and urgent against his, and he met them with all the emotions he'd bottled inside himself since opening the letter the afternoon before.

She threw herself into his arms as they kissed, her fingers winding through his hair, her legs tangling with his. All Tag knew, as they fell back onto the quilt, was that he never wanted to let her go, that he couldn't bear the thought of letting her go.

"I love you, Tag," she whispered against his jaw while one of her hands slipped up under his T-shirt and clutched at his chest.

"Oh, God, Susan, I love you, too."

She looked into his eyes then, and pulled away from his embrace. Before he could ask what was wrong, she was unbuttoning the little brown shirt that was part of her Dairee Dreme uniform.

"Susie..."

"Just hush, Tag Hutchins," she whispered with the stubborn set to her chin that he knew so well. But he had trouble watching her chin, for her shirt was off and she wore nothing beneath it. All he could see were her small, perfect breasts with their dusting of freckles, puckered into small, tight points.

Knowing better, he reached out and felt one of those small, tight points with the tips of his fingers. Susan closed her eyes and gasped.

Tag pulled his hand away. "We can't do this, Susie. We've waited all this time. We have to—"

"If you're going to make me wait to be your wife, we're at least going to know there's something real between us, Tag. You're taking something with you. And I'm keeping something here with me."

She slipped her skirt down around her ankles, then stepped out of a scrap of yellow bikini panties. Tag groaned at the nest of pale curls between her legs.

"Susie, are you sure you know—"

"I'm sure."

She dropped to her knees once again and pulled his head to her breast and Tag was lost. He took her nipple in his mouth, swirled his tongue around it, groaning again, but deeper this time as he felt her open the zipper on his jeans and take him in her long, elegant fingers.

He knew then it was going to happen because there was no way he had the strength to stop himself any longer. So he touched her, there between her legs, and felt the hot, damp place where he'd wanted to be for so long. He touched her, heard her breath become ragged and quick.

He pushed her back onto the quilt and threw his own clothes into the pile with hers. He kissed her then, all over, although she tried in her impatience to hurry him. By the time he finished kissing her, touching her, she was writhing and calling out to him.

"I'm going to go crazy, Tag, if you don't love me soon."

He knelt and let the tip of his erection touch the hot, wet place between her legs and struggled not to come right then. "It might hurt," he said. "I don't want to hurt you."

She arched up until the tip of him was just inside her. Then she wrapped her long, slim legs around his waist and pulled him into her in one swift lunge. She cried out and so did he. He held her buttocks in his hands, holding her still against him until he could be sure he wouldn't explode and spoil everything.

When they started moving together, slowly, tentatively, Tag watched her face until he was certain she wasn't hurting. Watched until her nipples puckered once again and a slow flush covered her freckles and her eyes grew hazy. Then he could contain himself no longer.

Afterward, he stayed inside her, growing hard again before he had fully lost his first erection.

When the moon went down hours later and they folded the Double Wedding Ring quilt and walked to the edge of the woods, he kissed her one more time before she ran back to her house to sleep alone.

"I'll be waiting, Tag. Wherever they send you, however long it takes, I'll be waiting for you."

Tag held on to those words for a long time, hearing them over and over in his heart like a prayer; they saw him through times when faith in Susan was the only thing sustaining him.

CHAPTER EIGHT

MALORIE FOLLOWED her grandmother to the car, wishing Addy Mayfield hadn't been available to stay with Susan. Wishing she knew where to find the gumption to stand up to Betsy Foster.

"I don't *want* to go to church with you," she would say. "I don't *want* to get to know anyone in this town. I don't *want* to get a life."

In your dreams.

For, as she buckled Cody's carrier into the front seat, Malorie knew the bitter truth. She was no more able to stand up to Betsy Foster than her mother was. She didn't even have the courage, at this moment, to brush Cody's soft cheek with the back of her hand, which she ached to do. And all because she didn't have the nerve to risk one of her grandmother's stern, disapproving glares.

Nagged by the certainty that she deserved her misery, Malorie climbed into the back seat as her grandmother started the pristine six-year-old Cadillac. Although Reid Foster had been dead and his dealership in new hands for five years, the new owners still treated Betsy Foster like a queen when she came in for service.

Cautiously, the way she approached everything in life, Betsy backed the car down the driveway toward the street. She had almost reached the end when the roar of a motorcycle destroyed the Sunday morning serenity of Mimosa Lane.

Betsy braked to a stop a bit too abruptly. Malorie looked over her shoulder to discover that Tag Hutchins' big black bike sat squarely in the Foster drive. It idled noisily. Tag stared through the rear window, one arm resting on the helmet that sat on his thigh. With the other hand, he slowly revved the bike's engine.

Despite herself, Malorie smiled. Her boss was not like anyone else she'd ever known. He, too, intimidated her. But somehow she didn't mind that as much as she minded being intimidated by her grandmother.

Betsy shoved the Cadillac into Park. "Well, of all the nerve!"

Malorie half expected her grandmother to get out of the car and confront Tag Hutchins. But she didn't. Instead, after a moment, Tag swung one long leg over his bike and slid off. Dangling his helmet from a thumb, he approached the driver's side window, leaned over and peered into the car.

"Mornin', Miss Malorie."

Malorie smiled. His words were polite, courtly even, but his voice was, as always, as rough as a gravel road. Indeed, Tag looked rough all round this morning. Heavy stubble darkened his lean face, his too-long hair was rumpled and his eyes were bloodshot.

"Good morning, Mr. Hutchins. You're looking well today."

He chuckled, something he rarely did. The deep, pleasant sound ended abruptly as he turned his eyes back to the woman behind the wheel.

"Thought you deserved fair warning," he said, his voice matching the coldness in his eyes. "I'm going to see Susan again. Now that I know…where things stand with her.''

A thrill of uncertainty traveled up Malorie's spine. What was it he'd said? See Susan *again?* How odd that no one had told her.

Mostly, though, she loved the way he was speaking to Betsy Foster. As if daring her to be her usual cranky self. Malorie shoved her hands into the folds of her loose gauze dress and clenched them tightly, waiting for Betsy's reaction.

''You'll do no such thing, Eugene Hutchins. You've set her back already.''

Malorie opened her mouth to protest, but had no opportunity to speak.

''She's a grown woman now, Betsy. You can't stop me.''

''She's barely competent. You don't want a thing to do with her.''

The words cut Malorie, and she could see Tag flinch at them, as well. ''You leave that to me to decide.''

He turned to leave, but Betsy Foster wasn't finished. She twisted and called after him in a shrill voice Malorie had never heard her use. ''I will not abide trouble from you, Eugene. Stay away from my house or I'll have the law on you. You hear me?''

Tag's only response was to swing into the seat of his bike, bring the engine to a deafening roar and wheel around in a U-turn. He exited Mimosa Lane in a flurry of noise that made Cody whimper and Betsy flush an angry red. Malorie tried to unclench her fists but couldn't quite manage to relax.

As she gave one more sideways glance in the direction of Tag's grand exit, Malorie noticed Bump Finley and his young nephew and niece, Krissy, all dressed for church, standing on the corner, also staring after Tag. Malorie almost smiled again, knowing how much her grandmother would hate having an audience to such a disorderly little scene.

Betsy rolled up her car window and backed out as if nothing had happened. "Stop whining, Cody. It's just a big noise and nothing for you to be afraid of."

Malorie pursed her lips and realized her nails were cutting into her palms. As the Cadillac purred up Mimosa Lane, she tried to swallow the questions she knew would not be welcome. Halfway to church, she discovered a small pocket of courage deep inside her that said she didn't care whether her questions needled her grandmother or not.

"What have you got against Mr. Hutchins?"

"What I think about that man is none of your affair."

Malorie felt a knot of apprehension growing within her. She plunged forward, before her courage was overcome completely. "Why don't you want him to see Mother?"

"I know what's best for Susan. I'll thank you not to question that."

Anger shot through Malorie with a force that surprised her. Frightened at what the unexpected anger might produce, Malorie decided she'd better keep quiet until it was gone. She forced herself not to think about the ugly way her grandmother had characterized her mother as mentally incompetent. She forced herself not to think about the way Betsy Foster thought she had the God-given right to make the rules in everyone's life.

She definitely wouldn't think about times she had let her grandmother call the shots in her own life. At the time, she had assumed her grandmother was right, that

Betsy Foster had only Malorie's best interests at heart. Now she wondered. Now that it was too late to turn back.

She didn't protest when her grandmother insisted on leaving Cody in the church nursery, although Malorie had hoped to hold the little boy on her lap, taking comfort in his warm, plump body and his unwavering affection. She simply listened to the sermon and sang along with the hymns. After the service, her grandmother took her by the elbow and maneuvered her through the clumps of people gathering in the churchyard.

"We'll fetch Cody in a minute," Betsy said. "I see someone I want you to meet."

I don't want to meet anyone. Malorie protested loud and clear in her own mind. But as everyone had always done with Betsy Foster, she kept her mouth shut. Betsy stopped beside two women, a smiling auburn-haired woman named Rose who had once been her mother's best friend, and an ebony-skinned woman with an abundance of braids and bright-colored clothes with an ethnic flair.

"Maxine Hammond." Betsy interrupted the two women without hesitation. "This is my granddaughter, Malorie. I'd like her to help you with that Christmas charity project of yours."

Maxine arched a brow at Betsy, directed a regal smile at Malorie and said, "But does your granddaughter wish to assist in our project?"

Malorie sighed. "Hi. I'm Malorie. I'd be glad to help."

"Would you, indeed?" Maxine exchanged a look with the other woman. "What do you think, Rose? Do we have need of such an *eager* young recruit?"

"I think we can use all the help we can get if some of the kids in this county are going to have a merry Christmas." The calm assurance that Rose Finley McKenzie emanated made Malorie instantly envious. "Why, Betsy, I'll bet you're planning to write a big old check to see to it we can get a few more gifts from Santa, aren't you?"

"Well, I—"

"Uh-oh." Rose gestured over Betsy's shoulder. "My Uncle Bump's headed this way and he's looking awful grouchy. You didn't do anything to set him off this morning, did you, Betsy?"

Betsy frowned and glanced around. Sure enough, Bump Finley was headed in their direction. Malorie had met him only briefly, at a wedding years ago and once or twice when he'd brought Rose's son over to play with Cody. With his flyaway white hair and colorful suspenders, he had always struck Malorie as funny and grandfatherly. But right now, as Rose had noticed, he looked very determined and very displeased.

"Don't be ridiculous," Betsy said. "Jacob Finley and I have nothing to say to each other."

Bump Finley obviously had other opinions on the matter. He walked right up to Betsy, favoring a bad right knee, and took her by the elbow. "You and me's got a bone to pick, woman."

"Jacob Finley, I suggest you let go of my arm right now and—"

"And I suggest you hush your mouth and come along or I'll speak my piece right here in front of God and ever'body." His watery green eyes shifted in Malorie's direction.

With a heavy sigh, Betsy Foster said, "Ladies, if you'll excuse me, it appears Jacob intends to do what he does best—behave unpleasantly. I will spare you all the scene."

Although Rose and Maxine chuckled as the two walked away, Malorie heard the sharp exchange between the pair.

"You have gone too far this time for sure, Jacob!" Betsy Foster hissed.

"Just because you do it with ever'body else, don't think you can steamroll all over this old coot, too," Bump replied, not bothering to lower his voice. "I saw the way you were acting this morning, and I aim to tell you what I think about the way you try to run the whole goldanged world."

Malorie felt her face growing warm and wished she could slink away. Whatever must these people think?

She felt a gentle hand on her shoulder and looked up into Maxine's warm eyes. "Pay them no mind. None of us do. They have bickered for years."

"They have?"

Rose laughed, a throaty, delightful sound. "The way I heard it from my mama, they bickered the whole time they were sweethearts. Breaking up didn't even slow 'em down."

"Sweethearts? Grandmother?"

Both the women, who looked about the age of Malorie's mother, laughed.

"We were all young once, my dear," Maxine said. "Now, if you are indeed willing to help us provide Christmas for needy children in our area, we would be most appreciative of the help. In fact, we have our first meeting in—" she glanced at her watch "—about ten minutes."

Finding she was grateful for an excuse not to accompany her grandmother home, Malorie agreed to stay for the volunteer committee meeting. Betsy picked up Cody, and Malorie followed Maxine and Rose into the Fellowship Hall in the basement of the church. In minutes she felt at ease with Rose and Maxine and was soon laughing along with their humor, which was alternately sharp and wry.

"So you see," Rose said, finishing a story about her twice-a-week commute to the University of Alabama, where she was working on a degree, "I had to tell that uppity young'un that he might be the graduate assistant and I might be a freshman, but I just happened to be full grown when Vietnam was going on, while he was likely still in diapers. So if he was as smart as he pretended to be, he'd better be listening to me."

Laughter died on Malorie's lips when she caught sight of Sam Roberts lounging against the table in the center of the room, talking to the group of six others who had already congregated for the meeting. Out of the uniform he wore each day when he worked with Susan, he looked more disconcertingly human than usual. His smile looked warm, and not just professionally encouraging. His eyes were bright, his fair hair rakish with his casual tweedy slacks and collarless shirt.

She wished she hadn't been reminded quite so unexpectedly that Sam Roberts was not just a physical therapist. He was also a man.

She almost turned and left the room. But Maxine was looking at her quizzically. And, worst of all, Sam had turned at the sound of their laughter. He had seen her, too. She didn't like the welcoming look in his eyes.

"Ah," Maxine said as she saw where Malorie's gaze had landed. "I see you know at least one of our volunteers. This is excellent. Sam will be glad to take you under his wing, will you not, Sam?"

Sam smiled and pulled an empty chair away from the table and offered it to Malorie. "It would be my pleasure."

Malorie had no choice but to sit next to Sam. The chairs, she discovered, were crammed too close together around the unsteady folding table. Sam's sport coat was draped over the back of his chair and his crisp white sleeves were rolled halfway up his forearms. She noticed, as she had before, the strength in those arms. She told herself she noticed only because she was grateful to know her mother was in such capable hands.

Malorie pulled her own arms closely against her body and waited for the prickly sensations to leave her.

"They're all nice people here," Sam whispered as the others scraped chairs on the linoleum floor and took their seats. "They'll like you."

Malorie frowned and turned to retort that she wasn't worried about not being liked by this roomful of small-town strangers. But as she looked into Sam's eyes, she found herself drawn deeply into their dark depths, and she couldn't quite mouth the flippant words. She found she didn't mind that he seemed to see her fear.

She smiled at him and nodded. But she didn't relax her arms. She didn't loosen her hold on all she'd bottled up inside.

BY THE TIME MAXINE Hammond had outlined plans for the church's Christmas charity project, Sam had pretty much decided he had fallen in love.

Falling in love with the daughter of one of his patients gave him a few moments of uneasiness. But Sam figured he had waited a long time to fall in love—not that there hadn't been plenty of other women along the way—and he had no intention of letting anything interfere now that he'd found the magic that kept so much of the world in turmoil.

At twenty-seven, Sam welcomed a little cockeyed thinking, and he had a hunch Malorie Hovis would provide just that.

He followed her out of the Fellowship Hall, up the steps and out into the autumn sunshine. He knew she knew he followed her, but she continued to ignore him, just as she had ignored him for the past hour, when she also knew his eyes were on her.

She hadn't fidgeted, although nervousness sparked off her like noon sunshine off a tin roof. Instead, she had wrapped her arms tightly around her and stayed perfectly still. As if she might be overlooked if she remained motionless.

Sam didn't see how it was possible that anyone wouldn't notice her, wouldn't be captivated by her presence.

Malorie Hovis struck him as a sprite, a fidgety, fly-away sprite who might be easily startled away from the blossom where she perched. By a sound. A movement. A touch.

Yes, certainly by a touch.

But the aura of intensity that clung to her skin like a faint perfume was the only thing about her that spoke of rigidity. Her hair was a tumble of unruly curls. The freckles that hadn't faded with the passing of summer said she couldn't be bothered with makeup. Her only jewelry was loose silver bangles on her left wrist, but she was so still they hadn't made a single sound for the entire hour. And her dress—a gauzy, flowered, flowing thing—said she didn't care whether men looked twice at her or whether the proper Baptist women approved of what she wore to church.

Even her legs, he had noticed as he walked up the steps from the basement, were bare, her feet tucked into little slippers that tied around her ankles with some kind of ribbon.

Sam assumed those little ribbons binding her ankles were designed to set men thinking about loosening them, and loosening whatever else might naturally follow. He hoped that was the intention, for that would make them mighty successful. He wanted to set her bangles ajingle, too.

Sam knew that meant he was in trouble, for he thought he'd never seen a woman less likely to want someone to loosen her ribbons or jingle her bangles.

"Would those shoes fall off if someone untied the ribbons?" he asked after watching her slender feet pick their way carefully through the clutter of fallen leaves littering the church grounds.

He would have sworn she didn't even crunch a leaf as she made her way to the street.

She paused but didn't turn to look at him. "I'd trip over them, that's all."

He caught up with her then and walked beside her, although he felt distinctly uninvited. "I could catch you."

She kept her eyes straight ahead; nothing about her faltered. "I think I'll keep them tied if it's all the same to you. Then I won't need catching."

"Won't you?"

Her crocheted purse hung across her body, the way women learned to wear them in cities like Atlanta, and she clutched it tightly to her with one arm. He wondered what she was really afraid of losing.

"I'll walk you home," he said.

"It's just a few blocks," she said. "I'll be fine."

"I know a better way," he said.

She looked up then. "You do?"

"I've lived here all my life. You doubt me?" He smiled, and was rewarded with a flash of the impish smile he often saw when she came in from work, full of stories to share with her mother.

"What's it like? Living here forever?"

He turned off Main Street, toward the park. The long way home. He hadn't said it was shorter. Just better. And it was. Especially now.

"Peaceful," he said. "Reassuring."

She pursed her lips and eyed him speculatively. "Don't you think that's putting your head in the sand? With so many cities in turmoil, aren't you just hiding away from all the problems?"

He shrugged, stopping at the foot of the sliding board. "Maybe if we all turned away from the turmoil, maybe if we all went searching for a little personal serenity, we'd look around one day and discover that a lot of the turmoil had simply disappeared. Maybe if we don't feed it, it'll starve to death."

He climbed to the top of the metal slide and hoisted himself into position.

"A nice thought." But he heard the doubt in her voice, despite being several feet above her.

"It's worked for me." *Until now.*

He shoved off then. The metal popped and rumbled under his weight. His Sunday best shoes landed in the sand at the foot of the slide. He looked around for her, prepared to coax her onto the slide, and realized she was already perched at the top, skirt tucked around her knees, waiting for him to clear the way.

Pleased, he stood and watched as she sailed down, the autumn breeze lifting her hair to the sun and bringing a glow to her cheeks. She closed her eyes, head raised to the sky as she came down.

When she stood, she looked sorry the ride was over.

"Has it worked for you? No turmoil for Sam Roberts? No unhappiness or tragedy or trauma?"

"Well..."

"I thought so."

"I lost my father in Vietnam. That was right after I was born, though. I never knew what it was like to hurt over it." Walking to the edge of the park, where a narrow path led to Jasmine Court, the road parallel to Main Street, Sam hesitated. He knew from Susan's records that Malorie's father had died less than a year ago. "Not like you."

She looked displeased that he even knew, much less that he might sympathize. "He'd been sick awhile. It was a blessing when it finally happened. Where does this lead?"

Since she was following him, Sam saw no urgent need to answer her. "That doesn't always make it hurt less, does it?"

Now she was the one to shrug. "He was a good father. He always...stood by me."

"When did he stand by you?"

"Whenever I needed him to," she said, looking around as the path opened onto Jasmine Court. "Why, look! It's Wonderland."

"Oz."

"Never-never land."

She whirled around, taking in the block-long street that was Sweetbranch's oldest neighborhood. Most of the rest of the town had been settled and built up between the world wars. But Jasmine Court had been settled during the Victorian era by displaced coal magnates hoping to get away from the grime in their mines to the south. The two-and three-story houses laced with gingerbread and crowned by turrets were almost incongruous in the working-class town Sweetbranch had become.

"They need work," Sam said, almost apologetically.

But he could see from Malorie's reaction that she didn't need his apologies. Like Sam, Malorie could see the possibilities in the white houses with their peeling paint, broken porch spindles and crooked shutters.

"They're wonderful," she said, and Sam took pleasure in the glitter in her eyes as she continued turning in a circle, her soft skirt swishing around her calves. "I'd paint the trim on that one teal. And that one, I'd find a carpenter who knew his stuff to duplicate those broken shutters and turn some new porch rails. Why, you could... Who owns them? Who lives here?"

"A widow and her two bachelor brothers live there." He gestured to one of the houses, thinking of all the times he'd made this walk alone because so many people in Sweetbranch only saw the imperfections in Jasmine Court. "That one was willed to the library last year, but the library says it can't afford the renovations and nobody in town wants to buy it. That one—"

"Nobody wants to buy it?" She sounded incredulous. "You're kidding?"

"No. Although, Kitty Macauley has made an offer on that one and wants to turn it into a bed-and-breakfast. But the bank won't give her the money because they say nobody would come to Sweetbranch to stay in a bed-and-breakfast."

"If I had the money, I'd buy one of them."

"Me, too."

She froze, as if it might have occurred to her that he'd brought her here because he hoped she would share his enthusiasm.

"I always wanted to live in one of them when I was a kid," he said. "I always thought, when I have kids, that's where I'd want to raise them."

Malorie started walking, back toward Main. He wanted to ask how many children she wanted, because he'd watched her with Cody and couldn't imagine she wouldn't want several. *Three,* he thought. *Would that be too many to expect in this day and age?*

He didn't think it was the right time to be asking about kids, though. So he followed her back down to Main Street, and they turned in the opposite direction from the church.

"Tell me about the rest of your traumas and tragedies," she said, her voice once again sounding closed and tight.

Her attempt to change the subject was transparent, but Sam decided to grant it to her. Pushing wasn't likely to be effective with Malorie.

"Does being an only child for thirteen years count?" he asked, knowing it really hadn't been a trauma for him. He and his mother had been close all those years they were alone.

"No. I like being an only child."

"Liked it, you mean? For what, nineteen or twenty years?"

She shrugged and kept her eyes on the ground. "I was grown by the time Cody was born. It didn't matter."

If he hadn't seen how devoted she was to Cody, Sam would have sworn he detected some bitterness in her clipped reply.

"Does that mean you have a stepfather?" she asked. "That must have been a trauma. Nobody likes stepfathers, do they?"

"I do. It was great just having another male in the house." Sam recalled the warmth and understanding with which Pete Roberts had approached the adolescent who had never known what it was like to have a father. "You know, I don't think I realized how much I missed having a 'real' family until I actually had a baby brother and a baby sister. I loved it. Still do. When you're that much older, there's an element of hero worship—pretty heady stuff. You know what I mean."

"Yeah. What about your uncle? Was it tough on Tag, being replaced by a stepfather?"

"Tag hadn't been around for a while, anyway. He... Tag was sort of a wanderer."

"You seem close."

"We are. But... I was pretty young when he came back from 'Nam, so I didn't really understand what he'd been through. What he still had to go through. But it changed my life."

"How?"

"He'd been a POW for, I don't know, three years or so. He had a lot of recovering to do—physically and mentally. After he got out of rehab, he stayed with us,

Mother and me, for a long while. And I . . . I made up my mind I wanted to help people do what I'd watched Tag do. Get their lives back. That's what it's all about to me."

They were nearing the end of Main. The now-defunct Dixie Drive-in appeared in the distance, with the giant red-and-white Property Available sign that had been posted so long it was almost orange and yellow. Sam prepared to turn, but realized Malorie had paused to face him.

"Can my mother get her life back?"

He heard the whisper of fear in her voice and wanted to touch her, just to offer reassurance. For a moment, he forgot he was supposed to be professionally noncommittal, coyly blending just enough encouragement with a safe amount of caution. "Of course she can."

"You're not supposed to say that," she said. "The doctors never will."

"I believe in all my patients. I have to. Sometimes I'm the only one who does."

"And does that work?"

"Sometimes. Sometimes if I believe enough, they start to believe, too."

He thought he saw mist in her eyes before she lowered them. "Thanks, Sam. Thanks for that."

He smiled. "Thanks for letting me take you the long way home."

"It was nice."

He liked the simplicity in the way she said it. It made it easy to believe she meant it. Sam thought of some of the other women he'd met and played at courting over the years. Especially in Birmingham, where some of the premed students seemed to think their future careers entitled them to limitless research in human anatomy. Perhaps it did, for they seemed to have no trouble attracting willing research subjects. Sam hadn't cared much for that. And he hadn't cared at all for the young women who seemed more interested in their dates' career plans than in what they thought or felt or believed. Sam had tried to fall in love with one or two of the nicer ones, but he couldn't quite muster what it took.

With Malorie, no effort whatsoever had been required. It had simply happened, like being caught by surprise in a summer shower or finding a butterfly content to rest on one of the shrubs beside his porch. He had simply looked around and there it was, filling him with joy and trepidation.

Now remained the task of coaxing that butterfly to stay.

CHAPTER NINE

SUSAN DRAGGED HER PEN laboriously across the small ivory-colored thank-you note, heaving a sigh as she completed her name. She dropped the pen onto the lap desk laid across the arms of her chair and looked up expectantly. Cody ate breakfast in his high chair, also confined by a tray across his lap. But in a few minutes, Susan knew, Cody would be free to run and play. And Susan would still be confined to her chair.

Betsy Foster stood at the kitchen counter, her back to Susan, peeling potatoes to go with the pot roast she was preparing for dinner. Susan waited, wondering if her mother refused to look her way on purpose. At last, feeling like a bother, she said, "I'm finished."

"Me, too," said Cody, holding up his cereal bowl so everyone could see. Milk dribbled over the edge of the bowl. The little boy grinned proudly.

Betsy looked over her shoulder, then took her time about wiping her hands on the dish towel tucked into her waistband as an apron. "You're making a mess," she reprimanded the boy, wiping the spot of milk from the high chair tray.

Susan thought about how Malorie always praised the little boy for finishing his food and wondered why her mother didn't do the same. But Susan was never sure that her perception of a situation was as clear as it should be, so she kept quiet. Betsy, surely, knew better than she.

Lifting Cody out of the chair, Betsy wiped his face and hands with her makeshift apron, then turned to Susan and her thank-you notes for all the flowers and gifts she had received when she was in the hospital. "I hope this is better than the last one."

Susan didn't know the answer to that, so she didn't answer. The big, looping scrawl looked as unwieldy as it had felt, even though she wrote with her good hand. But maybe it would meet with her mother's approval. She hoped so. Her hand hurt from the effort.

It never hurt from the effort she put into sewing when Addy came over. But it always ached after a writing session with Betsy.

Betsy picked up the sheet of notepaper and studied it. Her lips puckered a bit more with each second that passed. Susan's heart fell.

"I don't see how your pride would let you send out a thank-you note that looked like that, Susan." She dropped the paper on Susan's lap desk and turned back to her potatoes. "But if that's the best you can do, I guess that's the best you can do. You should let me do it for you."

The back of Susan's eyes burned and her throat felt thick. She hurt and she didn't want her mother to see, because she was worried that big, fat tears were going to plop right into the middle of the note she'd labored over for fifteen full minutes. She had timed it by the kitchen clock, because Addy had showed her the day before yesterday how to figure out what the movement of the hands meant.

But no matter how much time she'd spent, it wasn't good enough. Would never again be good enough, she supposed.

"Will I ever be good enough for her, do you suppose?" The young man's voice echoed in Susan's head. She squeezed her eyes shut. She didn't like the voice to come when Betsy was nearby. When it did, she felt afraid again. But the voice didn't always do what she wanted it to do.

It didn't this time, either.

"I don't know what she's got against me."

Susan did, but she didn't know how to say it because she knew he felt bad enough about his father's drinking. Ashamed, he'd told her, and she still remembered the look on his face. It twisted her heart to see it, and she wasn't about to tell him that her own mother looked down on him because of it, just the way he was afraid everyone in the whole town did.

Susan jumped as her pen rolled off the lap desk and hit the floor. She looked up, saw Betsy's irritation, looked away quickly. Could her mother see what she was thinking? Could her mother see the reflection of the young man's face in Susan's eyes?

His face came to her often now. She sank into these memories of talking to him, laughing with him, even touching him, all the time now. But she couldn't control the coming and going of the memories, of the feelings. They swelled up and filled her on their own time, then went away just when she most wanted them to stay.

"Here, Mommy." Susan looked down. Cody held her pen in the air, smiling proudly. "Me help."

She smiled and took the pen. "What a good helper."

Cody nodded. "Me pway now."

"Play quietly," Betsy called after the toddler as he headed for the side porch, where most of his toys were stored. "And don't drag out every blessed toy you own. Do you hear me?"

He didn't, of course. Even Susan knew that. She tried hard to figure out why Betsy wasted her breath telling everyone in the house, even a two-year-old, exactly what to do. The effort to figure it out started a throbbing in her temple.

"I'm tired," Susan said. "Going to rest."

"That's a fine idea. Would you like me to call Addy and tell her not to come today?"

"No."

Betsy put her hands on her hips. "There is no need to wear yourself out over this foolishness, Susan. What good do you think it's going to do?"

Susan didn't know the answer to that. And she worried sometimes that the answer was "None." That, she knew, was what her mother believed.

"I want Addy," she insisted, and wheeled through the kitchen door into her room. When she was in her room, she kicked the door shut behind her. She felt angry and hurt and frustrated. More than anything in the world, she wanted to leave this house, wanted to go where she didn't have to see her mother every day.

"Don't cry, Susie."

His voice was soft, a comfort to her, and she closed her eyes, welcoming its visit. She could almost feel his hand, tender against her damp cheek.

"It won't be like this forever."

"Tell me what it will be like, Tag."

He brushed his lips over her wet eyelashes. "Here's what it'll be like. We'll have this little house, all by ourselves. About two blocks from campus, with a lit-

*tle porch out front where we can sit and watch fireflies
in the spring. We won't even have a phone, so none of
our nosy relatives can call us and bug us. I'll hold you
close all through the night—"*

"Under our quilt?" And she smiled through the
drying tears as Tag's daydream filled her head, taking
the place of her mother's hurtful words.

"Under our quilt," he agreed, pulling her closer into
the safe curve of his chest. "And we'll wake up together and have Dr. Pepper and chocolate-covered
peanuts for breakfast—for the protein—and walk to
class together. Or maybe we'll ride bikes. Would you
like to have bikes, Susie?"

The comforting memory faded with the sharp rap on
her door. Susan looked up as Betsy, as usual, opened
the door without waiting for a response.

"I'm going outside," she said. "Got more work to
do to get the garden cleaned up before the first hard
frost. I'll watch out for Cody. You're sure you don't
want me to call Addy and—"

"Don't."

Betsy turned away. "Fine."

And she was gone, leaving Susan blessedly alone
with memories of a boy named Tag and the girl he
called Susie.

TAG POKED AT THE long-cold ashes in his fireplace.
Idly at first. But the longer he stood there, thinking, the
more pissed off he got. Finally, he poked so hard he
sent ashes flying all over the hearth.

"Dammit, Betsy Foster! Who the hell died and made
you God!"

Tag never had been one to do what he was told. Fact was, he was about a hundred percent more likely to do exactly what he was told *not* to do.

So when Betsy Foster issued her personal restraining order on Sunday morning, Tag's second impulse—right after he'd followed his first and roared off on his bike—had been to march right back up to the Foster house and demand to see Susan.

He hadn't done it, though.

The bewildered, fearful look on her face when he'd dashed into her house the week before kept stopping him. As beautiful as ever—fine-boned and fair, with all those short, soft curls clinging to her forehead and cheekbones—Susan had nevertheless looked different in a way that made him cautious. And the things Sam had told him kept coming back to him, kept replaying again and again in his head.

Extensive memory loss.

Some residual loss of motor skills.

Easily confused. Easily upset.

Some nights, when he was fool enough to stay here alone, Tag thought he would go crazy if he didn't see her, if he didn't reassure himself that things weren't as bad as Sam had made them sound.

Other times, Tag thought it might be the final blow, the thing that would finally make him snap, if he discovered that Susan was permanently, irrevocably impaired.

Go ahead, he egged himself on. *Put it on the table.*

"What if she can't—" He tossed the poker into the grate, sending more ashes flying. He turned away abruptly. "Ah, hell! What if she really never remembers me?"

That, he thought, might be more than he could bear. Because then it would be the same as if none of it had happened. As if it had all been nothing but his fantasy, his teenaged daydreaming.

Tag stalked through the living room and into the kitchen, where he splashed water on his face. He stood there, letting it drip off his lashes, his mustache, onto his T-shirt. His eyes felt grainy from another mostly sleepless night. The shower an hour ago hadn't helped. The pot of coffee he had methodically devoured over the past ninety minutes hadn't helped. He knew he had to get moving, get his day on track. Malorie needed help this morning; a new shipment from the nursery was due this afternoon and he needed to clear a space in the fenced area to the rear of the shop.

But here he sat, the way he had spent more of his life than he cared to think of, obsessing over Susan Foster. Susan Hovis. Susie.

"Dammit!"

He grabbed his helmet, straddled his bike and spit gravel in his driveway until he hit Mimosa Lane.

Despite his intention to go to the store, soon his bike was spitting more gravel. This time, in Betsy Foster's drive. He hung his helmet from the handlebars and stalked toward the house, not knowing what he would say, not even knowing what he hoped to find.

Betsy Foster stepped around from the side of the house before he made it to the front door.

"I thought I made myself clear," she said. "You aren't welcome here."

"I came to see Susan, not you."

A little boy toddled around the corner of the building. Tag vaguely remembered seeing the boy when he'd burst into the house before, and in the front seat of the car on Sunday. A little towhead with freckles.

"Susan isn't seeing company. And she certainly isn't seeing you."

Tag decided to take the risk. After all, how much worse could it get? "Did she tell you that, Betsy? Or was that your decision?"

Betsy smiled. "She can't tell me, Eugene. She doesn't even remember you."

The sickness spilled into his gut then, rose up through his lungs to choke him, pumped into his brain like a poison. *She doesn't even remember you.* So it was really true.

Betsy turned, took the little boy by the hand and started back around the house. "Come along, Cody."

Tag stood there, uncertain he could get his legs to carry him, unsure he had the will to keep this day going. Betsy disappeared around the corner of the house, but the words she had used to stab him remained, continued to destroy him.

Then it hit him. Betsy would say anything. From the very beginning, she would have done or said anything to keep them apart. Why should things be different now?

He started after her, an angry roar rising in his chest. "You're lying! Damn you, you're lying to me!"

He caught up with her at the side of the house and grabbed her by the arm, whirling her around to face him.

"Take your hands off me," she spat out, "or I'll have the sheriff come after you for assault."

"You would, too, wouldn't you." He flung her arm away from him.

"You're absolutely right I would. Why don't you do this whole town a favor and crawl back under whatever rock you've been hiding under these past twenty years!"

"I'm going to see Susan. You can't stop me."

"I beg to disagree. As long as she's in my house—"

"I'll be back." He backed away from her. "I'll keep coming back until you let me see her."

Betsy looked over his shoulder and again a brittle smile touched her face. "Go right ahead, Eugene. She's here right now. I think you'll find I'm not lying at all. Susan doesn't even know who you are."

Fear rose in his chest, stronger than his anger. He kept backing away from Betsy until he stood at the side porch. Then he turned and looked.

She sat in a wheelchair in the threshold between the porch and the room that had been the family room a lifetime ago. She looked frail and confused, maybe even frightened by the argument she'd just witnessed. Tag was overwhelmed by the need to go to her, to hold her in his arms, to comfort her and tell her everything was all right. He even took a step in her direction.

When he did, she flinched away, startled. Frightened.

Hurt tore through Tag's heart as her reaction sank in. "Susan?"

Her forehead wrinkled in a frown, and it was then that Tag once again noticed the pink scar that slashed across her forehead. What was he doing? He was in over his head here. He didn't know what he was dealing with.

Easily confused. Easily upset.

That was it. He had upset her. Betsy had upset her. Emotion made his throat raw, left him hoarse. He couldn't gentle his voice as much as he would've liked. "It's okay, Susan."

She closed her eyes tightly and shook her head. "No, no, no. Tell me. Tell me who. Who?"

Tag swallowed hard, opened his mouth. Even her voice was different. So uncertain, and softly slurred. Tag thought he'd been hurting for twenty-five years. Now he knew what real hurt was.

"You see, Eugene." Betsy's exultant voice stopped the words in his throat. "You see how it is now?"

Then he felt a tug on his jeans and looked down into the bright blue eyes of the toddler Betsy had called Cody. "Don' scare my mommy. Her not feew good. Okay?"

Tag looked from the appeal in the little boy's eyes to Betsy's mocking gaze and back to Susan's eyes. All he saw was confusion. His fears had been right all along. Nothing remained of the Susie he used to know.

He wheeled and walked away.

SUSAN'S BREATH ROSE and fell in tiny gulps, hurting her chest, hurting all the way to her temples, even, where something roared and pounded in her head.

She watched him walk away and wanted to do something to stop him. But her head was too full of the roaring and pounding to figure out what. What could she do? How could she make him turn back?

Even as he disappeared around the corner of the house, she tried to memorize him, so perhaps she could figure this out later. The shape of his broad shoulders burned into her memory, as did his long, tapering legs and the fists clenched at his sides. His dark hair was long, hiding the back of his neck. He wore jeans, but they didn't fit loose and baggy the way Buddy's did when he worked on cars under the shade tree in Atlanta.

Susan squeezed her eyes shut. Buddy? Who was Buddy? Why was this happening? She saw his face, kind and full-cheeked, eyes lost in a squint when he laughed. She felt happy about Buddy. And sad. The feelings were strong. But not as strong as the feelings she had when the man her mother hated stared at her through the porch screen.

She didn't even know what to call the feelings. She only knew they filled her, overpowered her, rendered her momentarily speechless.

Putting her head in her hands, Susan willed all these confusing things to go away, to stop. Buddy and the man with the dark mustache and the clenched fists and the boy named Tag—

"Oh!" Susan cried out, almost jumping from her chair.

Betsy, who stood at the bottom of the steps, urging Cody to play in the backyard, looked up as Susan did. "Whatever is it now?" she asked.

"Him," Susan said. "Tag!"

Betsy looked displeased. She spoke sharply to Cody, who seemed to want to go back onto the porch with Susan. But Betsy gave him a light swat on the backside and he went on his way, head down.

"Whatever are you blathering about now?" Betsy said. "I vow, I can't understand half of what you say."

Susan felt as if she'd been slapped. She said the name again, but her voice was drowned in the roar of an engine from the street. Betsy glanced in that direction, her expression more sour than ever. Susan took a deep breath, tried to marshal her thoughts while the sound of the engine faded.

"I know Tag," she said slowly, as distinctly as she could. "I want to talk to Tag."

Betsy squared her shoulders. "He's no good. That's what you need to keep in mind, girl. Don't even *think* about starting that up again."

Susan started to protest, but Betsy trampled on her words. "Didn't you see how he reacted? He was revolted. Can't you see that? Didn't you see how he ran out of here when he got a good look at you?"

Tears sprang to Susan's eyes. Giving the wheels of her chair a vicious tug, she spun backward into her room. Her mother wouldn't see the tears. That much Susan could do. She kicked the door shut as tears spilled onto her cheeks. *Lies, lies, lies!* she thought as her mother's words continued to play in her already overloaded brain.

But the truth of the man's actions wouldn't let Susan find solace in that. For the truth was, he had run away.

Now she couldn't even find comfort by calling him forth from her memories.

Dragging herself across her bed, Susan cried until exhaustion allowed her to sleep.

BETSY WAS SHAKING when she reached the garden, her stomach in knots. She thought she might take a seat on the little bench for just a moment and calm herself before she went at her hoeing.

The bench was taken. Bump Finley sat there, gnarled hands on his knees. The way he looked at her, she couldn't look back at him for long.

"That was a fine performance, Bet."

"You nosy old goat," she snapped, taking a whack at a yellowed row of corn that had long since played out. "You have no business lurking around my house eavesdropping."

"If there's a nosy old goat in the vicinity, it ain't me."

She gave the hoe such a thrust it stuck deep in the hard red clay. She struggled with it a moment, then turned on Bump.

Funny how an old fool's eyes could trick her sometimes. Just for a moment, her eyes told her Jacob Ebeneezer Finley hadn't changed that much. He sat on her bench, his auburn hair still thick and wavy, his eyes a sharp green giving her that same disapproving look he'd leveled at her the day she told him she'd accepted Reid Foster's proposal of marriage.

"He ain't right for you," Jacob had said, tucking his big, broad hands into his suspenders. They had been yellow, she recalled, the loudest ones this town had ever seen. "Too soft. You'll walk all over him, Bet. And neither one of you'll be happy. You need a man with a little fire in him, to match your own."

She had smiled at him, a part of her half hoping he would change her mind. "A man like you, I suppose."

But he had stood and shaken his head. "Not this one. I don't reckon I need to play second fiddle."

And he had walked away. At the time, Betsy had told herself she was glad he hadn't made a scene. Folks in Sweetbranch didn't call him Bump for no reason—Jacob was known for riding a pretty bumpy road through life. Betsy hadn't wanted that. She had wanted the stability—and the malleability—of a man like Reid Foster, who had sworn he would make his fortune selling automobiles.

But sometimes, over the years, Betsy had lain in bed at night and felt an empty longing. Maybe she *had* needed a man with fire.

Clutching the handle of her hoe to steady her nerves, Betsy glared at Bump. "I know what's right for my own family, Jacob."

He shook his head and stood, the same way he had all those years ago. "Hell, Bet, you ain't never even known what was right for your own self."

"You're an old fool," she called as he walked away.

His chuckle drifted over his shoulder. Left alone in her garden, Betsy told herself the opinions of an old fool like Jacob Finley weren't worth a plugged nickel.

TAG WAS HALFWAY ACROSS Willow Creek Bridge on the way out of town when he remembered that Malorie needed his help. Angrily braking to a stop, Tag sat on the bridge and cursed aloud until his pain and rage dissipated enough that he could force himself to turn his bike around and ride back into town.

When he walked into the store, Malorie was flitting cheerfully from task to task. Ringing up a sale with the impish smile that tore at Tag's gut. Helping an elderly man find the exact bird feeder he wanted for his wife's birthday. Adjusting the display of clay flowerpots for precisely the effect she wanted. Tag never could tell the difference, but he had learned that whatever Malorie did would be better.

"Good morning, Mr. Hutchins!"

Her voice was an affront. Lilting and clear, it was so much like Susan's voice. The way Susan's voice used to be. But no more.

"That's one opinion," he snapped, never slowing his step on the way to the back of the store, where he needed to clear a place for the afternoon delivery.

No matter how loudly he banged things around, Tag couldn't shut out the sound of her voice ringing through the store like a bright, clear bell as she greeted customers. It shredded his heart, reminding him of the voice that had haunted his dreams for so many years. A voice that no longer existed.

He had worked himself into a sweat and managed to accomplish a half-day's work by the time Malorie peeked out the back door ninety minutes later. Looking at her from the corner of his eye, his heart hurt. He had to look directly at her just so he could remember this was Malorie, and not his Susie.

"What?" he growled, tightening his grip on the pitchfork he'd been using.

"I was just wondering..."

"Well spit it out."

She drew a long breath and he could tell from her uncertainty that he had managed to intimidate her. He felt like a snake.

"Well, you lived in Sweetbranch all your life, didn't you? I mean, until you were grown?"

Was she going to ask him about Susan? About the summer they fell in love and the night she promised to wait for him? His heart began to pound painfully. What would he tell her? He wasn't even sure what he believed about those days any longer.

"So?"

"Did you... I guess you knew my grandmother. Since you lived across the street from her and all."

"So?"

"I just wondered, was she always so... bossy?"

He looked at her face, so solemn and expectant. For a moment, he was torn between wanting to laugh and wanting to cry. Then it occurred to him that Malorie could as easily have been his daughter as another man's if things had been different. If only... Didn't it always come down to that?

"Yeah, as a matter of fact, she was," he said, propping his chin on the pitchfork handle. "Why? She starting to get to you?"

"I suppose so. And I thought, well, everybody says you've always lived life on your terms. That you never let anybody push you around. And I...I wondered how you managed that." She shrugged. "You know, where you found the courage?"

Granted, she wasn't his daughter, but some part of Tag felt as protective of her at this moment as he'd always felt of Sam.

He reminded himself he'd been a lousy role model for Sam, and he was certainly no better equipped for that part now. Giving somebody like Malorie advice would be the worst thing he could do for her. But as he was about to blow her off, he had a vision of her going home each evening to Betsy Foster and that rigid code of right and wrong. And he knew he owed Malorie something, even if it was born of his own bitterness toward her grandmother.

"The best thing I can tell you is never listen to people like Betsy Foster. They're poison."

The irony, he thought, was that he'd never been able to figure out for himself how to take his own advice.

SUSAN BARELY HAD the strength to grip the bar running the length of the wall in the dining room. She didn't want to walk, because she couldn't handle the anxiety that came from feeling so vulnerable, so alone.

"Don't want this today." She didn't look at Sam, just dropped back into her chair.

"Okay. What do you want today?"

"Nothing."

He was silent, and Susan hoped that meant he would give up and leave. Today, even having Sam see her this way seemed unbearable. She was startled when a foam rubber ball landed in her lap.

"Squeeze," Sam ordered. "We'll work on your hands."

She tossed the ball back at him. It landed two feet short.

Aching, frustrated, weak from crying and refusing to eat, Susan wondered why she kept denying what her mother so obviously knew to be true. This was hopeless. Pointless.

"Susan, what's wrong?"

"No more of this! It's stupid. Just go. Leave."

"Tell me what happened?"

"I won't get better. Never. Don't pretend anymore."

"Susan, that's not—"

"Leave! Don't lie anymore! Just leave!"

She turned away from him, but she could sense him rising from the floor and walking toward the door. Susan wasn't certain if she felt relief or despair. If he left, that must surely mean what she'd said to him was true. He *had* been lying. She wouldn't get better. Ever.

His voice came to her from across the room, but she didn't turn to look at him. "You don't have to be this way forever, Susan. But if you give up, if you send me away, you surely will."

Then he was gone and Susan sat in her chair for a long time, feeling too weary and broken even to wheel herself back into her room, where she could at least hide in the dark and the solitude.

CHAPTER TEN

SUSAN LEANED ACROSS the round wrought-iron table and whispered, "I remembered something important."

Addy stopped drinking her milkshake and grinned. "You did? That's wonderful!"

What was wonderful, Susan thought as she gathered her thoughts, was this idea she had resisted so stubbornly when Addy first suggested it that morning. The idea of an outing.

"Why not?" Addy had badgered her. "There is no good reason on earth why you have to stay cooped up in this house day after day."

Susan had looked at her hands, knotted together in her lap. "But..."

"But what?"

"Won't people...I mean...the way I look...it's..."

Addy had dropped into a chair, a bewildered expression on her face. "The way you look! There's nothing wrong with the way you look! Where on earth did you get such a silly idea?"

Susan had shrugged, and Addy had gone hunting for a mirror. She finally found a small one in an unused compact of blusher. Wheeling Susan to the window, where the morning sun streamed in, she put the mirror in Susan's hand and said, "Look."

Susan frowned, but she looked. She shrugged.

"You're adorable! Don't you know that?"

"Adorable?"

"Those platinum curls. Those smoky blue eyes. My gosh, you're Jean Harlow with freckles."

"Who?"

Addy had laughed. "She was a sex symbol. A hot number."

Still, Susan had remained unconvinced. "But I have this scar."

"Just a little pink line across your forehead. No biggy. A little concealer and it'll barely show. A year from now, nobody will notice."

"Concealer?"

Addy shook her head and navigated Susan's chair back to the dresser, where she started rummaging through a vinyl bag of jars and tubes Malorie had brought from their little house in Atlanta. "Honey, I can see I have a lot to teach you besides sewing, don't I?"

After Addy had finished with her, Susan felt a little more confident about going out in public—although she was still haunted by the memory of Tag running away from her and how her mother had explained it. But what really convinced Susan that an outing was the right idea was the look on her mother's face when Addy suggested it.

Betsy Foster disapproved. And that was reason enough for Susan to do it.

So here they sat in the Dairee Dreme on Main Street, sipping milkshakes through straws. They had already been to The Picture Perfect, where everyone laughed in such a friendly way when the woman named Rose said Susan was to blame because she'd never fulfilled her lifelong dream of being homecoming queen. Susan had felt close to Rose right away, from the scraps of memory she was recovering about their childhood friendship. Rose had trimmed Susan's hair, shaping it around her ears and fixing it just so, and suddenly most of the ugly scar didn't show at all.

All in all, Susan felt almost like a normal person again. Even in this wheelchair, which nobody seemed to mind at all. She thought maybe when Malorie got home she would ask her daughter to dial Sam's phone number so she could apologize and ask if he would come back and help her.

"Well, don't keep me in suspense," Addy prodded. "Tell me what you remembered."

"I remembered Buddy."

And she had. Sometime in the middle of the night, after that awful day when Betsy got angry at Tag and Susan had gotten angry at Sam, Susan woke up with puzzle pieces of her memory falling into place in her mind.

That, too, had made her feel almost like a normal person. Maybe she *could* get better if she kept trying. Maybe her mother didn't know everything, after all.

"Your husband? You remember Buddy?"

Susan smiled. "Isn't that wonderful?"

Addy's smile was hesitant. "Do you remember... what happened to Buddy?"

Even that couldn't dampen Susan's joy in simply being able to recall, even when those recollections weren't always pleasurable.

"Malorie told me. He got sick. For a long time. Then he... passed away."

She didn't remember that part, exactly. But she felt a kind of cloud of mixed emotions that always seemed to precede real memories. So she felt confident that that memory, too, would return someday soon.

"But I remember lots of other stuff about him, too. From a long time ago."

Addy smiled and squeezed Susan's hand. "I'd like to hear what you remember, Susan."

Susan smiled, feeling shy about sharing now that she had her young friend's attention. "I guess it's not that important."

"Everybody's love story is important, Susan. Why, I'll bet there's nothing more important."

"Tell me yours, then."

Addy paused to spoon a chunk of cherry nut out of her milkshake. "Danny and I were high school sweethearts, and I worked in the grocery store in Auburn while he went to school, and we came home to live happily ever after." She chuckled. "Well, sometimes Danny says it's more like living in a nursery rhyme than it is a fairy tale. You know, the one about the woman in the shoe with all the children."

Susan didn't remember the nursery rhyme, but she did remember how much mayhem Addy's brood created when they came over to play with Cody. Sometimes the noise made it hard for her to think, but it was a happy noise that cheered her heart.

"But my fairy tale isn't nearly as important as yours right now," Addy said, stuffing her napkin into her empty paper cup and sitting back. "I'm waiting."

Susan drew a deep breath and wondered where to start. She wasn't even sure, sometimes, what order her memories belonged in—it was like sorting through a box of photos and being unsure which one had been taken the summer you were ten and which one the Christmas before that.

"Buddy was real sweet," she said, remembering again that plump, ruddy face with its warm smile. "He helped me when I was...confused. I...I can't remember everything, but I know when I first met him, lots of things were making me sad. And Buddy was a friend."

She remembered the garage apartment she had rented from Buddy Hovis the year she moved to Atlanta to begin college. The two tiny rooms over the garage where Buddy operated his auto repair business were clean and neat and plain. They were a place where Susan could hide away, and she remembered wanting to hide from something.

"But Buddy wouldn't let me," she said. "He made me come out and talk. He told me I'd lose my freckles if I stayed inside too long."

She hadn't remembered that until this very moment, and it made her laugh, as it had more than twenty years earlier.

Eventually, she recalled, Buddy had coaxed her out of her shell. Although something had happened that made her quit college and almost give up on everything in her life, Buddy wouldn't let her. He showed her how he'd made a go of his own small business, and soon she was taking in sewing—clothes, drapery, slipcovers, anything. She even started doing costumes for a local dance company, although she had lost the heart for her own dancing.

"Later, though, the dance instructor told me I could use the studio after hours if I wanted to. So I did. And it made me better, somehow."

"Better?"

"You know, healed me. From...whatever it was that made me hurt so much." She looked up and frowned.

"It's so hard. Sometimes I think if I don't find all the missing pieces, I'll just...explode."

Addy squeezed her hand again and Susan realized how grateful she was to have someone to talk to. Someone who didn't get so upset with all the blank spots in her past, the way Malorie did. Or someone who didn't tell her that she shouldn't even be trying to get well, the way her mother did. She remembered, then, about her mother and Buddy.

"I did it because of Mother, you know."

"Did what?"

"Married Buddy." She felt sad, now, remembering her wedding day. She had stood in the vestibule of the church, feeling shaken, torn. She had always known she wasn't passionately in love with Buddy, but he did love her so. And her mother had convinced Susan she was doing the right thing. A steady man, Betsy had said. Someone you can rely on, like your father.

So, because she didn't have the spirit to fight her mother, Susan had walked down the aisle in a champagne-colored lace suit that she'd made herself. She did remember fighting with Betsy about the suit. Susan had wanted pink, but Betsy had insisted on white. Neither of them won that round; neither of them felt happy about the champagne lace. But Susan didn't tell Addy that part. She told her friend only the happy things.

And there was the other thing Susan had remembered. The thing that had happened right after the wedding, in the little Fellowship Hall where they'd had the cake and the toast to the happy couple. Susan remembered most of that, now, too, but she didn't want to tell Addy about that, either. She wanted to worry that awhile, like a sore tooth, until she remembered all of it.

And when she did . . .

"I've got an idea," Addy said as they cleared their trash and went back out onto Main Street. "Isn't Malorie working down at the Lawn & Garden? Why don't we go surprise her?"

MALORIE WAS RESTOCKING birdseed when she heard the bell jingle over the front door.

"Good morning!" she called out over the aisles. "I'll be with you in just a sec."

Birdseed, Malorie figured, would be a big seller during the winter months, so she had placed a large order. She hoped she'd guessed right, and thought about setting up an eye-catching display on the sidewalk with some of those new bent-willow birdhouses and cedar feeders. Mr. Hutchins didn't seem to mind what she did, although he had seemed awfully distant these past few days.

Maybe she shouldn't have asked him about her grandmother.

Maybe she should ask Sam, instead. Except that Sam hadn't been to the house for a couple of days and her grandmother had told her to let it lie.

"Your mother is a grown woman and deserves to make her own decisions," Betsy said.

Once again, Malorie hadn't had the gumption to remind her grandmother that it was Betsy herself who was always harping on the fact that Susan still wasn't capable of thinking for herself. Malorie wished she knew which was right.

Maybe she should ask Sam that, too.

And maybe you'd better get Sam Roberts right out of your mind and get up front to see if your customer needs help, she chastised herself. *Maybe you'd better admit that advice is not really what you want from Sam Roberts, anyway.*

But no, maybe she was better off not admitting anything. Maybe she was better off just trying to put it all out of her mind. Mr. Hutchins and her grandmother and her sad, discouraged mother, and especially Sam Roberts.

"Oh, there you are."

Malorie turned at the sound of Addy Mayfield's voice, wondering if that meant her mother had "fired" their neighbor, too. What she saw next startled her, then filled her with quiet joy.

"Mother!" She knelt, clasping both Susan's hands in hers. "Oh, Mother, what a nice surprise!"

"We're on an outing. Addy's idea."

Susan looked so pleased with herself, there was so much sparkle in her eyes this morning, that Malorie wanted to hug Addy Mayfield. "What a wonderful idea. Why, it looks to me as if you've made a stop at the beauty shop."

"That's right." Susan turned her head, giving Malorie a better view of the soft new style. "And we had milkshakes."

"Oh, I'm jealous. I'll bet the Dairee Dreme makes great milkshakes."

Susan's eyes lit up again, this time with surprise. "I used to work there."

Malorie felt her throat tighten. Every moment like this one gave her hope and seemed to fill her heart to bursting. "You did?"

"Yes. A long time ago. Before you were born, I think."

At that moment, realizing the memories had been triggered by a visit to a familiar place, Malorie had what was surely a stroke of genius. "Come on. I know something else that may jog your memory."

And she pushed Susan's chair down the cluttered aisles of the store, pointing out a few of the things she'd done to spruce up the place. When she arrived at the office door, she knocked.

After all, whether or not Betsy Foster approved of Mr. Hutchins really wasn't Malorie's concern, was it?

Malorie heard the gravelly rumble that was Tag's invitation to enter the office and she opened the door. Tag sat, scuffed boots on the desk, head against the wall. He barely moved, didn't even glance at her.

Sometimes Malorie would have given anything to know what dark secrets her boss brooded over when she caught him at times like this. She fancied it was a broken heart that made him so crusty, but figured maybe she'd been watching too many movies.

"Mr. Hutchins, I wanted you to meet my mother, Susan. Mother, this is—"

"Tag."

For the second time in moments, Malorie was filled with delight. It had worked, just as she'd hoped it would. She looked down at her mother, and her delight fizzled at the troubled expression on Susan's face. Susan's pink cheeks had gone pale, her eyes dark. Her hands clutched the arms of her chair.

Malorie jumped as Tag's front chair legs hit the floor with a crack. Her eyes darted to him. He stood over the desk, glaring directly at her mother. Bewildered, Malorie looked at the only other person in the room. Addy, too, looked startled.

"So you do remember me?" Tag Hutchins said coldly.

Susan nodded. "Yes. Tag."

"Then I guess that means you're letting Betsy call the shots these days."

Susan hesitated. Malorie could tell how agitated her mother was, knew how confused and upset she could get when she felt things were beyond her control. "Yes, but—"

"No need to explain, Susie."

"Mr. Hutchins, I—"

"I'm glad you brought your mother in, Malorie. She and I go way back. But you didn't know that, did you? She never mentioned me to you, did she?"

"No, but—"

"No reason she should, I suppose. I was just the neighbor boy. Your uncle's best friend. It isn't like I was real important to her, is it, Susan?"

Susan shook her head in the jerky movement she used when she was trying to clear her thoughts. "No. I...Tag..."

"Well, it was swell to see you, Susie. I've thought about you over the years a time or two. Hoped you were as happy as I've been." He gave a short laugh that sounded anything but cheerful. Then he stalked past the three visitors and was gone.

Susan was still upset when she and Addy left, and Malorie had no idea how to calm her. No idea how to calm her boss, either, because she didn't know what was causing his bitterness. All she knew was that her idea of stirring up more hometown memories had backfired. Still shaking, Malorie realized that some memories might be better left buried.

Like the secret she and Susan shared.

SUSAN SAT AT THE DINNER table that night eating what was set in front of her without tasting it, barely aware of moving her fork from the plate to her mouth.

So many things had happened. Some of them made sense now. Some of them didn't.

Like her wedding day. The incomplete memory still haunted her, the same way these encounters with the man named Tag haunted her. In both cases, something important was missing. Something everyone understood but her. So the memories wouldn't let her go.

Susan slipped away from the celebration, not an easy thing when you are the bride and therefore the one everyone wants to fawn over.

But smiling was exhausting her. She needed a break from trying to look radiant, so she ducked out of the stark little Fellowship Hall. She turned down one corridor, then another, where the lights were out and she could lean against the wall, close her eyes and drop the forced smile that was wearing her out.

Had she made a mistake? Was this all wrong? Or was this nothing more than the kind of jitters every bride felt?

With her thumb, she felt for the new ring on her third finger, left hand. She hadn't been able to take the other one off until that very morning, when she was leaving her little garage apartment for the Atlanta church. She hadn't wanted to be married in Sweetbranch, either. Hadn't wanted to see all the old gang. Hadn't wanted the reminders. It was time to leave the past behind.

So right before she'd left her apartment, she thought of the perfect place to keep the ring, a place where it would be safe. A place where she could always think of it as being close to her heart.

She knew she couldn't stay away long without people beginning to wonder. But as she squared her shoulders and prepared to go, she heard voices, and realized the Fellowship Hall kitchen was only two doors down.

One of the voices she heard belonged to her brother, Steve. "Are you saying you didn't even tell her?"

There was a moment of silence, then Betsy's voice replied, "It really didn't seem necessary."

"Didn't seem— Mom, are you out of your mind?"

A rustling of fabric, the ugly green satin Betsy had chosen for her dress. "I don't have to listen to this from my own son."

"The hell you don't! This is the meanest, most deceitful thing I've ever—"

"I've deceived no one."

"You've deceived everyone! He's my best friend and you didn't even tell me because you knew I'd never have let her go through with this if I knew."

Trembling more than she had been when she walked down the aisle, the words resting heavily in her stomach, Susan started toward the voices....

The memory ended there, as it always did, and Susan stared at the black-eyed peas on her plate. The memory made her sad, even a little angry. She looked up at Malorie, who'd been upset ever since Susan's visit to the store that afternoon. Without having to say so, they had both apparently decided not to tell Betsy about the incident.

Although maybe, Susan mused, Betsy was the only one who could explain all of it to them.

Susan remembered how good she'd felt this afternoon, going out with Addy when it was clearly something Betsy didn't want her to do. She remembered how good it had felt, bringing her memories out one by one to examine them with Addy's caring help.

She stared at Betsy, who was admonishing Cody to keep his peas in his spoon. Cody apparently enjoyed watching them roll around on his high chair tray.

Suddenly Susan knew the anger in her memory was for Betsy. And she was angry right now, as well, for the way she didn't like to let Cody be a baby.

"Why did you keep a secret from me?" she asked.

Betsy and Malorie both froze.

"Whatever do you mean?" Betsy asked.

"On my wedding day. You kept a secret from me."

Betsy took her napkin from her lap and wiped her fingers, placing the napkin carefully on her half-full plate. "I don't know what you're talking about."

"You kept a secret from me. And from Steve. Tell me now."

Betsy stood and began clearing the table. "Malorie, I think your mother is finished."

"But—"

"I am not finished!" Susan said. "I want to know. You have to tell me."

Betsy continued clearing the table. Malorie stood and looked from one to the other uncertainly. "Grandmother, I think you should tell her."

Betsy stood with her hands in the sink and didn't turn around. "She's upset and she's not in her right mind. I should think you would understand that by now, Malorie."

The only sound in the kitchen for the next few moments was the sound of water running in the sink and Cody banging his spoon against his plate. Susan's shoulders sagged. She felt Malorie's hand on her shoulder and looked up into sympathetic eyes. Susan nodded and Malorie wheeled her toward the door.

"I'll remember soon," Susan called out as they left the kitchen. "You can't do anything to keep me from remembering."

CHAPTER ELEVEN

TWO DAYS PASSED before Susan realized that the image haunting her was a quilt.

The revelation came to her while she threw the orange foam ball back to Sam. In a flush of excitement, she tossed the ball over his head and all the way into the hallway.

Sam looked delighted. "Wow! Whatever that was, let's do it again!"

"My quilt!" Susan gripped the back of the chair to keep from toppling over as her concentration fled. "I want the quilt!"

Looking bemused, Sam came over and helped her sit. "What quilt? You're not cold, are you?"

"No." Susan shook her head. "I have to see it. The quilt."

She had woken up in the early hours of the morning the day after confronting her mother, with tiny squares of pink and green and white spinning in her head. Soon, the little squares had settled into a pattern of circles. Then the circles joined together. And with each new configuration of the squares of color, Susan grew more confident, more peaceful inside.

On the coattails of that confidence, she had asked Malorie to call Sam so she could begin her therapy again.

But now that those shapes and colors in her head had become something she could label, the peacefulness was beginning to slip away. She felt agitated. And she felt certain she wouldn't be able to rest until she held the quilt, could touch its weathered fabric.

For there was something about the quilt. Something she couldn't quite remember. But she would. She knew it. And when she did, things would be okay again. Her world would be right side up again. She just knew it.

"Which quilt, Susan? Tell me what you're talking about and I'll get it for you." Sam grinned at her. "Goodness knows, I'd get you a dozen of them if they give you that kind of strength."

Susan laughed with him, buoyed by his promise that he could get the quilt for her.

"It's green and..." She fought to retrieve the word she wanted. "Rose-colored. It has circles all around it. That's the one I want."

"Is it in your room?"

Susan was growing impatient with her inability to communicate. "No. I don't know. I just see it in my head."

The enthusiasm on Sam's face faded.

"But it's real," Susan added hastily, pleased with herself for picking up on Sam's expression and being able to interpret it. "I know it's real."

"Is it something you and Addy are working on?"

Susan shook her head.

"Maybe I should ask Betsy."

Susan shook her head again, this time more adamantly. "No! She doesn't know."

But when she said it, the words felt like a lie. Her mother might know, said the voice inside her head, but she wouldn't tell. Just as she wouldn't tell other things.

For Susan was convinced now that Betsy could fill all the holes in her memory, if she wanted to.

But her mother was hiding things. That made Susan angry.

"Okay," Sam said. "Tell you what. You keep working, and put the quilt out of your mind. Just let your body take over and soon it'll pull that memory right out for you."

Looking at him skeptically, Susan dragged herself back to a standing position. "Honestly?"

"I'm sure of it." He went after the foam ball and tossed it toward her, resuming their routine. "The brain doesn't like to be pushed. But you can trick it. If it thinks you don't care, it'll try to tease you into caring by giving you a little more information."

She caught the ball, fascinated by the idea of tricking her brain into cooperating. "Really? Even *my* brain?"

When he nodded, she threw the ball back. And tried not to worry about the quilt.

The next day, the quilt still occupied her mind, and her brain had not dished up another single fact about it. Growing slightly petulant, Susan once again badgered Sam about the quilt. Finally he called Addy, and she brought over every book of quilt patterns she had in the house.

"How about this one?" she would say, holding up a picture that Susan would reject.

Susan saw one or two that were almost like the one in her head. But none of them were quite right. They were different colors. Or the circles didn't fit together exactly as they had in her head. She was even beginning to see the tiny pattern of stitches, including the place near the center where a whole series of stitches had frayed and been replaced.

That was the quilt she wanted to find, not one from all these pictures.

"It's not any of these," she insisted. "The one I want is *mine*."

Addy and Sam exchanged perplexed looks. Then Addy opened one of her books one more time. "But does it look a little bit like this one?"

Grudgingly, Susan said, "Maybe. A little."

Addy and Sam sighed.

"So it might be a—" Sam leaned over the book "—a Double Wedding Ring?"

"What is going on here?"

All three of them jumped at Betsy's accusatory voice.

"We're trying to find out about a quilt Susan remembers," Sam said.

Betsy's perpetually displeased face looked perceptibly more displeased. "All this—" she waved at the piles of books scattered on the dining room floor "—all this over a quilt? Land's sakes! If Susan wants a quilt, all you have to do is say. I have plenty upstairs."

Susan was already shaking her head, but Sam stood. "Let's bring 'em down."

"Fine," Betsy said. "I'll go get one."

"Not one," Sam said, following her toward the stairs. "*All* of them."

"All of them? Why, you must be—"

"I'll help, Mrs. Foster. Just show me where they are."

Susan heard her mother protesting all the way up the stairs, then all the way back down again a few minutes later. Sam came into the dining room loaded down with quilts, which he dropped onto the floor at Susan's feet. Log Cabins in brown and yellow. A Texas Star in shades of blue. A Bicentennial sampler quilt in red, white and blue. A half-dozen quilts in all.

None of them was the one Susan wanted.

"She said it was one she made," Addy pressed, looking up at Betsy. "In rose and green. Maybe a Double Wedding Ring. Does that ring a bell?"

Betsy sighed sharply. "Am I now expected to remember every single project she ever worked on? This is ridiculous. If you want a quilt, take one of these and let it rest."

Frustrated, Susan said, "You could lie about this, too. I know you could."

"You are behaving like a spoiled child," Betsy snapped, then turned with rigid dignity and left the room.

Addy stayed after Sam left, clearing away the quilts and the books and wheeling Susan out to the side porch.

"Let's sit out here and watch the leaves fall while I tell you about Danny's big promotion," Addy said. "How about that?"

Susan barely listened to Addy's news about her husband's promotion to production manager at the paper plant. But she was grateful for her friend's presence.

That night, before she went to bed, Malorie came in to say good-night. No one had told Malorie about the incident that afternoon, but Susan wanted to. She remembered how much she and her daughter once talked. She wanted that back, but she wasn't sure right now how to go about it.

All she could think to say was, "Am I a spoiled child?"

Malorie immediately sat on the edge of her bed. "Oh, Mother, why ever would you think that?"

"*Am* I?"

"Of course not. You're brave and strong, and I don't see how I could ever fight as hard as you have."

"Then why doesn't anyone like me?" Betsy wasn't the only one who glared at her with that cold look in her eyes. Susan remembered the look in Tag's eyes, too.

"Oh, Mother, people love you. I love you. Cody loves you. And Grandmother loves you, too. I know she does."

Even in the darkness, Susan could see the glimmer in her daughter's eyes. "Are you crying?"

"Maybe just a little."

"I wish you were happy."

"I'm happy."

"You could be happy with Sam. Sam likes you."

Malorie was silent and looked away for a moment. "Sam isn't... It wouldn't be a good idea for Sam to like me."

"Yes, it would."

"Mother? Do you...do you remember...when Cody was born?"

Susan sighed. "I don't think so. Was I very happy?"

Again, there was a long silence. When she spoke, Malorie's voice had a choked sound. "I...I think so. Of course you were. Very happy."

MALORIE WORKED HARD the next morning to get the four-pack trays of pansies lined up perfectly on the shelves in the front of the store. If the rest of her life

was in chaos, the things under her control at Hutchins'
Lawn & Garden would be in perfect order.

Some days she prayed that her mother would hurry
up and remember. Everything. Because carrying the
secret had been easier when she shared it with her
mother. Then it had seemed to Malorie like a difficult
but wise decision. Better for everyone involved.

Now it just seemed like an ugly lie, lurking in the
darkness and growing uglier by the day. Waiting to
burst into the light and destroy everyone it touched.

*You watched too many soap operas while Mother
was in the hospital,* she told herself, pulling down the
torn sign below the bin of ornamental cabbages and
taking it to the front to letter another one.

Other days, she prayed Susan never remembered.
Because Susan was too unpredictable. If she remembered in the middle of Thanksgiving dinner just weeks
from now, she'd likely blurt it right out there for everyone to scoop up with their sweet potato casserole
and corn bread dressing.

Malorie's stomach was in a knot from worrying
about it. But the person she'd always confided in, always trusted to know what to do, had been taken from
her.

If there was anything she prayed for *every* day, it was
Susan's recovery. *Is a twenty-one-year-old supposed to
want her mother this badly?* she wondered.

She studied the sign. Buy One, Second Half-Price.
Tag had been skeptical when she'd suggested trying a
number of different special offers to see which one
sparked the most sales. But he'd given her the go-
ahead.

She'd tried, these past few days, not to be angry at
her boss. But it wasn't easy after the way he'd treated

her mother. He'd been almost mean, it had seemed to her. But then, she kept remembering the things he'd said, and the way he'd asked if Betsy Foster was still running the show. And the way Susan, in her confusion, had answered in the affirmative.

Something kept telling Susan to set him straight. But she was worried stirring things up would only hurt her mother. Might anger her grandmother or her boss. She was tired of having things stirred up.

She was tacking the new sign to the shelf when she heard the jingle of the bell over the front door. Grateful for the distraction, she dredged up her best store-manager smile and walked toward the front.

Sam stood beside the colorful display of gourds and pumpkins she'd spilled out onto a table, hoping to capture the fancy of anyone ready to decorate for Thanksgiving. Malorie's heart gave a leap. For a moment, she toyed with the coincidence that Sam had showed up just when she was wishing for someone to confide in. The crazy notion came into her head that his arrival in the store was no coincidence at all.

I could confide in Sam. He could be my friend.

Then he turned, saw her, and his face lit up with a smile that sent a tingle from the top of her head all the way to the tips of her toes. Her heart sank, for she knew right then that Sam could never be her friend. Other things, maybe, but never a friend. And she couldn't handle other things.

"Isn't it time to start closing up?" he asked, taking a step in her direction.

Malorie glanced over his shoulder at the old-fashioned clock. "In ten minutes."

"So close up early. I carry a little weight with the owner."

Malorie smiled. "I can't do that. What if someone is a block away right now, headed this way to spend a thousand dollars on gourds and pumpkins?"

Sam glanced at the display. "Then I think you're understocked." He took another couple of steps in her direction. "I'm here on a mission."

"Oh?"

He nodded. "Maxine called me today. Said she'd heard the Christmas trees were in."

Malorie pointed toward the rear of the store, where the glass door opened onto the fenced back lot. "The live ones are in."

"Good. Help me pick one out." He took her by the hand and started toward the back. "For the church. We want the best tree you've got for our angel tree."

With Sam's big hand closed around hers, Malorie could barely remember the discussion about the pink and blue paper angels that would be used to decorate the tree, each printed with information about a needy child in the county. Members of the congregation would be urged to select an angel—or several angels—and buy appropriate gifts to place under the tree. Being part of the project had excited Malorie. But not as much as being touched by Sam.

They stood in the back lot, where the sun had already dipped below the roof of the building, leaving them in dusky shadows. Sam had draped his arm around Malorie's shoulder. Casually.

She wondered if he felt casual. Or did he feel the way she felt? As if she'd been struck by a sudden power surge.

"Which one do you like best?" he asked.

Malorie wished she could trust her voice. She cleared her throat and said, "I'm always partial to the little scraggly ones. The ones with the bare spots and the lopsided tops."

Even in the shadows, she could see the sparkle of interest in his eyes when he looked down at her. She wished he weren't so close. She wished she had the courage to move away herself.

"Now why is that, Malorie Hovis?"

"I figure they're the ones that need the decorations most."

She grew warm inside as the slow smile spread across his face.

"Ah, a redemptive bent. I like that in a woman. Especially in a woman with freckles on her nose."

"When you have freckles on your nose, you can't afford to be too frivolous."

"I noticed that about you right away."

"You did?"

He nodded. "I think it was the day I came to the house and found you lying in the front yard letting Cody's puppy lick your nose while Cody tickled your feet. Bare feet, at that. In November."

Malorie ducked her head. "Shoes are for the timid, the stodgy, the unimaginative."

"A redeemer *and* an adventuress." Sam lifted her chin and looked into her eyes. "Are you adventurous, Malorie?"

His eyes challenged her, promised imminent adventure. Suddenly unable to breathe, Malorie backed away.

"Not really," she said. "I'm probably not at all who you think I am."

"Then, who are you?"

Again the urge to tell him swept over her, set her heart racing even faster than his touch. She called her-

self a fool and gestured toward the rows of evergreens.
"I'll turn on the light. I think I know the perfect tree."

Twenty minutes later, Malorie had locked up the
store, helped Sam load a ten-foot Scotch pine into his
van and was helping him haul it into the church vestibule. Working quietly in the hushed emptiness of the
church, they set the burlap-bound root ball of the tree
in the galvanized washtub Maxine had left out for
them, then draped the tub in the red-and-green
flounces Addy Mayfield had made.

"It looks better already," Sam said, stepping back
to regard the tree.

Malorie was careful to keep an arm's length away
from him. "Wait until we lavish a little attention on
it," she said.

"That's all it takes for most of us. A little TLC."

He took another step in her direction and Malorie
sought a diversion. "Like Mother," she said. "Is that
part of your prescription for your patients?"

Disappointment briefly flickered across his face.
"I'm glad you brought her up. I'd almost forgotten,
but that's one of the reasons I came by this afternoon."

"What's wrong?"

"Nothing, really." He frowned, and paced a few
steps into the sanctuary. "She's asking for a quilt.
More than asking, really. She's starting to obsess over
it. Sometimes people with this kind of injury can't let
go of an idea as easily as you or I can."

"The Double Wedding Ring?"

Sam's face brightened. "You know the one she's
talking about?"

Malorie leaned against the back of the last row of
pews. "I know the one. It was always her favorite. But

it's gone. Lost in the accident, I guess. We'd just had a picnic. It was in the car.''

Now another kind of disappointment settled onto Sam's face. ''That's too bad.''

''Should I tell her?''

''If she asks about it again, I think we'll have to tell her.''

Anxiety clutched at Malorie's stomach. ''It's going to upset her, isn't it?''

''Probably.''

''I don't want to set her back again. She's just getting her fight back.''

''I know. What happened? Do you know?''

Malorie shook her head. ''No, unless it was her outing with Addy.'' She told him about the afternoon the two women spent going up and down Main Street. She hesitated, remembering how the afternoon had ended. ''Do you know—how well Mr. Hutchins knew Mother?''

''Tag? They grew up across the street from each other. He was friends with your Uncle Steve. He and Susan dated when they were kids. Why?''

Malorie told him then, both about the Sunday morning Tag had argued with Betsy and the afternoon Susan came into the store. Sam frowned.

''I'll find out,'' he said. ''Tag doesn't need to be running around making Susan's life more difficult right now.''

''Thanks, Sam. I know I probably worry too much.''

''It's understandable. She's your mother. You want her to be better.''

''She was... I miss talking to her, you know? We were close. It's like losing my mother *and* my best friend.''

Sam stepped close again, but this time Malorie was trapped against the pew. "You shouldn't isolate yourself, Malorie."

"I know. But—" She shrugged.

"You need some substitutes for what Susan can't give you right now. I can't be a mother-figure. But I could be a friend."

"Sam, I—"

"Give me one good reason why I couldn't be a friend."

"You don't know me, Sam."

"You won't give me a chance."

She looked up at him, wishing she knew how to explain. But sometimes it didn't make sense, even to her. People make mistakes. They do what they can to fix them. Why was it the thing she'd done to fix her mistake seemed to have left her more trapped than the mistake itself?

"I like you, Malorie," he said softly. "I don't put the rush on the daughters of all my patients, you know. Just give it a chance."

She wanted to tell him she liked him, too. But then what defense did she have? How, then, to explain that she could be neither friend nor lover?

"Susan trusts me," he said, moving closer and putting one hand on her shoulder. With the other, he touched her hair. "Why can't you?"

"It isn't that."

"Then, what?"

His fingers brushed against her temple, lightly feathering her curls away from her face. A tickle of sensation curled low in her belly. She closed her eyes, afraid for him to see her weakness. Afraid to feel it, even.

The touch of his lips on hers didn't surprise her. For a moment, she allowed herself the pleasure of that warmth, that softness. She didn't lean into the kiss but she didn't, for the moment, retreat, either. She let her lips soften against Sam's, felt the heat sinking deeper into her, sending sensations rippling through her.

How sweet it would be...

And how impossible.

The instant she felt his lips part, she drew away. "I'd better go."

He stepped back, shoved his hands deep into the pockets of his white slacks. "If that's the way you want it."

She couldn't even answer. She only nodded and walked past him as quickly as she could, afraid that if he tried to stop her she wouldn't have the courage to keep going.

HOW MANY TIMES, Tag asked himself, had he sat beneath this very tree staring at the Foster house, waiting?

Too many times to be doing it again, he told himself.

So many that one more wouldn't make much difference, a more hopeful part of him countered.

But maybe it *would* make a difference. Maybe if he could stop being so damned stubborn and prideful for a few minutes, he might find that things were a lot different than he'd thought.

Sam's visit a few hours earlier had been a slam to the gut. He hadn't been expecting his nephew. In fact, he'd been expecting to leave the house in another fifteen minutes, on his way to God knows where. Hours on his bike, feeling the bite of the autumn wind on his cheeks, in his hair, that was how he killed most of his free time these days. And at night, things didn't look quite so stark. Everything was in shadows, and that was the way Tag liked it. Sometimes his wandering turned up a diversion—a sign advertising a Saturday afternoon dirt track race or a drag race in some rural county.

Sometimes his wandering just accentuated his loneliness.

But Sam had caught him this time. And his first words had stalled Tag in his tracks.

"What are you trying to do to Susan Hovis?"

Tag had whirled around, letting his helmet drop into an armchair. "What do you mean?"

"I've heard about your little scenes with Betsy and with Susan. I want to know what you're up to, Tag."

"Has Betsy got you on a string now, too?"

"What's eating you, Tag? This is my patient you're messing with, and I want to know why."

"None of your damn business." He snatched his helmet up and stalked toward the door, but Sam grabbed him roughly by the arm.

"Susan is my business. And when you get her so upset she doesn't want to continue her therapy, that's my business."

"So sorry she's upset. Maybe it's time I upset her life for a while."

"I'm not leaving until you tell me what's going on between you two."

So they had sat for nearly twenty minutes, glaring at each other across the silent room. Tag had finally recognized a stubbornness that matched his own.

Besides, there was a small part of him that desperately wanted to hear what Sam could tell him about Susan.

He shifted his eyes from Sam's face, stared at the dark rug on the floor, the same rug he'd stared at when he was growing up and his old man chewed his butt out for something. "We were friends. A long time ago. I told you that before."

"Friends, Tag? I thought it was some kind of puppy love."

"Yeah. That's it."

"Is it really?"

"Okay, okay. We were...engaged."

Only silence greeted that admission and Tag knew he'd taken his nephew by surprise. "Before I went to 'Nam. She promised to wait. She didn't. That's it."

"Aah. So she jilted you and you've been ticked off about it half your life?"

Having his pain belittled angered Tag. He fought the urge to sweep his mother's red-and-gold Tiffany lamp right off the table and onto the floor with one swift swipe of his arm. "Come back when you've been in love, Sammy, and we'll talk about it then."

"Okay. Fair enough. But, Tag, you were gone, how long, four, five years? Nobody knew if you were dead or alive. She was young. Are you going to hold that against her forever?"

"I tried to see her. She doesn't want to see me. She...she pretended she doesn't even know me."

"She probably doesn't. Her memory was pretty much wiped clean, Tag. It isn't like she zeroed in on you for special treatment."

"No?" Tag felt himself begin to soften and melt at the reminder of Susan's illness. Hearing about it like this, he could be sympathetic, understanding. But seeing it face-to-face made him crazy. Anger was easier to deal with than the pain of the truth.

"She didn't remember Malorie, either, at first. Or Cody."

"Cody? That's the little boy?" Something about the little boy had given Tag an extra pain in his heart. As if seeing the tyke had reminded him of everything he'd missed.

"Whole parts of her life are missing, Tag. She's learning to read all over again—and she'd be doing a lot better if Betsy didn't think it was a waste of time."

"What?" His fury at the woman grew.

Sam shook his head. "I've never seen anything quite like it. Susan is her daughter, but she seems to be doing everything she can to convince Susan she'll never recover. Susan gets discouraged just listening to her. And it's easy enough for Susan to get discouraged, anyway."

"But she will get better, won't she?"

He remembered the way Sam had talked about it before, his mention of miraculous recoveries. The word *miraculous* had lain in his mind for days until he allowed it to take root. He wouldn't have said that was what he was hoping for, because that would have been too optimistic.

But a part of him kept saying it *could* happen.

He didn't bring it up again because he didn't want Sam snatching away that thin thread of hope.

Sam voiced the noncommittal phrase of the professional who neither wants to raise hopes nor dash them. "She's getting better all the time. Her physical therapy goes well—when she's feeling encouraged enough to stick with it."

"No thanks to Betsy."

"And you."

Tag heaved a sigh. "What can I do, then? How can I help?"

"Since you can't seem to keep from blowing off steam, I'd say you'd better keep away from her."

Tag had made up his mind to do just that. But just as Sam was leaving, his nephew said something that changed Tag's mind. He'd been talking about how rapidly Susan was recovering her memories and how arbitrary her brain was in offering them back to her.

"She's got her mind set on finding this old quilt right now," Sam said. "I don't know how she's going to feel when Malorie tells her it was lost in the accident."

So here Tag sat, waiting for the last light to go out in the Foster home, determined that the only one who was going to tell Susan about the quilt was him. For it had to be *their* quilt. The Double Wedding Ring. He just knew it.

And if she wanted the quilt, didn't that mean that buried somewhere in her injured mind were good memories about Tag, about the two of them?

At last the lights went out. Still he waited, hoping everyone in the Foster house slept soundly. Then, when he was too impatient to wait any longer, he walked up to the side porch. The screen door to the porch was unlatched. And the window beside the door into the house was also unlocked, as were half the windows and doors in Sweetbranch. He opened it as quietly as possible, reached inside and freed the door lock. He was inside in minutes.

He stood, letting his eyes adjust to the darkness. Slowly he began to see shapes. The piano. A wheelchair. A bed beside the fireplace.

Then Susan's voice came to him in the darkness. "I've been waiting for you, Tag."

CHAPTER TWELVE

Atlanta—1973

THE NIGHT STARTED like a hundred others.

Stretching her back and rubbing her neck, Susan turned out the light on her sewing machine, folded the wool plaid suit she was altering from a size 16 into a size 14 for Mrs. Wickham. Quitting time.

Through the screen door, she could smell the charcoal burning as Buddy fired up the grill. Susan smiled, knowing if she stuck her head out the door and looked down into Buddy's backyard, he would call up, "You hungry? Just so happens I've got an extra burger here."

So she did just that, and went down to join him.

Burgers on Buddy's back patio—overlooking the clutter of his auto repair business and the neatly painted garage Susan had been renting since her freshman year at Georgia Tech—was a better deal than another night alone in her apartment. Susan had spent enough of those to last a lifetime before she started accepting her landlord's overtures of friendship.

A bed and overstuffed floor pillows had been her only furnishings during her freshman year, when she had spent her time either studying or writing letters to Tag in Vietnam. The Double Wedding Ring quilt was with her, of course, but carefully wrapped and stored in a box in the top of her only closet. Over the years, she had added furniture—a couch from the Salvation Army, a kitchen table and chairs that were a yard sale find. The quilt was now folded across the bottom of her bed. She'd dropped her classes more than a year ago. And the letter-writing long before that.

"I see Mr. Snipes's Lincoln is back," she said, setting the folding metal table with paper plates and napkins while Buddy flipped the burgers.

"Yeah, and it'll keep coming back unless I convince him to replace that carburetor." Buddy shook his head. "Shoot, maybe I'll just fix it, anyway. He's too old to get stuck out on the highway if the blasted thing gives out on him."

"You wouldn't let me get away with giving away my time," Susan protested.

"Do as I say, not as I do." Buddy looked over at her, his eyes sparkling. "Besides, I'm not out to make a fortune. Just so I have enough to get by. You know that."

"I know that."

She also knew that Buddy Hovis was a smarter businessman than he liked to let on. Hadn't he shown her all the ropes in getting her own alteration and seamstress business off the ground? With his help, she had gone from doing a little work on the side to supplement her scholarship to working forty-plus hours a week, with customers willing to wait until she could get around to their curtains or couch covers or bridesmaids' dresses.

But Buddy's heart was bigger than his ambition. Susan also knew that firsthand.

They'd eaten the burgers and recapped their day and were watching the first fireflies of the season flit around the backyard when Buddy shifted uneasily in the webbed lawn chair.

"Susie, I've been thinking." He spread his big, thick-fingered hands on the table and stared at them. Susan noticed that he'd scrubbed so hard tonight they were clean. No grease, no stains. Not easy for a mechanic to accomplish. "I've been thinking a long time, actually. But I guess I'm pretty much a coward."

Susan grew uneasy.

"But I've made up my mind and I just want to plow right on through this, get it out here in the open, where you can tell me I'm an old fool or . . . or not." He blotted his upper lip with the back of his hand. "You know how I feel about you, Susie. You're the sunshine in my day. And I know you . . . had your heart set on other things. And maybe you won't ever be able to put those other things out of your heart completely. But that doesn't matter to me. I'd like you to be my wife, Susie. And I'd do everything in my power to make you happy again."

BUDDY HAD BEEN THERE in 1970, when word came that Tag was missing in action. When Susan almost fainted, Buddy caught her safely in his arms.

The only haven Susan knew for the next few years was her friendship with Buddy. For months after receiving the news, she was paralyzed by fear, able to do little more than sit and wait for news about her fiancé. She barely passed her courses at Georgia Tech. She couldn't even begin to think of dancing, for she no longer possessed the joy that once gave lightness to her feet.

She had no one to talk to about her pain except Buddy. Most of her friends on campus were on the antiwar bandwagon, and Susan couldn't bring herself to ask them for sympathy or understanding. Turning to her family was even more out of the question.

"The worst of it is Mother," she told Buddy, one of those long, lonely evenings when she sat on the floor in Buddy's living room, knees curled up to her chin. "She keeps saying..." Susan's chin wobbled, and with it her voice. "She keeps saying I should get on with my life. That it'll be a...a blessing if he... That I wouldn't want him to be a prisoner. And that's true, but... Oh, Buddy, I don't know what to think. Some days I just don't think I can get up in the morning."

"Anybody would feel that way, Susie. What you're going through is hell, and nobody expects you to act like nothing's wrong. Nobody expects you to quit hoping, either."

"Mother does." And Susan no longer had the heart for battling her mother. She felt like giving up.

"You just let old Buddy be your mother for a while. How's that?"

And she had done just that. Although only ten years older than Susan, Buddy had a weathered, trampled look about him that said life had dished out a lot, but he'd stood up to it. Stocky and ruddy, with eyes that out-twinkled anybody's idea of Santa Claus, Buddy was a workhorse, not a racehorse. That stability, that reliability, gave Susan something to hang on to while the rest of the world careered out of control.

During the next two years, Susan gave up many of the dreams she and Tag had shared. Dance became as much a fantasy of her childhood as tales of sleeping princesses and the princes who saved them. She quit college, concentrating instead on building her business. She refused to go home, taking only small pleasure in defying her mother.

The only dream she held on to was the dream that Tag would return, whole and unharmed and ready to whisk her right back into the happily-ever-after dream world they had built for themselves on the banks of Willow Creek. She wore her engagement ring and caught herself staring at it, lost in the sparkle of its tiny diamond, a dozen times a day. And at least once a week, she took the Double Wedding Ring quilt down from the closet, out of its box, and spread it on the bed. Sometimes she lay on it, facedown, imagining the smell of Tag's skin still clinging to the rose-and-green squares.

Mostly, however, the quilt only grew mustier and more tear-stained with each week, each month, each year, that passed.

Sometimes, Buddy Hovis was Susan's only link with sanity. He discovered new albums he thought she would enjoy and brought them home for her to listen to. He took her to funny movies and coaxed her into reading him the Sunday comics every week. He taught her to bake bread and how to use a corkscrew. He was gentle and compassionate and he let her talk about Tag whenever she needed to. Buddy was her one true friend.

Tag had been missing more than two years when Susan's hope began to waver.

The U.S. was scaling down its efforts in Vietnam. Reports surfaced almost daily about the inhumane treatment being handed out to prisoners of war. Few had survived.

"And I'm not sure I would have wanted him to," Susan confessed in a whisper against Buddy's often-bleached workshirt. His arms tightened around her. "I don't want to think he had to endure those things. Is that awful, Buddy?"

He patted her back and whispered against her hair. "To hope he didn't suffer? No, Susie, that's not awful. That's no more than any of us would wish for the ones we love."

"And I do love him, Buddy. Even after all this time."

"I know you do."

"I think I always will."

"I think so, too, Susie."

She had straightened up then, backing out of his arms and looking him straight in the eyes. "But maybe it's time I started letting him go."

THAT HAD BEEN ALMOST a year ago. And on the surface, Susan knew she'd done a pretty good job of convincing the world she'd let go of her memories of Tag. She might've fooled everyone, but she didn't think she'd fooled Buddy. He knew her too well.

At least that's what she'd thought until this moment.

"Buddy, I...I hope you know how I feel about you, too." And she saw from the look in his eyes that he did. But she still felt the only fair thing to do was say the words out loud. "You're my best friend. My family. My rock. I love you. But the way I love you..."

"I know it isn't the way you love Tag."

Susan looked down at her hands, clasped in her lap. The tiny diamond still winked at her from her third finger, left hand.

"Notice I said 'love.' I know it's not past tense, Susie. I know it probably never will be. But Tag's gone and I'm here. And maybe I'm just patting myself on the back a little too much, but I think he'd want you to be with somebody like me, who'll love you just as much as he did."

Tears came to Susan's eyes then, because she believed that was so, too. She knew Tag wouldn't want her to be alone forever. And she knew he would want someone as fine and decent as Buddy to take care of her.

She reached for one of the paper napkins she had anchored under the catsup bottle and wiped the tears that were trickling down her cheeks.

"Buddy, I can't imagine ever finding a better husband."

EVERYONE WAS THRILLED with the news. Especially Susan's mother, who seemed more than gratified with the way her daughter had quit resisting. But as the days passed, bringing her wedding day closer and closer, Susan grew more uncertain.

Tag haunted her. The stubborn line of his jaw, the determined jut of his chin. The gleam in his dark eyes and the hope in his young voice.

Sometimes she could almost imagine that she saw him—not her young Tag, but Tag as he would be today, older and harder from what he'd seen in the war, with an edge to him that almost frightened her. And whenever she saw him, he was reminding her.

You promised, he seemed to say. *You said you'd wait forever.*

But the lace suit had been made and the cake ordered and the invitations sent. Even a new ring bought.

The morning of her wedding, Susan slipped off Tag's ring for the last time. A pale indention marked her finger. She held the ring in the palm of her hand and looked at it one last time. Then she took the Double Wedding Ring quilt from her bed, opened a seam in the back and tucked the engagement ring inside the soft, fluffy batting. Then she sewed the seam shut.

CHAPTER THIRTEEN

SUSAN LAY IN TAG'S ARMS, weeping for the losses and laughing for the promise of his presence.

She told him the story as it came back to her, uncertain memories spilling into her head from who knows where. He grew tense, then relaxed, then tense again as she talked. He brushed her hair with his fingers, her forehead with his lips.

"I wish I'd known," Tag said when she finished, his voice soft in the darkness. "I wasted a lot of time on anger."

"I'm sorry. But I never knew where you were. And...I wasn't sure it would be...smart. To see you again."

She heard the rustling of his head on the pillow as he nodded. She took a moment to marvel at feeling so...normal. Lying here with him, curled against the length of his body, his breath on her forehead, the accident might never have happened. Twenty-five years might never have passed.

"You loved him."

She hesitated. "We had a good life. A daughter." She breathed in the scent of him. He was denim and soap and night air. "Was yours good?"

"No. It wasn't."

She kissed him now, on the jaw, jumped at the rough whiskers on his chin.

"Careful," Tag said. "Sam says I'm a bristly sort."

"Are you?"

The beat of his heart beneath her ear took on resonance. She lay still and listened to the sound, grateful they were both alive to find this moment of peace together after all these years.

"You wouldn't have liked me when I got back from 'Nam," he said. "And I wouldn't have been as good a husband as Buddy, that's for damn sure."

Susan's heart constricted. She wanted to contradict his words, but more than that she wanted to listen to him talk. Telling her own story had been healing; she hoped it would be the same for him.

"They held me almost three years," Tag continued. Susan winced, a shaft of pain going through her with his words. "I wasn't a pretty sight. My left leg was so mangled I could barely get around. The docs at VA ended up breaking it again just to reset the damn thing. I've got this one ear I can barely hear out of." He chuckled, but it had the sound of bitterness to it. "At least it muffles the sound on the track when I'm racing."

"Racing?"

"Motorcycles. Stock cars."

The hint that he led an exciting, physically challenging life gave her a moment of dismay, but she decided not to worry about the future or where this would lead. She would enjoy the moment. One of the many lessons of her accident was that she was promised only this moment; nothing more.

And for now, the pleasure of this moment was more than enough.

"'Course, the docs tell me that kind of noise won't do my other eardrum a lot of good," Tag continued.

"But I'm kind of hard to reason with sometimes. Lotta times, actually. I don't pay much attention to what people like doctors tell me I'm supposed to do."

The silence grew long.

"I guess I used up what little bit of obliging nature I might've had—and then some—over in the Hanoi Hilton."

He told her then about the years of captivity. Susan lost herself in his words—how he watched the others die, sometimes swiftly, mostly with agonizing slowness. She felt with Tag the despair of sitting by while others lost their faith, their courage, their will to hang on. She experienced with him the smirking of their captors playing videotapes of protesting students in the U.S., their impassioned young faces filled with distaste for returning soldiers.

"I wondered, sometimes, if anybody would welcome me if I ever made it back," he said. "But I knew you would. That was the only thing . . . the only thing I had to hold on to for the longest time. The only thing that kept me sane. Remembering you. Knowing you were waiting."

Susan felt the tears running out of the corners of her eyes, felt his T-shirt grow damp beneath her cheek.

"When I got back, they said I'd need about a year in rehab, but it didn't matter. I was back and I knew you were waiting. I wanted to tell you myself, wanted to hear your voice for myself. But when I called your house, Betsy answered."

Susan's heart grew heavy and cold in her chest.

"She said you were engaged. That you were going to be married in a week. That I wasn't to interfere."

Susan shot up in bed, awash in a tangle of emotions. "She knew! She knew you were back and she didn't tell me!"

She listened, horrified, as he told of the days he spent trying to get in touch with her. But he was stuck in a veteran's hospital bed in Virginia and no one would tell him how to reach Susan. Even his own mother agreed with Betsy Foster that he owed it to Susan to let her get on with her life.

"Almost a year passed before I even found out you were in Atlanta."

Knowledge of the lost years filled her. She sank back into his arms.

"I feel as if we've been robbed," she whispered.

"What are we going to do about it?"

She looked at the face just inches from hers. "What do you mean? What can we do?"

He leaned forward, and his lips touched hers. Startled, Susan grew very still. His lips were soft on hers, warmer than anything she could ever remember feeling. This was new, different from all the other new sensations she had experienced since the accident.

She liked this one better than all the rest.

She let her lips move the way his moved, a response that felt instinctive once she started. In fact, instinctive responses began to ripple through every part of her. Heat seared her. She raised a hand to touch his hair, but found that a gentle caress wasn't enough. Without thinking, she threaded her fingers through the silky strands of his thick, long hair, pulling him closer.

His lips barely parted from hers, he whispered, "We can take back what's ours, Susan."

"Yes," she whispered.

He touched her then, while his lips hovered over her face, her throat, her ears, in the barest of whispers. His big hand explored the curve of her breast beneath her nightshirt. Her body's response was immediate, stunning in its intensity. She gasped. His hand moved on, following the shape of her ribs, her belly.

"I'd know this anywhere," Tag whispered. "This is just how you felt then."

"I'm not seventeen now."

The whisper of a chuckle floated on the darkness. "Thank the Lord for that."

His touch swept along the swell of her hip, the slender length of her thigh. She tensed.

"What's wrong?"

She turned her face into the darker shadows where his shoulder and chest came together. "My bad leg."

"Does it hurt?"

"No. It...maybe it isn't pretty. Maybe it doesn't feel right."

She ached, waiting for his response, hoping for reassurance. When he moved, he lifted her nightshirt. She felt the cool night air on her thighs, then the whisper of his fingers on bare skin.

"You're beautiful, Susan." Now his touch moved to the inside of her thigh. "Not perfect. But still beautiful."

Again, tears smarted against Susan's eyelids. She relaxed. "Thank you."

"Hush. Just feel this. This is how beautiful you are to me."

And his hand continued to move along the length of her leg, until he reached the juncture of her thighs. He covered her with his palm, pressing against her. She opened slightly.

Tag's voice was hoarse. "I'm going to make love with you, Susan."

"I...I don't know if I...if I remember how."

He slid her panties off her hips, tossed them to the foot of the bed. "I'm not sure if I do, either."

He slipped her nightshirt over her head, then stood and swiftly dropped his own clothes to the floor. Susan's breath caught in her throat at the sight of him. His muscles weren't like hers. They were hard and defined, covered with dark skin and dusted with dark hair. His nipples were tiny, hard pebbles and she wanted to touch them. His maleness reached out, swelling and hard. She wanted to touch him there, too.

"We'll remember together," he said, putting his knees between hers.

He leaned forward to kiss her, but not on her face. He kissed her shoulder. Her breasts. Her belly. Susan was surprised to realize she had raised her legs—even her weak left leg—to press against his body, to try to bring him closer.

"Can I touch you?" she asked.

"Wherever you want."

So she did. Tentatively, she felt the crisp hair on his chest, let her fingers linger over the ripple of muscles along his back, the matching ripple along his stomach. His legs, his arms, everything was new and wondrous to her.

Then there was the hard shaft that seemed to seek her touch. She hesitated. He lowered himself, touching his erection to her belly. His flesh was hot. A wave of heat deep inside her responded to the touch.

With trembling fingers, she felt the length of his hardness. He groaned.

"Does it hurt?"

He laughed softly. "Not . . . not the way you think. I hurt from wanting you so badly. That's all."

The words were a revelation. This remarkable way she felt must be the same thing. She, too, hurt from wanting him so badly. She savored another tiny promise that she was normal, after all.

Feeling more sure of herself, she touched the swollen tip of his erection, felt the dampness, felt the throb of his response. She looked up, saw his eyes on her. They were dark with twenty-five years of the same unspoken emotions that filled her to bursting.

"I always loved you," she said. "Every day."

He kissed her, a long, slow kiss made up of promises renewed and regrets abandoned. She moved against him, brushing her breasts against his chest, her belly against his.

She felt him then, the swollen tip pressing against her, slipping inside her, and a moment of panic gripped her. But he moved slowly, filling her inch by inch until she realized there was nothing to fear.

They were one. The way it always should have been.

Tag moved within her. She moved with him. Slowly the intensity of their movements built, as did the physical sensations, until movement and sensation seemed to disappear. All that remained in the dark room was soaring emotion and a place where Susan felt a part of Tag and he a part of her.

THEY LAY STILL for a long time, murmuring softly to each other. The words hardly mattered, for each knew what the other said.

Susan felt whole in a way she never had, even before the accident. Scars and weak muscles, the tangled web of her mind, none of that seemed to matter. Even the lost years didn't matter, for right at this moment, all that had been lost was found.

"I feel too many things," Susan said, wishing she knew how to explain the jumble of emotions filling her. "I don't have that many words yet."

Tag brushed a kiss over her forehead, where she knew the fine pink line still marked her injury. "Nobody ever has that many words."

"Really?"

He nodded. "Even if nobody's ever conked you on the head, there's never any way to explain about love. All you can do is feel it. And give it away."

Susan liked the sound of that. She smiled. "Then I give mine to you."

Tag smiled, too, and she thought it was the nicest she'd ever seen him look. Almost like the boy he still was in her memories.

"And I give mine to you."

"Do you?"

"I promise."

She could see the bittersweet expression in his eyes as he spoke those words.

"I'm sorry I didn't wait."

"I'm sorry, too. But...you waited longer than most would have. I wouldn't have wanted you waiting forever." He smiled, another rueful smile. "I thought that's what I wanted, a lot of times. But this is how it's supposed to be. Maybe we were too young then. Maybe I came back so crazy and messed up that even if you'd waited, I would have driven you away. Maybe this is the only way we could keep it."

Susan struggled to understand. "By waiting?"

"Maybe I needed to grow up." He chuckled. "Maybe I still do."

The moon set and the night grew darker. They lay together and talked and touched and found the parts of themselves buried in each other's memory. They relived almost every minute of the years they'd been together, all of it fresh and alive again.

"Oh, no!" Susan looked up, dismayed.

"What's wrong?"

"The quilt. Malorie told me about the quilt. It's gone." Another wave of loss assaulted her. "Lost in the accident. It's gone." She clutched his hand—and realized she was using her weak one.

"It's okay," he whispered. "We'll make another."

"No, but...I used it all the time, after I decided you weren't coming home. I kept it in a box before that, saving it. But when I thought you were gone, when I thought I'd never see you again, I took it out." She realized she was talking completely unselfconsciously, as if Tag's acceptance made it all right that her speech was no longer perfect. She could talk all she wanted to without worrying how she sounded to anyone else. "Using the quilt was like... having part of you there with me."

"I'm glad, then."

"I almost wore it out. Using it on picnics. Taking it to the beach for Malorie to play on when she was little. Wrapping her in it when she had the flu. Oh, Tag, it can't be gone."

He wiped the lone tear escaping from her eye.

"Right before I...before the wedding...I sewed your ring into the lining, Tag. Because I still couldn't give it up. Even knowing I was going to marry someone else, I couldn't give up the idea that I was promised to you. And that...that promise was more real to me than any of the promises I gave Buddy."

He wrapped her in his arms and it was better, even, than being wrapped in the quilt she had treasured for so long. "The promises are still real. Even without the ring or the quilt, we still have the promises, Susan."

BETSY FOSTER WATCHED from her upstairs bedroom window as Tag strode away from the house in the gray light of predawn.

Seeing him leave, she hated him for walking tall, for not having the common decency to sneak away or feel the shame of taking advantage of Susan at her most vulnerable. Bitterness toward him burned in her gut, and fear whirled around her racing heart.

She had awakened in the dead of the night, jabbed by a sense of foreboding. Something was wrong in the house and she knew it. Unable to shake the feeling, she had risen, finally, and crept through the house.

She looked in on Cody, found him sprawled on his tummy, covers kicked to the foot of the bed. The moonlight silvered his fair hair and shadowed his plump cheeks. She wanted to touch him, to feel his soft baby skin, but she couldn't bring herself to do it. Just looking at him brought out feelings she couldn't control and couldn't express. Disgust and shame, she used to think.

Now she wondered if it wasn't her own guilt that kept her from caressing this little one. Had she ruined his life, too?

Standing outside Malorie's door, she had listened for the even breathing that would reassure her, and when she heard it, she slipped down the stairs. As always, Susan was at the heart of her greatest fears. That was what drove everything in her life, her fears for the precious daughter she had always loved more than anyone or anything in the world.

Betsy heard the soft murmur of Tag Hutchins' voice.

Clutching her robe close to her throat, she stood for a long time, unable to move, barely able to breathe, certain her heart would give out on her. But it didn't, and she mounted the stairs and posted herself in the straight-back needlepoint chair at her window. Sleep wouldn't have come in a million years, so she waited and worried.

Hadn't she always known the kind of man Tag would turn out to be? Hadn't she watched his father ruin the life of her best friend? How many times had she counseled Eula Hutchins, giving her the best possible advice?

"Leave him, Eula. Take those boys and get out now, before it's too late."

"You talk to a lawyer, Eula. You'll see I'm right. You don't have to live like this the rest of your life."

Over and over she had urged her friend. Until finally their friendship had suffered, while the troublesome marriage endured.

Betsy had known, of course, that what she urged Eula to do wasn't easy. Hadn't she learned that herself when she walked away from Jacob Finley? But she'd been right. Look what that rascal had done with his life, while she'd had all the security in the world with Reid Foster.

And what about being happy? a little demon in her head asked as Tag Hutchins disappeared into his house across the street. *Have you ever been happy?*

Or have you caused more heartache than you've ever prevented?

Betsy dropped her face into her hands, afraid for a moment that the sob rising in her chest might escape. She caught it just in time.

CHAPTER FOURTEEN

TAG OPENED THE STORE not long after daybreak.

Showered and shaved—he even trimmed his mustache, although he stopped short of his impulse to trim his hair off his collar—he had dressed in a fresh pair of jeans and the only sweatshirt he owned whose printed design hadn't faded beyond deciphering. Wide-eyed and wide awake despite his sleepless night, Tag had been unable to hang around the house. Any minute, he feared, he would be pounding on Betsy Foster's front door.

Later there'd be time enough for a little justifiable homicide.

Instead he went to the store, just hoping some poor early riser would be seized by a compelling need for peat moss before his morning coffee kicked in.

Nobody came, of course. And Tag found he was no less fidgety here than he had been at home. He paced. And as he paced, he began to discover all the little things Malorie Hovis had done in the past month.

Not a speck of dust to be found anywhere in the store, he discovered, although he well remembered the coat of gray that had dulled every surface a few short weeks ago. She had even rearranged the shelves, grouping like products and moving the slower-selling products to the top shelves and the big-sellers to eye-level. Neatly hand-lettered signs alerted browsers to special buys. And the table in the front, with its colorful display of gourds and pumpkins and multicolored corn gave even crusty old Tag Hutchins a festive feeling this morning.

Malorie Hovis was turning around Hutchins' Lawn & Garden. Making it a place where people might enjoy shopping again. He was proud of her. Wanted to give her a big hug the minute she walked in the door this morning.

"Slow down, Junior," he told himself, boosting himself onto the counter, where he sat and viewed the cheerful-looking store. "Don't start acting like she's your daughter yet."

But he knew the warning was pointless. Susan was his again. And this time, the whole world could go straight to hell before he'd let her go. He could finally stop running, could finally slow down and make a life for himself. He hadn't realized, until the thought came to him, how much he had ached for a real home, a normal life, people to help. People to love.

In fact, he had an idea. Betsy Foster be damned, he was going to do it.

Jumping down from the counter, he turned off the lights, locked up once again and went back out to his bike. By the time he got to Birmingham, the stores would be open. And if traffic was light, he could get back by midafternoon. He would surprise Susan. And Sam. And Betsy, damn her black-hearted soul.

SUSAN DIDN'T WAIT for her mother to come down so help would be within calling distance while she showered and dressed. She didn't wait for her mother to make the coffee, either, and was sitting in the kitchen, staring into the dregs of her first cup when Malorie came down.

"Mom! What a nice surprise." Malorie dropped a kiss on her cheek, then poured herself a cup of coffee. "Already up and raring to go? You mus'"ve rested well last night."

Smiling at her daughter's exuberance, Susan said, "The best night in a long time."

"Is that so?" Betsy's brittle voice said from behind her.

Susan didn't turn as Malorie greeted her grandmother, and she didn't respond to Betsy's ill-tempered question. "Sit down, Mother. I have a few questions for you."

Malorie looked at her quizzically, then glanced uncomfortably at Betsy. Betsy remained at the counter, behind Susan, presumably pouring coffee.

"I don't have time to sit around and chitchat, Susan," she said. "I have breakfast to make for all of us and a baby to wake and dress and—"

"You don't have to do a damn thing but answer my questions!"

Malorie's cup clattered into her saucer.

Some of the determination had gone out of Betsy's voice when she responded, "Watch your tone, young lady."

Susan had hoped to keep her fury in check, but her emotions ran too close to the surface this morning. If she'd had any other choice, she would have left this place immediately. But she was trapped and she was angry and she teetered on the verge of hating the woman she called mother. And Betsy's imperious attitude this morning wasn't helping one iota. "Watch yours, Mother. I'm not a little girl anymore."

Noticing that Malorie stared at the table, too uncomfortable even to get up and leave, Susan reached out and covered her daughter's hand and gave it a squeeze. Betsy walked around, sat at the table and faced Susan for the first time.

"All right. Whatever it is, you might as well get it off your chest."

Now that she had her mother's attention, Susan feared the confrontation more than anything else she had faced in the past three months. When she lost Tag, she lost her spirit. And ever since, she had simply accepted her mother's domination, caved in whenever Betsy passed judgment on all their lives. Did she really have the courage—now, of all times, when she couldn't even balance her own checkbook—to throw her mother's deceptions in her face?

The memory of all she and Tag had shared the night before was the only answer, the only bolster, she needed.

"Why didn't you tell me Tag had been released?"

Pity scrabbled at Susan's heart as she saw the color drain from her mother's already pale face. Betsy looked old and drawn.

"I don't know what you're talking about."

"He came home weeks before the wedding, Mother. And you knew it. You and Eula Hutchins were best friends. Of course you knew it. And you didn't even tell me."

"To what good purpose, for heaven's sake? To stir everything up? Everything was settled." She moved to stand. "That's all another lifetime, Susan. Stop obsessing over the past. Don't you have enough problems to keep you busy today?"

"I loved Tag and you knew it! You knew how long I'd waited. You knew how much I hurt."

"Well, Susan, I'm not a mind reader. If—"

Susan picked up her empty coffee cup and threw it across the room. It shattered against the wall. Malorie and Betsy jumped.

"Don't lie to me anymore! I talked to you the night before the wedding. I told you I wasn't sure! And you... you knew! And you didn't say a goddamn word."

"I know you aren't exactly stable right now, Susan, but that is no excuse for airing this unpleasantness in front of Malorie. Now, if you—"

"She deserves to know all this. She deserves to know what lengths you'll go to just to get us all to live our lives your way."

"I know what's going on here, Susan. And I won't see this start up again. You're still living with me, you know. This is still my house. And I warn you—I will do everything I can to keep Tag Hutchins out of your life."

Susan was the one who was startled when Malorie jumped up, sloshing her coffee across the table. "What *is* this? What is all this about?"

"Don't worry..." Susan began.

"This man has—" Betsy started.

"Stop it! Just stop it!" Malorie looked from one to the other. Color was high on her cheeks. Before Susan could speak again, before Betsy could continue, Malorie turned and ran out the door.

Betsy glared at her daughter. "Satisfied?"

"No, Mother. Not yet."

Then she wheeled herself out of the kitchen and left her mother to clean up the mess.

ONLY AFTER SHE STOPPED running did Malorie realize she had come out without her jacket. The cool fall air cut through her cotton sweater. A few blocks from the house, she felt chilled all over. She wrapped her arms tightly around herself and wondered where to go. Too early to go to the store. Too late to go home.

Too late for a lot of things, she supposed.

How had she let these things happen? How had she allowed her grandmother to manipulate her into making an even bigger mess of her life than she had made of it on her own? She longed to talk to her mother. Maybe soon she would be able to do that. Memories were recurring at a lightning pace, it seemed. This morning, Malorie had been so proud of her mother, so thrilled to see a side of Susan she'd never seen before. Even so, the confrontation had frightened her so much that all she could do was run away.

Your typical response, she thought. *Run away. From Cody. From life. From Sam.*

Oh, God, why did she have to remember Sam right now? Getting him and his kiss out of her mind even for a few minutes had been a blessing. A short-lived one, apparently.

A little girl's voice startled her. "You're s'posed to not forget your coat."

Malorie looked down into a pair of round, dark eyes belonging to Krissy McKenzie, Rose's stepdaughter. The dark-haired little girl clutched a book bag to her chest. The concern on the girl's face drew a smile from Malorie, despite her preoccupation with her own fears.

Malorie shrugged. "My mommy forgot to remind me. Does your mommy have to remind you sometimes?"

Now the little girl shrugged. "My mommy isn't here." After a solemn moment, her face broke into a grin that revealed a missing front tooth. "But my stepmommy remembers me to do a lot of stuff."

The little girl looked back down the sidewalk. Rose McKenzie was only a few steps behind. Calling out a greeting that was cheerier than she felt, Malorie stopped to wait for her mother's long-time friend.

"The lady forgot her coat." The little girl said by way of an update, then skipped off ahead of the two women.

"That's Krissy for you," Rose said. They followed the child at a slower pace. "She's learned from spending so much time with my Uncle Bump that sometimes grown-ups need taking care of, too."

Malorie forced a chuckle. "She's smart."

"How's your mother getting along? We really were tickled when she came into the shop the other day."

Something in the motherly warmth of Rose's voice made Malorie want to talk, spill all this to someone wise and tender and compassionate. She fancied she saw all those things in Rose's green eyes.

"She's . . . better, I think."

"Sam's a good therapist, I hear."

Sam. An inner tingle crashed head on with the goose bumps she already had from the morning chill. Perhaps she should work late again tonight, maybe start on the preholiday inventory. Just to make sure Sam was gone by the time she got home.

"Mrs. McKenzie . . . ?"

"Lordy, honey, call me Rose. I'm not ready to feel that old yet."

Malorie smiled again; this time it wasn't quite the effort it had been moments before. What a comfort to talk to someone like Rose. Someone loose and easy-going. It hit her then that Rose might know more about some of the things Malorie barely understood. She looked over at her neighbor.

"Okay. Rose. Do you... I'm not trying to be nosy or anything... Well, I don't know, maybe I am. But I wondered if you might remember anything about Mother and... Mr. Hutchins. You see, my grand-mother... That is, Mr. Hutchins acted... Well, it just seems like everybody knows what's going on but me."

Rose chuckled. "You're just right in the middle of a twenty-five-year-old feud, that's all."

"I am?"

"Mmm-hmm. You see, Betsy never did want Susan to have anything to do with Tag. I don't think it had a thing to do with anything Tag ever did. I think Betsy just had her own ideas about how Susan ought to live her life."

Malorie grunted. "Some things never change."

"But they fell in love, anyway."

"They did?" A shiver of anticipation coursed through Malorie. She had wondered, of course, when Sam said they dated all those years ago. But to hear it confirmed by someone who had been there made it all so real. "Mother and Mr. Hutchins?"

"Then he shipped off to Vietnam, although as I re-call they got engaged first. But Tag... he was a POW for... I don't remember how long. A lot of years, anyway. And when he finally got home, Susan had married somebody else."

A sick uneasiness invaded Malorie's belly as her mother's accusations that morning grew clear. Her grandmother had known Tag Hutchins was already home the day Susan married Buddy Hovis. She had let the wedding go on. Malorie felt light-headed with dismay. Did that mean her mother had never loved her father? Did that mean her mother had been sad and miserable all her life?

"Oh, God," she whispered.

"You okay, honey?" Rose put a hand on Malorie's shoulder.

"Yes. I mean, no. Not really." She looked up at Rose, not bothering to hide the tears welling in her eyes. "I'm realizing how much my grandmother has manipulated everybody's lives, that's all."

They continued on around the corner to the elementary school. Krissy already stood on the front sidewalk in a circle with three other children her size, comparing lunchbox contents. Waving goodbye to her stepdaughter, Rose turned and gave Malorie a hug.

"Don't hate Betsy for it. She's doing what she thinks is right."

"But it isn't. It's wrong!"

"The only defense is for everybody to stop letting her manipulate them."

"But how? I'm so confused. It's scary."

"I know. I remember how I let myself be coaxed into staying here, seeing after my father, then my mother. You know, I was forty before I realized I'd lived my life for everybody else but me."

"You were?"

"Yep."

"Then what did you do?"

"Well, shoot, I just started figuring out what *I* wanted for a change."

"You make it sound easy."

"I know. And I know it's not." Rose raised her face to the early-morning sunshine and breathed deeply of the crisp autumn air. "But you know what? Just a few years later, I'm working on a college degree, I have a stepdaughter I adore, a son—imagine that, a son of my very own—who makes me feel younger every day...well, except when he keeps me up all night...and a husband who's also my best friend. Honey, today I have the most perfect life I ever dreamed possible. And all because I decided I'd better start figuring out for myself what I wanted and how to get it."

"Gee."

"Yep. Gee is right. And if I had it to do all over again, there's only one thing I'd do different."

"What's that?"

"I'd start doing all that stuff a lot sooner. Say about—" she gave Malorie a speculative look "—oh, twenty or so, maybe."

They were standing in front of The Picture Perfect. Rose stopped, keys to the beauty shop jangling in her hand.

"Thanks for listening."

Rose shrugged. "No problem. Us wise, middle-aged folks like to give advice. Makes us think we didn't do all that messing up for no good reason."

Malorie laughed softly.

"It's a while before you open up. You planning to walk some more?" Rose asked.

"Maybe. I don't know."

Rose slipped off her jacket and draped it around Malorie's shoulders, giving her a pat as she did so. "You keep warm."

Malorie thanked Rose and slipped her arms into the jacket. She felt warmer, inside and out.

ROSE STOOD INSIDE the door of her shop, watching Malorie headed down the sidewalk, head lowered, once again deep in thought.

"You're a fine one to be dishing out advice," she muttered into the room. "Like you've got it all together, you old fraud you."

The truth was, she'd been teetering on the edge of panic for the better part of a month.

Sighing, she flipped on the overhead lights and started through the shop to begin the morning rituals. By the time she reached her station, the front door whipped open again. Alma had arrived.

"Hey, Finley, I b'lieve the weather's turned for good this time, don't you?"

Alma, who had worked at The Picture Perfect since Rose's mother owned the shop, refused to consider calling Rose by her married name. She insisted she was too old a dog to be learning new tricks, although Rose knew for a fact that Alma and her current main squeeze were learning country line dancing at a nightspot in Tuscumbia once a week.

"It's time," Rose said. "Thanksgiving's barely a week away."

"Well, you don't sound exactly enthused at the prospect of the holidays."

Alma removed the pink chiffon scarf that held her hair in place, stuffed it into the pocket of her cardigan and stared at Rose. Rose continued rinsing the plastic rods she'd used yesterday afternoon for Missy Grady's perm.

"I've got a lot of work to do before the end of the year, that's all. Exams are coming up."

Alma grunted, a response Rose had heard often enough to know it indicated a lack of conviction.

"Still haven't heard anything, huh?"

Rose turned the water off with a fierce twist of the faucet, then grabbed up a double fistful of rods and shook them. "I don't want to talk about this right now, Alma. I've got too much to do to be worrying about . . . stuff."

Twisting from side to side in the yellow vinyl chair at her station, Alma continued her steady examination of her co-worker. "It won't go away just because you don't think about it, Finley."

Rose stopped her busy work and faced Alma, hands on her hips. "Krissy's mother will turn up. I'm not worried, so there's no reason to talk about it."

"You think she's drinking again?"

Although it would certainly short-circuit any plans Cybil Richert might have of trying to regain permanent custody of Krissy, Rose nevertheless hoped the woman hadn't started drinking again. Krissy's mother's drinking had been a big part of the reason she'd tolerated her second husband's abusive behavior toward Krissy when she was just a toddler. A big part of the reason Ben had actually kidnapped his own daughter and brought her to Sweetbranch where Maxine ran an underground network for abused children. Rose prayed Krissy would never have to be exposed to anything so traumatic again.

"Alma, I don't know what to think. All I know is, she's walked out on her job and nobody's heard from her."

"How far is it from here to Winston-Salem, reckon?"

"Far."

"But not far enough, huh, Finley?"

"No. Not nearly far enough."

CHAPTER FIFTEEN

TAG STOOD OUTSIDE the dining room, box in his arms, and watched as Susan grunted and strained to lift her stronger right leg and stand upright only on her left one.

"Hang in there," Sam urged.

"I... am!" Susan panted through gritted teeth. Perspiration stood out on her forehead, her scar showing a brighter pink from the exertion. Her left leg, thin and laced with its own pink scar, trembled with effort.

The scene tore at Tag's heart, filling him with too many emotions to sort through. Pride for her effort, love for her courage and pain for her pain. His own bad knee twitched just from watching her. He'd been there. He knew it all firsthand.

"What are you doing in my house?"

He didn't bother turning to respond to Betsy's sharp inquiry. "I'm not here to see you, Betsy."

Susan and Sam, having heard their voices, stopped and looked. Susan teetered and Sam caught her.

"Tag!"

Susan's exclamation sounded delighted; Sam's surprised. Tag smiled at them both, but his eyes were for Susan only. "Brought a little surprise if you two can take a rest."

Sam looked at Susan, and seemed to see her pleasure in Tag's presence. He immediately adopted a mock-serious tone. "I don't know, Tag. When I got here this afternoon, Susan told me she wanted us to step up her program. Something about making up for lost time?"

Betsy stepped into the dining room, positioning herself between Tag and the other two. "I've warned you before, Eugene—"

"And I'm through listening to you," Tag snapped in a tone to match hers. "Your days of ruining other people's lives are over, Betsy."

He was astonished at the venom in her eyes until he realized it was only a thin veneer. What lay beneath was fear.

"If I have to call the sheriff, I will certainly do it."

"No!"

At the sound of Susan's voice, Betsy closed her eyes and took a deep breath. For the first time, Tag really saw her: the iron-gray hair that had no life, the shoulders that showed no sign of yielding, the grim lines etched at the sides of her mouth and between her eyebrows, all testimony to the attitude she'd brought to life. Then he had a vision of himself, equally bitter, equally determined not to give life a chance these past twenty years. Betsy Foster became a vision of what Susan's return to his life had saved him from.

"Stop it, Mother. Right now!"

Everyone looked at Susan, who stood on her own two feet, bracing herself on her wheelchair and looking as determined as she had looked back in the days when she was willing to take on anyone—especially her mother.

Tag's heart twisted in his chest. He took a step in Betsy's direction, stood so close the box he held almost touched her chest. "If I have to, I'll take Susan with me."

She studied him for a long minute, then swept past him, pausing only to say under her breath, "This isn't over."

But Tag knew it was, and he turned his attention to the two people he loved most in the world—the people who, amazingly, still seemed to love him.

"Come on, you two. This rehab's about to go high-tech."

Within half an hour, while Susan watched and Sam proved himself more at home on the information highway than his uncle, a computer whirred to life on the table in Susan's room. Tag was glad Sam knew what he was doing. Disconnecting the computer in his office at the store hadn't been too tough; reassembly might have been more than his experience in motorcycle maintenance had prepared him for.

"But what am I going to do with a computer?" Susan asked.

"Ah!" Tag dug a shopping bag out of the box. "I'm glad you asked that."

Once again, Sam saved the day. Soon, software installed, the computer screen filled with a series of icons lined up across from a series of words. Tag saw from the pleased and grateful look on his nephew's face that Sam knew exactly what the software was for. Susan, however, inched forward in her chair and stared, confused, at the screen.

"That's a dog," she said. "Like Butch. And look!"

She pointed at the screen and looked over her shoulder at Tag. "It says 'dog.' Right there."

Without waiting, she keyed in the word from the list beside the icon. Both she and Sam started when the computer announced, amid the chime of bells, "Good job!"

Susan laughed, and Tag couldn't decide what to do with his pleasure. His heart told him it was okay to feel a little misty, but he didn't think he was ready to go that far yet.

"Tag, where did you get this?" Susan exclaimed, already eagerly keying in a word beside the next icon on the screen.

"In Birmingham. It's to help people learn to read and write again after injuries like yours." He squatted beside her, couldn't help but join her when she once again laughed at the positive feedback from the computer. "I thought you and I might make more progress this way than you and Betsy were making."

He and Sam exchanged a glance. Tag had been furious to realize that Susan had actually lost ground with her reading and writing while working with her mother. He was determined that situation wouldn't continue. He'd bought the most basic of reading and writing programs, as well as some intermediate programs. She would be needing them soon if he had anything to do with it—and if her immediate enthusiasm for the new computer was any indication.

"Oh, Tag, I love it. Now reading can be fun, just like sewing with Addy is fun." She turned to Sam with the impish smile Tag had only seen in his hungry, tortured memories for twenty-five years. "If we had a computer to take Sam's place, maybe that would be fun, too."

Sam laughed. "No way. I'm here to make you miserable and nobody's horning in on that."

How long they stayed hunched over the computer, laughing over Susan's exploration of the lessons at her fingertips, Tag wasn't sure. Even young Cody joined them. Tag boosted him into Susan's lap and the game continued.

They were all surprised to hear Malorie's soft voice from the doorway. "I see there's a party and I wasn't invited."

She sounded strained to Tag, and he looked up to study her. Her face confirmed what he'd heard in her voice. Although she was clearly striving to look and sound normal, her face was paler than usual, and there was no sparkle in her eyes.

He also noticed the mix of emotions on her face. Sympathy and concern as her glance strayed from her mother to her boss and back again. A sad, hurt look at little Cody, who pounded happily on the keyboard. Then she glanced at Sam and immediately looked away. But Tag didn't miss the flicker of feelings she exhibited. She had the wary, excited, secretive look of a young woman in the agonies of falling in love, and battling it every step of the way.

A quick look at Sam told Tag his nephew was in the same boat. Except he wasn't fighting the current at all.

Sam took Malorie by the hand and drew her into the room. "Take a look. My uncle's embarking on a new career. What do you think of Tag as a teacher?"

"Wait a minute," Malorie said. "That's *my* computer. What about inventory? Orders? Billing?"

Tag shrugged. "Emergency conscription?"

Amid Malorie's playful complaints about the downward spiral of efficiency at the store, they explained the new software and Susan demonstrated her efficiency. Even Cody took a hand at mimicking her and thrilled himself and everyone else when the computer declared, "Good job!"

Worried that Susan might be tired, Tag suggested that they quit for the day. But Susan wasn't ready to stop. Then Tag noticed she was leaving her left hand in her lap, keying in her responses one-handed. He realized that her speech had also grown slower, a little less distinct, in the past half hour. He questioned Sam with his eyes; his nephew nodded almost imperceptibly.

Tag knelt beside her. "Let's not wear out the computer on its first afternoon, how about?"

Susan looked at him, unable to hide her weariness despite her enthusiasm. "Do we have to stop?"

"I'll be back in the morning," he promised. "We'll spend as long as you like. I've got enough software here to have you writing *War and Peace.*"

At her quizzical expression, he amended, "A real big book."

She laughed softly. "Okay. But don't leave yet. Let's sit on the porch first. It's... we don't have to go to supper yet, do we, Mal?"

Malorie leaned over to kiss her mother's cheek, then lifted Cody out of Susan's lap. "You guys sit and visit. I'll take Cody for a walk. I think he needs a little time to calm down from all this excitement."

"I'll come with you," Sam volunteered.

Tag watched the silent interplay between the two, looked down to see if Susan noticed as well. She did. The struggle between the young people was hard to miss. Malorie was trying to escape, Sam determined to pursue. Malorie relented.

As the young people left, Tag was grateful that things would be simpler for him and Susan. They both knew what they wanted. They had both been without it too long to be indecisive now, he told himself as he pushed her onto the side porch and sat in the wicker rocker facing her.

"They like each other," he said.

"She's stubborn," Susan said. "Something's holding her back."

"What?"

He saw her hesitation. "I don't know. I keep thinking I should. But..." She tapped the side of her head. "If the reason's up here, it's still hiding."

She let her hand drop and closed her eyes. Her shoulders sagged. "I wanted to work as hard as you did. That's what I told Sam when he got here today."

Tag thought back to his first weeks in therapy, when he believed he had to recover quickly so he could go in search of Susan. He remembered what a setback he had suffered when his old man told him she was married. He'd almost quit right then. "It's easier when you have something to work toward. Something worth fighting for."

"I do," she said, her voice tired but determined. "I have to get away from Mother."

Tag leaned forward, took her hand in his. She gripped it weakly, but he knew the effort it took. "I'll take you away, Susan. Come with me and—"

She was already shaking her head. "When I'm back to normal. Then I'll come with you."

Uneasiness flirted with the euphoria he'd felt all day. All that Sam had told him about her injuries whirled in his busy mind. "Susan, you don't have to be perfect for us to be together."

She opened her eyes. "Oh, yes, I do. And I will be. I'm going to work so hard I'll be all well in no time at all."

Tag didn't know what to say that wouldn't discourage her. All he knew was that he didn't intend to wait another twenty-five years for Susan to figure out that she might never recover completely.

CODY SCRAMBLED ALONG the edge of Willow Creek, stumbling over his puppy and squealing in delight as his chubby fists splashed in the water.

"Be careful," Malorie called out from farther up the bank, where she stood with Sam. "Maybe I should get him before he scrapes his knee or something."

"He'll be fine," Sam said, taking her hand to restrain her. "Kids are supposed to scrape their knees. That's how they learn to slow down and watch where they're going."

Malorie looked up at him, knowing he couldn't understand her fears, but irrationally expecting him to do so, anyway. "I thought that's what mothers were for."

"And big sisters?"

She looked away. "Yes. And big sisters."

She walked off and sat on a big, flat rock, keeping a careful eye on Cody. All these changes were hard for her to handle. Her emotions were upside down, and Sam's presence didn't help a bit. As if doing his best to be contrary, Sam dropped to the ground at her feet, propping his elbow on the corner of the boulder.

"Susan was different today."

Malorie nodded but said nothing.

"What happened? Do you know?"

Darting an uncertain look at him, she clasped her hands on her knees. He was so close, too close. What would she do, she wondered, if he kissed her?

Run.

She tried to steer her thoughts back to the things that were really disturbing her. Sam was a distraction, that was all. "She and Grandmother had a big fight."

"Mrs. Foster seems to fight with a lot of people."

Malorie shook her head. "I've never seen Mother argue with her. It was scary."

"I suppose Tag has something to do with all this."

She wondered how much he knew and toyed with the idea of sharing her secret with him. The idea gave her a lift. "You wouldn't believe what Rose McKenzie told me this morning."

"I might."

She looked at him, saw the amusement in his eyes. "You knew? And didn't tell me?"

"We both knew they were friends," he pointed out. "I just didn't know how friendly until Tag told me the other night."

Malorie sighed. "Do you think they'll fall in love again?"

"I'm not sure they've ever been out of love."

Hurt flickered through her heart. If that were true, what did it say about her parents' relationship all those years? Wasn't it bad enough that her whole future was in question? Did she have to lose everything she'd ever believed about the past, too?

Sam put a hand on her wrist. "I'm sorry. I didn't mean that. I meant, I'm not sure Tag's ever been out of love with Susan."

His hand on her wrist felt so comforting. Too comforting. She pulled away. "I never thought my parents were unhappy, but—Cody! Be careful!"

She had glanced up just in time to see him lunge into the water and sprawl, facefirst, in the shallow creek.

Malorie's heart gave a fearful leap, but when Cody looked up, he was grinning gleefully.

"Fwogs, sissy! See the fwogs!"

Sam laughed. "Bring one up here for sissy to see, Cody."

"Don't encourage him," Malorie said, peeved that she seemed to be the only one who saw the darkness waiting to ruin their lives.

"Why not? Maybe he needs a break from Betsy's brand of vigilance." Sam touched her again, tracing the pale veins on the back of one hand. It felt just as it had before, soft and warm and comforting. She wanted to shrug off the touch, but found herself frozen. "Maybe he isn't the only one."

"Don't touch me like that." She heard the quaver in her voice and hoped it didn't rob her words of all conviction.

He kept touching her, tracing her fingers until he gave her goose bumps. She should have run when she first thought of it, because it was too late now.

"Are you cold?" His voice was teasing.

"No, I—I mean, yes. I am. We should go back."

He put one hand on the back of her neck. He was almost close enough to kiss her, and she was still paralyzed by feelings she was too confused and fearful to name. "You can't keep running away, Malorie."

"I don't want this," she whispered.

"Yes, you do." He clasped her head in his hand, letting his fingers tangle in the soft waves of her hair. "You can't run away forever."

"I'm not running away," she said. *But I should be.*

"Then kiss me."

"I don't want to kiss you." *Liar.*

He laughed softly, and she knew he, too, could see straight through her to the truth. And that, after all, was the danger, wasn't it? That he would get to know her too well, see too clearly all the things she had to keep hidden?

Then he dropped his hand. She faced him uncertainly. What would a normal person do now? she wondered.

"It was good to see the change in your mother today," he said, his voice still intimate. "It's clear she's decided she isn't going to let her injuries rule the rest of her life. She'd going to grab hold and take what she wants. You should look for a little of your mother's courage, Malorie."

The words hurt. There was too much truth in them. But for the life of her, Malorie didn't know what to do about it, didn't know how to steer away from this course of fear and deception.

Before she could reply, Cody dashed up and dropped something into her lap.

"Sissy, a fwog! Can I keep the fwog?"

Malorie couldn't even look down at the rambunctious little boy and his prize. Her eyes were still on Sam.

Sam's smile was no longer teasing when he said, "Even Cody is braver than you."

And now that she was pushed to the wall, no one knew that better than Malorie.

CHAPTER SIXTEEN

BETSY FOSTER TESTED her daughter's determination daily for the rest of the week.

"Why is she doing this to me?" Susan asked Tag as he installed a new cord for the computer. The original had turned up missing after Betsy's intensive cleaning of Susan's room.

Tag pushed the Power button and shook his head. "All I know is, sometimes I tried punishing the people I blamed for making me miserable. I think I've finally figured out the one I was punishing most was myself."

The computer whirred to life. Susan closed her eyes and squinted, focusing her thoughts on what Tag had said, trying to reason out what he meant. "Does that mean she's unhappier than we are?"

Tag leaned closer and kissed her tightly shut eyelids. They fluttered open and Susan looked into his gently smiling face.

"Yeah," he said. "Something like that."

Susan tried to reconcile that thought with her ever-worsening opinion of her mother. She tried to feel grateful that her mother was willing to take care of her while she recovered. But it was so hard to feel anything but impatient to get out of here, to get well enough to begin her own life again.

Sometimes, that day seemed so far away.

Glancing down at her hands, Susan said, "Do I sound . . . dumb sometimes?"

Tag lifted her chin. "No, you don't sound dumb. You'd sound dumb if you pretended to understand everything everybody said. Or if you didn't care enough to try and figure things out." He leaned closer yet and whispered, "Or if you acted like you thought for one single moment that anything you could do would keep me away from the woman I love."

Susan laughed softly. "Like Mother."

He nodded and kissed her again, this time softly on the lips. "Exactly. Now, are you ready for Advanced Kitchen Vocabulary?"

Shaking off the way his touch tingled through her, Susan sat up straight in her chair and faced the computer. "Ready."

Concentrating on the daily lessons was extra hard with Tag so close. Sometimes Susan had to use every bit of her concentration to pay attention to the words spelled out on the computer screen, because Tag's nearness distracted her so. They hadn't made love again since that first night. Tag hadn't even brought it up, although he told her with a million little looks and touches that it wasn't for lack of wanting to. And all those little messages kept Susan atingle. When he was with her, she wanted Tag to touch her again far more than she wanted to match the icon of the stove with the squiggles that spelled out the word.

And at night, when she was alone, she longed for him. Longed for his hands, stroking her body in a way that made her feel far more than whole. She came alive to his touch; she felt young and beautiful and perfect again. She longed to feel him moving inside her, longed for the heart-stopping shudder of his body as he climaxed. Longed to rest her head on his shoulder and fall asleep to the rhythm of his breathing.

"Do you still want me?" Even she hadn't expected the question. She wished she hadn't asked and wondered why, this particular time, it had been so easy for her brain to find words for the feelings inside her. She squinted at the screen and tried to pretend she hadn't said a word.

"Look at me, Susan."

She shook her head. "No. That was a silly question. I want to learn some more now."

Tag reached out and turned the screen on its swivel base so she could no longer see it. Then he picked her up and drew her onto his lap. She let out a startled cry.

"I want you every minute," he said, softly touching her hair with his fingers. "Why is it so hard for you to believe that?"

She shook her head.

"Tell me, Susan."

"You won't make love with me again," she whispered.

"This is Betsy's house," he said. "I won't risk any kind of ugliness with her, not about that. Move out, Susan. Come home with me."

She shook her head again, this time more forcefully. "Not now, Tag. I won't come until I'm...better."

She wanted to be able to walk and talk and drive and take care of his house and Cody and everything, just the way she had before. She would accept no less, no matter what Tag said.

So, every morning, they plugged away at her reading and writing while Betsy plugged away at blocking Tag's visits. She clipped the wires to the front doorbell. She kept the double doors to Susan's room flung wide open whenever Tag came over and commenced her vacuuming or any other noisy activity to thwart their conversation. She sent Cody in to play while Susan and Tag tried to work. She opened the door leading from the kitchen to Susan's room and rattled pans for hours on end. She invited Addy to come over an hour earlier, until Addy figured out what was going on and resumed the previous schedule. She even started inviting Bump Finley to bring his nephew over in the mornings so Cody and Jake could play their rambunctious games on the side porch.

The only thing she didn't do was speak—to either one of them.

Susan's concentration suffered. So did her emotional state. Some days she desperately wanted to pull the covers over her head and avoid the hostility that emanated from her mother. But that way, she knew, lay defeat. And she refused to be defeated by her mother.

"Not again," she would whisper to herself, then begin the painstaking process of dragging herself out of bed and bathing and changing clothes. "Never again."

Some days the strain gave her headaches. Some days she was so weary from it all, she could barely keep herself moving for late-afternoon therapy.

"Is something wrong, Susan?" Sam asked one day when she felt too weak to drag herself out of the wheelchair.

Afraid to tell him for fear he, too, might ban Tag from the house, Susan shook her head. "I'm fine."

"No, you aren't. Is it Tag?"

"No!" She tried to swallow back the panic. "No, really. I . . . I don't sleep well. That's all."

"Why not? What's on your mind?"

Frustration welled up in Susan. Sometimes she felt badgered on every front.

"Malorie," she said, wondering where that had come from.

"What about Malorie?"

She saw the interest in his eyes and felt guilty for the fib. Except, as she thought about what to tell him next, she realized it was no fib at all. She did worry about her daughter. On top of everything else, she saw how wan and edgy her daughter seemed these days. She had seen her daughter sink into that state before. If only she could remember when and why, perhaps she could prevent it from happening again.

"I don't think she's happy."

"Do you know what makes her unhappy?" Sam settled onto the floor, hooked his arms around his knees and looked up at her.

Susan shook her head.

Sam seemed engrossed in the subject. "She seems afraid of something to me. I wish I knew what."

"I keep thinking I should know. But I can't remember."

He put a reassuring hand on her knee. "Don't worry. It will come to you. And, Susan? When it comes to you...will you tell me?"

"Why?"

"Because I like Malorie. I might be...I might like her a lot."

"That would be nice."

"So you'll tell me? So I can help?"

Memories tickled the back of Susan's mind and she hesitated. But in the end, the look of genuine concern in Sam's eyes won out over the uncertainty of what the past held and how that might affect the future. Susan nodded.

BUMP FINLEY FINALLY caught on.

This past week, he had grown fond of sitting in the wicker rocker on the side porch at Betsy's, tuning out the shrill bickering and giddy fun of the two young'uns, Jake and Cody. Although he had occasionally come over so Jake and Cody could play in the weeks after Susan came back to Sweetbranch, Bump's spat with Betsy at church a few weeks back had brought that to an end.

That's why Betsy's call inviting him to bring Jake over in the mornings had taken him by surprise at first.

"Now, you must be sure to come in the morning," Betsy had insisted, sounding far more cheerful than he'd heard her sound in a coon's age, "because things get hectic around lunch, what with Susan's therapy and all."

So Bump had taken to coming. Tuning out the young'uns was no trouble. He could sit for an hour or more and hardly notice as they rammed their plastic trucks into one another or battered each other with ragged-eared stuffed rabbits or created the sounds of battlefields with their little toddler voices.

He pondered, one morning, how it was that Susan and her feller, Tag Hutchins, got much studying done on that computer right inside the door. They'd told him that first morning what they were up to—computer reading lessons for Susan.

It came to him finally. Betsy, the old cuss, was up to her tricks again.

Swearing a blue streak under his breath, Bump struggled up out of the chair, gave his trick knee—aw, hellfire, it wasn't trick at all, just crippled up with arthritis, was all—a chance to straighten out, then stuck his head inside the door.

"'Scuse me, Mizz Hovis, Tag," he said, and waited for the two to look over their shoulders. "It's just occurred to this old, befuddled brain of mine that these young'uns must make it right hard for the two of you to concentrate."

Susan and Tag exchanged glances, and Bump knew all he needed to know.

"Blast it all!" he said. "Beggin' your pardon, Mizz Hovis. Let me get these two noisy whippersnappers out of your hair right now. Come on, Jake, Cody. Pick up them trucks and we'll take 'em over to the park for a while. How's that?"

While Tag helped retie shoelaces and snap the two little boys into their jackets, Bump went into the yard in search of Betsy. He found her at the clothesline. Two blindingly white sheets already billowed in the November breeze, and a row of pink-and-white towels snapped as the wind whipped them around.

"Betsy Foster," he said, and took a perverse delight in watching her start. "You're just a black-hearted, mean-spirited old woman. How in the devil I ever figured to be sweet on you, I'll never understand."

Hands on her hips, Betsy glared at him. "I didn't invite you over here to remind me that never for one single minute of your sorry life did you regret giving me up without a fight, Jacob Finley."

Not to be distracted, Bump said, "No, but I know why you did invite me over here."

With a huff of frustration, Betsy turned back to the clothesline and snapped a pin onto the corner of a green-sprigged housedress. "What are you ranting about, Jacob?"

"You're still thinking to run Susan's life, aren't you." He walked up, plucked a bibbed apron from the clothes basket and handed it to her.

"I don't have any earthly idea what you're talking about."

"Oh, I b'lieve you do. And I ain't gonna be part of it anymore. I'm taking the boys to the park, Betsy. Givin' those young people a little peace and quiet for those lessons."

"You're an old fool if you think he's here to give her lessons!"

Bump chuckled. Couldn't help himself. Some cantankerous part of him delighted in spats like this. "And you're an old fool if you think you can stop him."

Betsy whipped a towel in the breeze to snap the wrinkles out of it. "Get on out of here, Jacob."

"I'm gettin', I'm gettin'." But before he got far, he turned and looked back. Still a fine-looking woman, Betsy was. "Sometimes I almost wish things had turned out different, Betsy. Maybe I wouldn't be such an old grump."

"That would be a blessing."

He chuckled again. "And maybe you wouldn't be such an old busybody."

Her outraged muttering set a swift rhythm for his stiff-legged retreat across the leaf-strewn lawn.

THANKSGIVING DAY at the Foster house proved to be as bleak as the weather. Beyond the off-white lace curtains at the dining room window, Susan could see the ledge of dark gray clouds hanging low over near-bare trees. The drizzle had stopped midmorning, just after her brother and his family arrived. But the clouds continued to look ominous; Susan's heart felt the same.

Steve and his wife, Debbie, had brought card tables and set them up in the dining room where Susan usually worked out. Chatting cheerfully about their jobs and their grandchildren's forays into kindergarten, they covered the ugly metal tables with festive paper tablecloths trimmed with cartoons of pumpkins and turkeys in Pilgrim hats. They set out paper plates and napkins in the same motif. And by noon the five adults silently passed the platter of turkey and the bowl of corn bread dressing and a small serving tray of cranberry sauce. Cody sat in a high chair between Malorie and Betsy, gaily splattering giblet gravy all over his plate.

Susan felt bad for Steve and Debbie, who both looked uncomfortable as the strain in the air dampened the festive mood they were trying so hard to generate.

"So, Susie-Q, how's the therapy going?" Steve asked. "You look great."

As she often did, Susan wondered just how great she looked. In honor of the holiday, Malorie had helped her dress in a soft rayon skirt and a cranberry-colored tunic instead of the comfortable fleece workout clothes she usually wore. Susan felt pretty. She wished she could look into Tag's eyes and see his approval. That often made her feel pretty, even in gray fleece.

But Betsy had made it clear. Tag Hutchins was forbidden to ruin her family holiday. Tag had said it didn't matter, had assured Susan he had other plans, anyway. But she had seen the bleakness in his dark eyes when he'd left yesterday.

He sat in that house alone, she was certain of it. Contemplating the possibility, Susan was not one whit grateful for her mother on this day of gratitude.

"She still can't walk," Betsy said into the silence.

"She can," Malorie insisted. "Can't you, Mother? I saw her two days ago, when I came in from work."

"Clinging to that rail," Betsy said, nodding toward the metal bar. "What good does that do, I ask you, a step or two at a time?"

"It's progress," Susan said, staring into the plate of food she didn't feel like swallowing and hoping she wouldn't cry.

Debbie touched Susan's arm. "Well, of course it is. My goodness, that seems like a lot of progress to me."

The tone of Debbie's voice sounded to Susan a lot like the tone Betsy used to compliment Cody on an impossible-to-decipher drawing. Telling herself Debbie meant well, she managed an upbeat smile for her sister-in-law.

Another few minutes of silence followed before Steve could think of another way to coax a conversation out of them.

"Mal, I hear you've got a job. How's that going?"

"Fine." Malorie sounded inclined to let that be the end of it. Susan looked up, their eyes met, and Malorie added, "I'm working at the Lawn & Garden. It's fun, actually."

Steve looked surprised. "At Hutchins'?"

"That's right."

Betsy thrust a bowl at her son. "More sweet potatoes?"

"Thanks, Mom." He scooped out a heaping spoonful. "I thought Mrs. Hutchins died a few months ago. Who's keeping the place open?"

"Shall I bring more rolls from the kitchen?" Betsy asked.

Malorie raised a stubborn chin and stared at her grandmother through narrowed eyes. "Her son owns the place now. You probably know him, Uncle Steve. Tag Hutchins."

"Tag?" Steve put the serving spoon back in the sweet potato soufflé and looked incredulously from Malorie to Susan. "Tag's back in town? Why didn't somebody tell me?"

Susan saw the excitement in her brother's eyes and knew she had an ally. "He's been helping me read."

"Helping you read? Really?" Steve's smile grew broader yet. "Is he staying at the house?"

Malorie patted her lips primly with one of the Pilgrim-hatted turkeys on the corner of her napkin. "Why, yes. I suspect he's there right now."

"Well, I'll be. I'll have to run over there after dinner. Deb, you've got to meet Tag."

Betsy shoved abruptly away from the table. "I'll bring another pitcher of tea."

She stalked out of the dining room. Steve looked around. "What's her problem?"

"She doesn't like Tag," Susan said simply.

"Still? After all this time?"

Malorie leaned across the table and lowered her voice. "He's been so sweet to help Mother, and he gave me a job and everything, but Grandmother refuses to be civil to him. I'll bet you anything he's sitting over there alone right now, and—"

Steve's fork clattered to his plate. "You're kidding? Alone on Thanksgiving Day? When we've got a twenty-pound turkey in the kitchen and enough food to feed an army?"

He stood. "I'm going to get him."

Debbie reached for his sleeve. "Now, Steve, if Betsy—"

"Tell Mother to set another plate."

He was out the door before anyone could react. Going to the shopping bag her uncle had brought in, Malorie retrieved another paper plate and napkin. Susan noted the tremble in her daughter's hands as she set the place and hated herself for allowing her daughter to grow up with such a weak mother for an example. Even Debbie glanced anxiously in the direction of the kitchen.

"Oh, dear," she said softly. "Betsy isn't going to like this, is she?"

Malorie dropped back into her chair, running a hand over Cody's blond curls as she did. "Betsy has run the show long enough."

Susan took courage from her daughter's tone of voice. Debbie shrank into her chair.

When Betsy returned with a pitcher of tea, she glanced at Steve's empty chair and the extra place Malorie had set. She circled the table refilling glasses, then sat again stiffly. No one spoke. No one ate except Cody, who had just discovered the raisins in his sweet potatoes. Betsy didn't even bother to correct him as he mined for raisins.

All four of the women stiffened further when the front door opened. Steve's boisterous voice carried into the room, and Susan looked up to watch Tag walk in.

He was dressed haphazardly, heedless of the holiday in frayed jeans and a University of Alabama sweatshirt that had been washed so many times the Crimson Tide was pink. His hair was uncombed save for a distracted sweep of his fingers, although it shone from his morning shower. His mustache captured Susan's attention; she remembered the soft feel of it against her lips when they kissed.

Suddenly the room brightened, although the sky outside was still the color of dull pewter.

Tag's first glance was for Susan—his eyes were hungry and solemn and apologetic—but he first went to Malorie and greeted her with a kiss on the cheek. A family kind of gesture, it seemed to Susan. Then he turned to Cody, who had crowed with delight the minute Tag appeared, and spent a moment or two pretending to steal the boy's plate of food. He met Steve's wife, displaying all the Hutchins charm. Then he turned to Betsy and, standing behind the chair that had been placed at the table for him, said, "Thank you, Betsy, for the invitation."

Betsy's cheeks grew red, whether with anger or embarrassment or both, Susan wasn't certain. Betsy stared at the centerpiece Malorie had made and brought home from the store. Susan noted that Steve, too, stood behind his chair, as if waiting for Betsy's reaction.

If Betsy noticed that her son was waiting for Tag to be made welcome, she gave it no mind. She nodded curtly, and Susan supposed that was the most she could unbend.

"Mom." Steve's prod held a warning tone.

She glanced up at her son. "Please, everyone, sit."

Tag sat, although Susan doubted he felt very welcome. She wondered if he was only trying to get Steve to sit, to avoid the confrontation. Beneath the table, she reached for his hand and squeezed it. He squeezed back, although his smile was uncomfortable.

Steve, once seated, pretended to be oblivious to the tension in the room. He started grilling Tag on his escapades, and Tag obliged with subdued stories of drag racing and dirt track motorcycle races and treks across the southeast to do stunt work for movies being shot on location.

"Mr. Hutchins, I had no idea you were so glamorous!" Malorie exclaimed.

"I'm glad Steve never had that kind of adventurous streak in him," Debbie said, her smile still nervous. "I'd be scared to death."

Tag chuckled. "Didn't your husband ever tell you what all his buddies called him in the old days?"

When Debbie shook her head, Tag gave Steve a devilish look and said, "We all called him Crash. And it wasn't because he could learn all the algebra he needed the night before an exam, either."

The conversation grew lively, despite Betsy's bitter silence. Despite Susan's relative silence, too, for she couldn't help but hear these additional details about Tag's life with renewed trepidation.

He had mentioned all of this before, briefly, the night he came to her room. But they hadn't really discussed it. In fact, Susan realized now, she had purposely let it drop, allowed herself to shove her concerns to the back of her mind. But hearing about Tag's life this way made the gulf that lay between them all too obvious.

Adventure and excitement had accompanied Tag wherever he went, whereas her life had been nothing but dull routine. She had even given up her dancing, except for her late-night sessions after the dance school closed. That was all she had allowed herself, lest the hunger for what might have been grew too strong.

Now even that would be denied her. Now she would be trapped in a body that did her bidding only haltingly and imperfectly.

She tried to imagine Tag tied to her and her limited future. Pictured him settling for that. How could she even think of trapping him with her limitations? She supposed she must be recovering some of her mental faculties, she thought with bitter irony, for the reality struck her full force.

"You okay?" Tag whispered when Debbie and Betsy returned to the kitchen for servings of pecan and pumpkin pie.

When he looked at her like that, she was perfectly okay, so she nodded. When he looked at her like that, she felt capable of flying, so how difficult could it be to walk and talk and read and drive?

"I'm sorry about this, but your brother wouldn't take no for an answer."

"I'm glad you're here."

He grinned. "Me, too. Actually, I didn't fight him real hard. I...I hadn't realized how tough it would be, sitting over there all by myself. I used to be able to handle it. I guess I'm not such a tough guy anymore."

The way he said it made her feel that he credited her with the change and that it was a good change. Susan smiled.

Betsy and Debbie set generous slices of pie in front of each of them—and a slice of both pumpkin and pecan in front of Steve.

"A man named Crash needs plenty of fortification," Debbie teased as she sat and took a small bite of her sliver of pecan pie.

Standing beside her chair, Betsy grimaced. "I certainly hope this doesn't mean we're going to resurrect that contemptible nickname."

Debbie's cheeks flamed at the rebuke.

Steve and Malorie spoke at once.

"Grandmother!"

"Mom!"

Betsy looked at Malorie, then put an end to further comment by circling the table with her imperious gaze. She stopped on Tag. "We're good, decent people. We haven't squandered our lives on race cars and film crews and heaven knows what else." She looked around the table again. "If it suits everyone, I would just as soon we kept it that way."

Tag was already balling up his napkin, tossing it onto the table. Steve pushed his chair back. Susan felt such anger she wanted to overturn the table. Cody looked bewildered, and Debbie stared into her lap.

But it was Malorie who stood, rattling the table and almost overturning her chair with the suddenness of her movement.

"I don't know about the rest of you, but I'm finished being a coward," she announced, looking at them all with an expression as fierce as Betsy's had been cold. "Grandmother, you've ruled our lives with manipulation and guilt for as long as I can remember." Her glance went to Tag, then Susan. "And a lot longer than that, apparently. Well, I'm done. The rest of you can do what you want. But I'm taking my life back."

When Malorie whirled and dashed out of the house, Susan thought she'd never been so proud of her daughter as she was at that very moment.

Before anyone else could say a word, Betsy snapped, "I wash my hands of this."

Then she, too, disappeared, her sensible shoes thudding heavily on the stairs as she retreated to her room.

The four adults who remained stared awkwardly at one another. Then Steve raised his glass of tea in the air and said, "Here's to Malorie for having the guts to say what the rest of us have been too chicken to say for the past thirty years."

Slowly the others raised their glasses in a tentative toast. And as they sipped, Tag raised his in Susan's direction and said, "And here's to taking our lives back."

She drank to Tag's toast. But as she did, she wondered if it was possible in her case. And if it wasn't, how many hearts would be broken in facing the truth?

THE TREE DECORATING was in full swing by the time Malorie arrived at the church.

After storming out of the house, she had walked for more than an hour. She had tracked Willow Creek all the way back to the covered bridge, where she sat on the bank and studied the calming ripple of the water, looking for answers. Looking mostly for serenity in the face of a turbulent reality.

She had meant what she said. She was ready to take the reins of her own life. She wasn't yet certain what that might mean. And it definitely didn't mean she faced the prospect without trepidation. But anything was better than knowing next Thanksgiving and the one after that and the one after that would be as sterile and meaningless as the one Betsy Foster had wanted all of them to experience this year.

She tossed a stick into the icy, clear water and watched it bounce and bobble its way downstream, buffeted by forces it couldn't control.

"Not me," she said.

Then she walked back to town, through the park and over to Jasmine Court. She looked longingly at the down-at-the-heels Victorian houses and made up happy stories about each one.

It was while she meandered the street that Sam had introduced her to weeks earlier that Malorie remembered the tree trimming. The volunteers had decided to make a party of decorating the church's angel tree, where gifts for needy children would be collected. Rose had suggested doing it Thanksgiving afternoon as a reminder of how much they all had to be thankful for.

"Beats falling asleep on the couch after overdosing on pecan pie," she'd said. Everyone had laughed and agreed.

Malorie backtracked to the church. Already a half dozen cars had gathered in the parking lot. She felt lighter of heart as she approached the building. Laughter floated through the open front door. She was smiling as she climbed the steps.

The first person she saw when she stepped inside the vestibule was Sam. He was helping Maxine's little boy, Rex, untangle a string of lights. They were laughing. Sam stood by patiently as Rex insisted on taking the lead. Thinking how patient Sam had always been with Cody, Malorie felt stabbed by a sharp sense of loss.

"Welcome!" Maxine's melodious voice rose above the holiday music wafting from someone's boom box. "We need all the hands we can get. God—and the good people at Hutchins' Lawn & Garden, I understand—sent us an enormous tree. We have one crew filling out more angel cards, because we hadn't prepared enough for such a fine specimen. And that means we'll be able to help more children than we had anticipated."

Malorie was instantly infected with Maxine's enthusiasm. "That's wonderful."

"Yes. Indeed it is. Perhaps you would like to help with the angels." Maxine's eyes swept the vestibule as she put her hand on Malorie's elbow to steer her toward the stairs to the Fellowship Hall. Her eyes lit on Sam, then she turned back to Malorie. "Or perhaps you are needed up here, after all. Would you mind terribly helping Sam? It occurs to me that two adults are needed to keep one impulsive child from creating disaster with strings of lights."

Malorie drew a deep breath, nodded and walked over to Sam. When he looked up, the patience in his eyes turned to pleasure.

"Rex, I think we're in luck," Sam said. "A woman. Did you know that women have a real gift when it comes to straightening out the messes men make?"

Rex looked up at them skeptically. "Nobody told me that before."

Malorie smiled. "He's exaggerating. Women do a pretty good job of making a mess of things, too."

But she sat down on the floor beside Rex. "Now, let's see what we've got here." She began guiding his small fingers in the task of untangling the lights.

"I'm glad you came," Sam said, beginning the same task on the other end of the strand.

"Me, too," she said. She wanted to tell him that she'd decided not to be a coward any longer. But all she could do was look into his eyes. And from the way he looked back at her, she believed he understood even though she couldn't say a word.

CHAPTER SEVENTEEN

BETSY HELD CODY TIGHTLY because he persisted in squirming. Malorie insisted he should be allowed to walk whenever they went out, but Betsy knew keeping the two-and-a-half-year-old under control would be impossible if she let him out of her arms.

A tiny voice inside her head asked if it would be so terrible if the toddler *did* head off in a dozen directions. Betsy ignored that voice.

"Keep still," she said for the umpteenth time since she had bundled the two of them up and headed out the door.

"Wanna pway wif Tag," Cody whined. "Pwease, okay?"

"Not today," Betsy snapped, irritated to realize that the man had even managed to charm an innocent child. "Just be still.

"Down," the little boy commanded.

"Not yet."

Then when? came the voice.

Betsy pursed her lips and continued determinedly down the sidewalk.

She was taking her grandson to the park, although her thoughts kept straying to the Finley house—now the McKenzie house to most folks in Sweetbranch—just around the corner on Dixie Belle Lane. They could stop by there first to see if Jake wanted to play.

Impatient with her thinly veiled self-deception, Betsy pulled Cody's knit cap farther down on his head. If she detoured down Dixie Belle Lane, it wouldn't be to inquire if young Jake could come out to play. It would be to see Jacob Finley. Surely she could be that honest with herself. Jacob's criticism had struck her to the core. He thought her manipulative and nosy and Lord only knows what else.

Of course, Jacob's assessment of her had hurt all the more since Thanksgiving Day, when it seemed that her entire family had turned on her, wagging their accusing fingers and passing the same judgment as Jacob Finley had.

She might *be* manipulative, she told herself. But didn't she have an *obligation* to see to the happiness and well-being of her children and grandchildren? She looked down at the pouting toddler held tightly in her arms. Wasn't Cody a prime example? Wasn't he better off than he might have been? Weren't they all, whether they had enough gratitude to admit it or not?

She had reached the corner without reaching a decision.

"Well," she muttered. "I'm no coward. Never have been."

So she turned onto Dixie Belle Lane, marched right up to the Finley house, opened the gate and knocked on the front door.

She heard the thunder of a toddler running to the door. Cody wiggled around, looking for the source of the sound. The sound of Jacob's approach was more halting. Betsy's heart began to pound a little harder. The front door creaked open and Jacob stood there, frowning out at her.

"For heaven's sake, Jacob, have you even combed your hair this morning?" she said, hoping her strident tone covered her breathlessness.

His frown deepened. "Dad blast it, woman, if I wanted to be nagged, I'da married a long time ago."

"You probably should have. Might've kept you civilized."

"Might not," he countered.

"I brought Cody to play."

"Fine. Fine." He pushed the screen door open. "Bring him in. We'll turn 'em loose in the backyard."

Hesitating, Betsy bent to set Cody down. The two little boys were off in a flash, chattering away in a language Betsy couldn't decipher. She remained standing in the doorway.

"You coming in or you just gonna stand there and let the flies in?"

Betsy saw no point in reminding Jacob there were few flies to worry about in early December. "I can come back for the boy later."

Although where she would go, she couldn't have said. Ever since Thanksgiving, she felt like a pariah in her own house. Everyone shunned her. And Tag was there now, for another lesson on that foolish computer of his.

"Suit yourself," Jacob said, stepping onto the porch. But as Betsy backed away and started to turn, he said, "Got some fresh coffee. In case you need a little warm-up before you head back."

Betsy weighed the disapproval and isolation awaiting her at home against the bickering and companionship awaiting in the Finley kitchen. "You have cream?"

Jacob shook his head. "Skim milk. Rose is the boss."

She didn't like the idea of skim milk, but she understood the importance of a woman making the rules in her own home. "Fine. But none of that powdered stuff."

"IT'S TOO EASY NOW," Susan said as the computer once again sounded a cheerful "Good job!" The commendation was growing monotonous; she longed for one of the silly sounds that signaled an error. She pushed away from the keyboard. "I want harder ones."

Tag smiled and kissed her on the nose. "Good! I...I have to be out of town a couple of days, anyway. I can pick them up then."

His eyes flickered when he spoke of being away, and Susan wondered where he was going. What he would do. She longed to ask but wasn't sure such questions were appropriate. Would it be nosy? Would asking make her like Betsy? She kept quiet.

"Sit with me in the love seat?" Tag asked. She nodded, and he picked her up and took her onto the side porch. She cuddled against him and he pulled an afghan over them for warmth.

"I wish—" She hesitated. Wishing was pointless.

"What?"

"Nothing."

"Tell me. Don't you know you can tell me anything?"

"I wish we had the quilt to cover up with."

"I know."

"I wish things had gone exactly the way we planned them." She buried her head more deeply into the crook of his shoulder, found the place where she could hear his heartbeat.

"Then there would be no Malorie," he reminded her, dropping a kiss as light as butterfly wings on the top of her head. "No Cody. I wouldn't want that."

"You like them."

"I like them a lot," he said. "Malorie's a bright, funny girl. And Cody—well, Cody's great fun."

Misgivings flashed through Susan's mind. She felt the same way, sometimes, when she watched Tag playing with the boy. She remembered Tag's delight Thanksgiving afternoon, when Cody insisted on learning how to climb a tree. Tag guided the boy up the trunk of a young dogwood, one hand lifting his bottom, the other showing him which little fist to move where. Tag made sure Cody got credit for "climbing" the tree, while keeping the adventure perfectly safe. In the days since, Tag and Cody had shared more than one adventure. Cody wouldn't leave Tag alone, and Tag seemed to welcome his company.

The first time she'd seen them together, Susan had felt warmed by their bonding. But the closer they grew, the more her anxiety grew. Something bothered her, and she couldn't put her finger on what.

"I've always wanted a son," Tag whispered, and the words shot through Susan like an alarm. Tag must've felt her reaction, for he said, "What's wrong?"

"Nothing," she said. "Just a shiver."

And the truth was, she didn't know what was wrong. She only knew that the alarms were growing louder. Worries she had put out of her mind were crowding forward. "The racing sounds exciting."

She didn't really want to hear about it, but it was the first thing that came to mind to distract her from the unnamed worries filling her head.

"Nah. Not really. Damn foolishness, mostly. Like a lot of the stuff I did."

"Why did you do it?"

He was silent, and she wondered what thoughts whirled around in his head. Sometimes it seemed to her that other people had just as much trouble as she did sorting through their thoughts, figuring out what was what.

"Is it fun?" she prodded.

"Sometimes," he said. "Yeah, I guess it's kinda fun. You're moving fast, taking chances, just skirting the edge of danger."

Susan closed her eyes and tried to imagine that being fun. She couldn't, quite. "Did you ever get hurt?"

He laughed. "Oh, yeah. Remind me to point out all my scars sometime."

Her anxiety grew. He had lived in a world she not only hadn't shared, but couldn't even imagine. "Tell me more. Tell me a story."

"Why?"

"Because. I want to feel like I was there."

She heard the reluctance in his voice as he launched into a story about the year he spent on the rodeo circuit. He started out downplaying the excitement and the danger. The travel in his battered trailer was monotonous, the work hot and brutal. He spent most of his time sweaty and dusty and bruised. But, eyes closed, concentrating only on his voice, Susan heard his tone change as he talked about riding the bull, about holding on for dear life and feeling the charge high in his throat when he went flailing through the air, never sure whether or not the landing would be a safe one. Excitement crept into his voice. She could almost feel the currents sparking off his skin.

"What a wonderful life," she whispered.

"It might sound glamorous," he said. "But it's not. It's just something you do to keep your mind off the things you really want. You know, family and a house and a puppy like Butch."

They laughed as Cody's puppy twitched an ear from his sunny spot in the corner. But Susan wondered if Tag was being totally truthful. He didn't sound convinced, somehow. Susan wondered again how she could ever hope to keep up with that kind of life-style. How could she ever recover enough for that?

"Why did you do it, really?" she asked.

"Sometimes I think I just didn't give a damn. You know, if I battered and bruised this sorry hide, who would care?" He raised her chin and looked into her eyes. "But that was before."

"Before what?"

His eyes were dark with emotion. "Before you came back. Before I realized there is something to live for, after all."

She kissed him back when he lowered his lips to hers. But she didn't believe him. She was certain he was only saying it so she wouldn't worry. He loved the excitement, and she had no way of sharing it with him. Where did that leave them?

The nagging fear stayed with her for days, although she did all she could to hide it from Tag and even from Malorie, who always seemed to show up after work in time to talk with Sam. One day the two young people even walked by the creek together in the lowering dusk, stirring hope and relief in Susan's heart. Perhaps her forebodings about Malorie were nothing, after all, just more of the irrational fear that her jumbled-up brain insisted on inflicting upon her. Fear that had been fed by her mother's sour outlook.

Even the absence of Betsy's carping did little to ease Susan's mind, however. Betsy moved briskly from room to room, never pausing long if anyone else was around, speaking only when necessary. Susan's heart hurt for her mother, even as she hurt for her own losses.

On the day that Tag left town, Susan's fear grew from an insidious whisper into a screaming monster consuming every empty corner of her mind.

"Where are you going?" she had asked, despite her resolution not to pry.

"I have some business," he'd said, and that was all.

She'd listened to him roar off on his motorcycle in the early hours of the morning. She lay in bed and closed her eyes and tried to feel the wind in her hair, on her cheeks, tugging at her sleeves, the way he must be feeling it. She tried to feel the graceful dip and curve of the machine as it took every bend in the road, a fluid sensation that Tag had tried to describe. She tried to see the open road leading anywhere, everywhere.

When she opened her eyes, she was still trapped in the house, her room, her chair.

"My body," she whispered to herself.

She told herself that if Tag needed time to himself to pursue the active interests he couldn't share with her, she shouldn't begrudge him that time. But jealousy and fear won out over her generous nature, and she spent most of the day steeped in self-pity.

Tag was back two days later, in time for Malorie's birthday. He and Sam and Susan and Cody spent the afternoon decorating, planning to surprise Malorie when she came in from work. Betsy baked a cake without being asked, but excused herself from the festivities when Tag exclaimed, "Coconut cake! My favorite! I don't know when I've had a coconut cake. Thanks, Betsy."

Her only acknowledgment was a curt nod.

But Susan and Tag were determined that Betsy wouldn't put a damper on Malorie's twenty-second birthday. A crepe-paper garland and metallic confetti and pink-and-white-striped candles transformed the bare dining room. They invited Rose McKenzie, Addy Mayfield and Maxine Hammond. When those three brought their broods, the house was suddenly full of children and laughter and Susan thought there was no way to avoid having fun.

When Malorie walked in the front door, they all jumped out of the dining room and shouted "Surprise!"

"I always wanted to do that," Susan told Tag as they watched the cake being cut at the kitchen table.

"Then, I'm glad we did it."

"Me, too."

After the cake, the children ran out into the yard to play, the older children charged with keeping a watchful eye on the younger ones. A few presents were opened and everyone sat around talking and making jokes. Susan thought she'd never felt anything so happy, so friendly. So normal.

"I remember when you were born," Susan said, happy in the memory.

"Oh, tell us," Addy said wistfully. "I love new baby stories."

Malorie smiled. "I wasn't eager to get here, was I?"

"No. Thirty-four hours in labor." Her daughter's smile spoke of shared memories, filling Susan with a quiet joy. She supposed she had told the story before and was glad for yet another sign that she and Malorie had been close. It had been different since the accident, but she hoped they would be close again. "I threatened to send you back, but they told me it was too late."

Rose groaned. "And I thought Jake took forever. Thirteen hours sounds like a breeze compared to thirty-four."

"Of course, I expected it to be difficult," Susan said. "Mother told me it would be, the whole nine months."

Everyone laughed.

Sam directed a private smile of his own at Malorie, then said to Susan, "No wonder you waited twenty years to try again. How tough was Cody's birth?"

Malorie said, "She doesn't remember that one yet. Do you, Mother?"

"Yes, I—" Susan stopped, because suddenly it was true. She stared at her daughter and watched the color drain from Malorie's cheeks. "Yes, I remember. It was even harder."

Because watching her daughter give birth had been far more difficult than going through it herself.

Malorie looked away. Susan leaned over and took her daughter's hand. It was cold.

SUSAN LAY IN THE DARK that night and waited for Malorie to come, as she always did, after putting Cody to bed. Her daughter came at last and stood by the door.

"Come here," Susan said, and reached out for her daughter.

Malorie didn't move. Her voice was laced with anguish. "You remember."

"Some of it. What happened? Why are we doing this?"

"Do we have to talk about it?"

"Please. I need to understand. He's your baby, not mine. Why are we pretending?"

"We thought— It seemed like the right thing. For him. For me, too. That's what...that's what everybody said."

"Buddy said that?" Susan wished she could see her daughter's face, but the soft light from her bedside lamp didn't carry as far as the door. All she could see was shadows. "Is it what I wanted? What you wanted?"

"Dad went along with it," Malorie said. "We just... I was only nineteen. And...I don't know. We just did it. Okay?"

"Were you in love with someone?"

"Mother, don't. Please don't."

"But—"

"I'm going up to bed now, Mother. Please, let's just let it be now. I'm trying to...to start over. Please?"

Susan thought of the secret smiles Sam and Malorie had shared that afternoon and knew what her daughter was asking. Don't let her past come back to haunt her now, just when the future looked so bright. How could she explain that she had learned the hard way how the past would forever haunt the future as long as it was based on lies?

She sighed. "I understand. I love you, Malorie."

Malorie ran over to the bed, grabbed her mother for an intense hug. In the golden light, Susan saw tears glistening on her daughter's eyelashes. Malorie ran out of the room before Susan could think of words of comfort.

MALORIE HAD AGREED to the date with Sam before her mother remembered the truth. Otherwise she might not have said yes.

But she wanted it so badly. She hadn't dated in more than three years and she ached to live normally. So she prayed Susan would say nothing and went on with her plans, eager to pretend her life wasn't littered with landmines waiting to explode.

Still, she was glad there was no hint of romance about the date Sam had suggested. They would be alone in a canoe on Lake Mabila, but there would be no candlelight or starlight or champagne. Bundled in jeans and sweaters and heavy socks, with a canoe strapped to Sam's van, they set out on Saturday morning. Sam had even coerced his uncle into opening the store in Malorie's place.

The December dawn broke as clear and cold as an icicle. Peeking through the towering pines, the sky was as blue as Sam's eyes. White clouds billowed upward and sunshine gradually warmed their cheeks and glinted off the water. Alone on the lake at midmorning, they stopped rowing. Malorie thought the morning fit the mood she wanted to have, if not her actual mood. Looking up, the sky went on forever; looking down, the water was bottomless.

Looking at Sam, the possibilities were infinite.

"You're strong," Sam said, taking her oar and stacking it with his against the side of the small boat. He poured two cups of hot chocolate from a thermos jug, handed one to her and sat back to sip and stare.

Laughing, Malorie bent one elbow and made a fist. "There's muscle under there somewhere."

His eyes grew serious. "And courage. More than I gave you credit for. I hope someday you'll tell me where all that strength came from."

Malorie pretended to rearrange her hair, which hadn't budged since she secured it beneath a knit cap three hours earlier. "Does it have to come from somewhere?"

From the corner of her eye, she saw him nod. "We aren't born with courage. We earn it from walking through the fire. It's waiting for us on the other end."

In her heart, Malorie knew she didn't have the kind of courage he was talking about. "What fire did you walk through?"

"Growing up without a father, I guess." He looked around at their magnificent surroundings, as Malorie had done minutes earlier. "Although, seeing what I see in my work every day, I think I haven't seen much fire in my life. Not yet. Maybe I'm lucky. Maybe I get to learn a lot secondhand from the people I work with."

"Maybe that's what happened to me," Malorie said. "Going through this with Mother, maybe that's changed me."

"I'm sure that's true." He looked at her speculatively. "Maybe that's part of it."

Malorie didn't want to leave the conversation where it was. The day was too beautiful, too perfect, to worry about where that discussion might take them if she left it to follow its own course. She sought a diversionary tactic.

"Why do you stay in Sweetbranch? Do you think about leaving?"

"I used to think about leaving. All the time. Then I went away to school and I realized I couldn't wait to get back."

"Why?"

He put his hands behind his head and stared up as if the answers were in the treetops. "I think I hated being someplace where I had no connection. I grew up worrying that my family was going to be yanked out from under me any minute, and suddenly, after I moved to Birmingham, I was right. It was yanked."

He smiled at her. "Then, when I got back to Sweetbranch, I realized how much family I had. You know, in the Dairee Dreme I'd been going to all my life and the church I'd hated getting dressed for on Sunday mornings and the dinky little stadium where we watched high school football. It was all there. Nobody was going to take that away."

In the short time she'd been in Sweetbranch, Malorie knew the feeling. But she also knew it wasn't hers to keep.

Sam sat forward, passed her oar back. "I knew it was the kind of place I wanted to raise a son."

Their eyes met over the handle of her oar. A knot of fear sprang up in Malorie's chest. She nodded, not trusting her voice.

As they continued navigating the lake, Malorie found herself thinking about raising a son in Sweetbranch. Her fear ricocheted around those visions.

That Saturday was the first of many dates. Dates to movies and dates for cherries jubilee milkshakes at the Dairee Dreme and even dinner at Sam's little farmhouse on the outskirts of town. Malorie loved the little house. White frame, with cheery green shutters, it was cozy and tidy and surrounded by the quiet of the countryside.

She thought about raising a son here, too. She even thought about unearthing a lot of the feelings she'd fought so hard to bury almost three years earlier when she found herself abandoned and feeling disgraced.

When Sam kissed her, she found nothing to taint the purity of their passion. In his arms, she felt whole and cleansed and ready to give again. The fear was slipping away, and Malorie let it go gladly.

Best of all, Sam always knew when it was wise to stop. Malorie was grateful and wanted to tell him so, but didn't know how. Then he did that for her, as well.

"I just don't want to go too far," he said. "I hope you don't think this is too old-fashioned, but...I'd like us to be committed first."

Emotion clogged Malorie's throat. "I don't think that's old-fashioned."

"Maybe more than committed. I think I'd like to wait until... Well, I think it's best for a couple to wait until they're married."

Her fear came roaring back. And with it, a heavy load of guilt. How could she ever tell him the truth?

CHAPTER EIGHTEEN

SUSAN HELD HER BREATH as the ski lift began to rise. She clutched Tag's hand—how many times had she done that today?—and tried to look in every direction at once. She'd done that more than once today, too.

"Scared?" Tag asked as the ground grew farther away and the sky came closer.

Susan shook her head. "Excited."

Tag laughed and put an arm around her shoulder. "Good."

Reluctant when Tag had suggested an overnight outing, Susan had given in only when Sam and Malorie ganged up on her and urged her to go along. Whatever objection she came up with, they had a ready answer.

So they loaded up Susan and Malorie's new van, despite Betsy's white-lipped disapproval, and took off for the Smoky Mountains of Tennessee.

Tag had promised it would be beautiful this time of year, and he'd been right. The little towns along the way were alive with bundled-up, red-cheeked people going about their holiday shopping. The mountaintops were lightly dusted with snow, and towering pines brushed a sky so bright it almost hurt Susan's eyes. She gloried in the drive through the national forest, as thrilled as someone who'd never before seen such natural wonders.

The road out of the mountains dropped them right onto the main thoroughfare of picturesque Gatlinburg. Although Susan remained apprehensive as they parked and Tag unloaded her chair, she tried to focus on the row of quaint shops sitting at the foot of the mountains. She felt the nip of cool mountain air on her cheeks.

Soon she began to realize there was nothing she couldn't do with Tag's strong arms to back up her own determination. They had shopped, loading up Susan's lap with holiday gifts for everyone. They had eaten lunch at a chalet-style restaurant nestled at the foot of a mountain. While warming up over hot chocolate, Susan had spotted the tourists taking the ski lift to the top. And when Tag saw the wistful look in her eyes, he was determined that they, too, would take the lift to the top.

Far below her now, Susan could see her wheelchair sitting on the deck. She'd thought the effort to get from chair to lift would be too tough, might embarrass everyone, but no one seemed to begrudge the extra effort. Least of all Tag. His face shone with the same excitement she felt as they inched their way to the top of the mountain. She couldn't help but notice he was barely looking at the spectacular scenery.

"You really don't mind," she said, without realizing she'd said it aloud.

"Mind what?"

"That things are...harder. With me around, I mean."

The pleasure in his eyes softened to tenderness. "Why in the world should I mind? Do you know how different the whole world looks to me with you at my side?"

She nodded, because she knew it felt that way to her. Her life with Buddy had been good, but the contrast between that life and the way she felt with Tag was the difference between Willow Creek and the Atlantic Ocean. Willow Creek was quiet and pleasant, a perfectly good place to spend the day. But the Atlantic filled your senses and sent your emotions soaring and never let you forget for a moment what a blessing it was to be alive.

Someday, Susan hoped, she would be able to find the words for all those feelings so she could tell Tag. She was determined that day would come, just as the day would come when she could walk at Tag's side.

"It won't always be this way." The simple promise was all she knew to offer him.

He looked at her, his dark eyes solemn, then kissed first the corner of one eye, then the other.

"It doesn't matter if it is," he whispered. "You don't have to be perfect for my life to *feel* perfect."

How many times had he said something similar these past weeks? But Susan didn't even try to believe it. She *would* be perfect again. And then they could get on with their lives.

"You'll see," she said, pressing her lips to his cheek. If she tried really, really hard, she thought, maybe that could be her Christmas present to Tag.

And to herself.

DOWNTOWN ATLANTA fascinated Cody, and his enthusiasm fascinated Malorie. The little boy wanted to greet the bedraggled Santas ringing their bells on street corners. He wanted to ride one of the noisy, smelly city buses, although he covered his ears and squinted every time one passed. He wanted to explore the street construction and the sidewalk hot dog vendors and every single window of every single store, as well as the dark alleys leading off the street between the department stores.

"We aren't here to explore," Malorie said, grateful when Sam finally picked the boy up to carry him the rest of the way. "We're here to buy Christmas presents for everybody. Won't that be fun, too?"

She and Sam exchanged a wry grin when Cody's only reply was to look wistfully over Sam's shoulder at the battered orange cones barricading a storm drain worksite.

"Trust me," Malorie said as they approached the revolving doors at one of the department stores. "You're going to love the T-O-Y department."

Cody looked back at her and said, "T-O-Y. Toy."

She groaned. Sam tugged on the bill of the toddler's cap. "Something tells me you've been sitting on your mama's lap while she works on the computer."

Cody grinned widely and nodded.

Bursting with pride, Malorie paused at the perfume counter just inside the door of the department store, pretending interest in the displays so she could compose herself. She'd spent so little time with Cody the first two years of his life that at times like this her love for him seemed to grow by leaps and bounds. He was smart and funny, and just looking at him made her heart glad.

And sad, for all that was lost.

But seeing him with Sam was hardest of all, she thought as she pretended to sniff at the samples on the glass countertop. Seeing the son she couldn't acknowledge in the arms of the man who wanted to make a future with her, that was a bitter pill to swallow. She hadn't realized how tough it would be to see the two of them together when she'd agreed to a shopping trip.

"Wanna see toys," Cody said, tugging on her sleeve.

Drawing a long, silent breath, Malorie looked up into their faces, expectant and happy and flushed from the cold.

"Okay," she said, kissing Cody's chubby knuckles. "Toys it is."

They spent longer than they should have in the toy department, but both Sam and Malorie took as much delight in watching Cody as the boy took in petting stuffed dinosaurs and setting toy trains in motion. All three of them were reluctant to leave, but Cody finally agreed without a fuss when Malorie promised another toy department in another store later in the day.

By lunchtime, their arms were loaded with shopping bags filled with cuddly bathrobes, color-splashed neckties and a dozen other items that would soon be brightly wrapped and stashed under a tree. Malorie's favorite purchase was the pink-cheeked baby doll for the little girl whose tag she had taken from the angel tree at church.

"Okay," she said, passing an overstuffed shopping bag to Sam. "You hold on to this and watch Cody while I run into the ladies' room. Then we'll grab some lunch and—"

She glanced around, and the blood froze in her veins. "Where's Cody?"

Sam looked down. "Right... He was right here. I—"

"Cody!"

Sam dropped shopping bags and packages to the floor. He took her hand in his. "Now, don't panic.

He's just wandered away. He's right around here somewhere, you'll see.''

"Okay. I'm sure you're right.''

But her voice was shaky, and so were her knees. She didn't want to let go of Sam, but it made sense for them to separate. She could hear Sam calling to the boy as he headed toward the luggage and she headed toward the linens. Her mouth was dry and her heart all but pounding right out of her chest.

When Sam returned twenty minutes later, he was empty-handed and so was she.

Cody was gone.

THE WINDOW FROM THE ROOM at the lodge looked out over a winter wonderland. Nestled into the foot of the mountain, it overlooked a stream Tag said was the Little Pigeon River. The night sky glittered with stars and the snow-covered slopes rose until the darkness swallowed them. The sparkle of holiday lights defined the rustic rails of the lodge and the faint sound of carolers wafted up to the room.

Susan couldn't take her eyes off the scene.

"You aren't eating," Tag said.

She smiled at him. "But it's so pretty out there.''

"It's pretty in here, too," he said, and his eyes told her what he thought was pretty.

The room was pretty, too. The massive sleigh bed covered in crochet lace was one of many antiques furnishing the room. Tiny pink flowers dotted the wallpaper. And room service had rolled in an elegantly outfitted table, complete with white linen tablecloth and napkins, a silver candlestick and a crystal bud vase with one perfect white rose. They had warmed themselves with hot soup and mulled cider.

A touch of melancholy crept into Susan's heart as she realized they would have to go home the next morning. Back to the big house that echoed with bitterness and betrayal. Back to the struggle for recovery.

"You look sad," Tag said.

"I'm not. Wishing it didn't have to end, I suppose."

They sat in silence, holding hands across the table, listening to the faint strains of "Silent Night."

When the caroling came to an end, Tag pushed away from the table and walked over to the canvas duffel bag he had set in a wingback chair. From the bag, he took a huge wrapped package, which he set in the middle of the bed. Then he swept Susan out of her chair and deposited her on the bed beside the package. He sat on the corner of the bed, looking at her expectantly.

"Open it."

She smiled. "It's not Christmas yet."

"And this isn't a Christmas present."

Feeling the excitement in her fingertips, Susan began tugging at the wrapping paper. Soft shades of rose and green peeked at her as she peeled the paper away. Recognition bolted through her. She tore at the paper now, shredding it, laying bare the frayed but familiar Double Wedding Ring quilt.

Tears blurred the quilt. She ran her fingers over the well-worn fabric.

"Oh, Tag. How did you do this?"

He was close beside her now, helping her as she struggled to unfold the quilt, as if she needed to reassure herself that every inch of it was actually here.

"When I found out how you'd lost it, I decided I'd try to track it down. I found the junkyard where they'd towed your car after the wreck, and there it was.

Somebody had stashed it in the back seat." He shrugged. "No big deal."

"No big deal?" She looked up at him, dumb-founded, tears still making her vision blurry. "Tag, that must've been somewhere in South Carolina."

Again he shrugged, and Susan remembered the days he had been gone on his secret mission. The days she had fretted that he was off on some adventure he would never be able to share with her. Now she knew. He had done this just for her. For them.

She kissed him, drawing his lean, lined face close to hers. She explored the sharp contours of his cheek and jaw, the thick softness of the hair spilling over his collar, the quickening pulse at his throat. She felt the wet warmth of his mouth, the strong insistence of his shoulders and thighs and chest as his body leaned into hers.

Illuminated by the candle, they lay back on the Double Wedding Ring quilt and made love, as they had so many years ago.

This time, Susan's heart told her, it was different. This time, their bodies were older, less perfect. But the fullness in their hearts was sweeter and their joining more poignant than youth could ever know.

MALORIE SAT IN THE HARD, molded plastic chair in the police station, fists balled tightly in her lap, eyes un-focused, back straight. She had shut down. It was the only way she could cope. Even Sam's steady presence wasn't enough to keep the fear at bay. Her only de-fense was to shut everything out.

The outside door would swing open from time to time, revealing the darkness that had fallen hours ear-lier. Malorie wouldn't look at the clock, though; she didn't want to add up how long Cody had been gone, because she knew every tick of the clock lessened the chances that Cody would come back to her safe and sound.

That, she knew, was to be her punishment.

The young policewoman who had talked to them earlier came out, and Malorie jumped up. The officer shook her head as she approached. Malorie noticed her name tag for the first time. Detective Litanna Watkins. "Maybe you folks should go home. We'll be in touch as soon as we have something to report."

Sam put his hand on Malorie's arm, and she knew he was about to agree.

"No! No, I can't leave! I won't leave without him!" Why couldn't they understand? And she could see in their eyes that they didn't. Not the young woman, who maybe had no children of her own. Not even Sam, who was supposed to care so much.

Detective Watkins exchanged a look with Sam. "I know how you feel, Miss Hovis, but you really need your rest. You won't be one bit of help to your little brother if you wear yourself out like this."

The words taunted Malorie. *Little brother.* For an instant, it struck her that they would never find Cody if they didn't even know who they were looking for. Then she realized how irrational that was and wondered if the policewoman was right. She needed to rest. She was no help like this.

That didn't seem any more rational than her previous thought.

"Maybe I should go back out there and call him some more," she said, looking at Sam, pleading with him to understand. "If he hears me, he'll come."

Sam looked questioningly at Detective Watkins. She shook her head. Anger washed through Malorie. "You can't stop me! If that's what I want to do, you can't stop me!"

Sam put his arm around her shoulder and held her against him. Just for a moment, she let herself sag against his solid chest. But in letting her defenses down, Malorie felt her control slip. She squared her shoulders and glared at them both.

Detective Watkins said, "Maybe it's time to call the boy's mother."

"No!" Malorie had already explained that Susan was away. She didn't intend to involve Betsy, either. She'd let Betsy keep her away from Cody for more than two years, and she wouldn't let it happen again. This time, she was here for him. When he came back, she would be here. "I'm telling you, I can handle this myself."

If he came back.

She made up her mind. She turned, yanked her coat off the back of her chair and headed for the door. "I don't care what you say. I'm going after him myself."

"Malorie—"

"You can't stop me! I'm his mother and you can't stop me!"

The words spilled out before she realized it. But once they were said, Malorie wouldn't have called them back. Not even after she saw the look of shock in Sam's eyes and knew that her reckless words had no doubt cost her all her hopes for the future.

Suddenly calm, she said, "Cody is my son and I'm going to look for him myself."

As she walked out the door of the police station into the cold, damp night, Malorie felt free for the first time in almost three years.

COZY, COMFORTABLE SLEEP, with Tag's chest for a pillow, beckoned Susan. She was about to give in to it when a memory tweaked her and she started upright. She looked down at Tag, who had already fallen asleep, his long, brown legs twisted in the quilt, his bare chest dark against the sheets. His hair spread over the pillowcase, and she smiled at the realization it was longer than her own.

Not wanting to wake him, she looked around the room, spotted her overnight bag and struggled with herself.

In the end, eagerness overcame anxiety.

Swinging her legs off the side of the bed, Susan put her weight on her right leg and began to maneuver herself across the room, hanging on to the side of the high mattress. By the time she reached her overnight bag, she was perspiring and trembling. With shaking hands she found the tiny pair of manicure scissors she sought, took a deep, weary breath and struggled back to the bed.

When she reached the bed, she realized Tag was gazing at her questioningly.

"You've been watching me," she said, embarrassed at being caught, more so as she contemplated the awkward picture she must have made.

He nodded, yawned. "I kept hoping you'd need my help, but looks like you made it fine without me."

"Yes, I did."

She climbed back onto the bed, then began running her fingers around the edge of the quilt until she found what she was looking for. With the manicure scissors, she snipped a few stitches at the back of the quilt, parted the cotton batting and spilled a simple gold ring with a tiny chip of a diamond onto her palm.

Tag was sitting up now, too, and she looked at him as the ring shone in the darkness. She wasn't sure what she had expected, but she realized that he now looked as uncertain as she felt.

"Well . . ." Tag said.

For more than twenty years, the knowledge that this ring remained close by had given Susan a serene confidence that the young love she and Tag had shared had been real and strong and permanent. But with the ring between them once again, she felt a new tension that hadn't been there before. Where did they go now? Could they really put behind them twenty-plus years of pain and loneliness and betrayals, real and imagined?

She was no longer certain. And from the look of him, neither was Tag.

CHAPTER NINETEEN

MALORIE WANDERED the dark streets in the vicinity of the department store, calling her son's name. Oblivious to the cold drizzle beginning to fall, even to the danger of being a woman alone in the dark, she knew one thing and one thing only.

Finding her son was all that mattered.

She didn't notice the van that pulled up to the curb behind her on the nearly empty street. Paid no attention when the door slammed and footsteps came up behind her. When Sam spoke her name, she was beyond being frightened. Some things, she'd learned, were worse than risking your neck.

Pushing back the damp hair plastered to her forehead, she turned at the sound of Sam's voice. He stood outside the halo of the closest streetlight and the blinking lights marking the nearby construction. She couldn't read his expression, but at this moment, even that mattered little.

"You shouldn't be out here alone," he said.

"I'm not leaving."

He walked to her side. "I'll stay, too."

"You don't have to, you know."

He nodded, and his face appeared in momentary flashes, there and gone before she could register the set of his jaw, the emotion in his eyes. She started walking, and he followed.

"Cody!"

An answering sound came back to her, weaker than the mewling of a lost kitten. She froze and called Cody's name again. A high, thin sound seemed to fill the deserted street. She dashed in the direction from which it had come and cried out again.

"Mal, pwease," said a tiny voice from somewhere beneath the street.

Malorie dropped to the ground beside the construction work. The grate covering the storm drain had been torn out. And there, far beneath street level, looking up at her from a muddy tunnel leading beneath the street, sat Cody, nursing a scraped and bleeding knee. His face, too, was scraped, and he looked soaked through with rain and mud.

"Oh, Cody, baby!" Malorie fought the sob in her throat as Sam scrambled down into the ditch after the baby. Hot tears mingled with the cold drizzle on her cheeks.

When Sam reached up and placed Cody in her arms, the toddler snuggled close and whimpered, "Me cold."

Malorie felt as if she was holding him for the first time in her life. Never again would she let go.

BETSY IMPARTED THE NEWS to Tag and Susan as if it pleased her that disaster had occurred while they were away together.

Susan talked to Malorie at the hospital in Atlanta. The doctors wanted to keep Cody twenty-four hours, to make sure dehydration was the only fallout from his experience. Malorie said there was no need for them to come, but Susan heard the ragged exhaustion in her daughter's voice. No mother could have stayed away.

The drive seemed interminable. Tag insisted on driving and Betsy refused to acknowledge his presence the entire way.

While the windshield wipers smeared her vision of the dreary day, Susan focused sharply on the tension of her unresolved relationship with Tag. Tag had studied the engagement ring, then handed it to her. But it was clear neither of them quite knew where to go from there. Susan had slipped the ring into her makeup bag and wondered if it hadn't been better off lost in the back seat of a junked station wagon somewhere in South Carolina.

Somehow, she had believed everything—twenty years' worth of wrongs—would be okay now. Maybe things wouldn't be that easy, after all.

THEY FOUND SAM in the waiting room across from the elevator on the ninth floor of the hospital. He looked haggard, and as strained as the three of them had been during the trip from Sweetbranch. He pointed in the direction of Cody's room and said in a scratchy, bone-tired voice, "Malorie wanted to be alone."

Susan wondered at the look he gave her, and said, "I'm going in."

Betsy stepped up behind her chair. "I'll go with you. You'll need some help."

"No, Mother. I can manage by myself."

"Well, I hardly see—"

Tag stepped up and put a hand on Betsy's elbow. "We'll wait here," he said, giving Susan an encouraging smile. "You see about Mal and Cody."

With part of her questioning the wisdom of leaving those two together, Susan rolled herself down the hall and into Cody's room.

Malorie had pulled the only chair in the room close to the bed. Her eyes were closed, and her head drooped to one side. One hand rested on Cody's arm, which was hooked up to an IV. Susan winced, noting that they'd taped the restless toddler's arm to a side rail to keep him from dislodging the needle.

As Susan rolled closer, Malorie started awake.

"Mother." She rubbed her eyes, which looked swollen and red. "Oh, Mother, I was so afraid."

Malorie's voice quavered. In one swift movement, she was at Susan's side, kneeling with her head in her mother's lap. Susan touched her daughter's soft blond hair, felt her shoulders shake with tears.

"I thought it would be my punishment," Malorie murmured. "I thought he would die because I gave him up, because I lied about him."

She looked up at her mother, eyes glistening with tears. Susan thought her heart would break from the anguish in her daughter's face. The pain of childbirth, she thought, was nothing but preparation for a worse pain—seeing your child brokenhearted.

"I kept remembering, over and over, how Grandmother told me I'd have to live with the disgrace forever. How the shame would ruin everybody's life. Even Cody's." She wiped away the last of the tears on her cheeks. "But she was wrong. Wasn't she wrong?"

"Yes, she was wrong. And so was I, for not being able to see that. For not being able to stand up to her." Susan shook her head, touched Malorie's cheek. "I keep thinking I had to be forced into a wheelchair before I could learn how to stand up to my own mother."

Malorie nodded, then bit her lower lip. "Sam knows."

Susan remembered the defeated look on the young man's face and felt dread.

"He had to know," Malorie continued. "I can see that now. But ... I don't know how he feels."

"Ask him."

"But he wanted to marry me. And now—"

"Don't think you can make his decision for him."

Malorie gave a shaky laugh. "I'm not sure I can make my own decisions."

"I think you can."

Cody stirred, whimpered, and Malorie looked over her shoulder at him. "I guess I have to, don't I."

TAG'S FIRST IMPULSE when Betsy returned to the waiting room with her cup of coffee was to leave. But he told himself he could be civil even if she couldn't. Besides, he wanted to be here when Susan returned.

"Sam didn't go in, did he?" Betsy asked sharply, clearly prepared to be miffed if she had been barred from the hospital room while an outsider was admitted.

"He's taking a walk."

He'd acted strange, Tag thought, troubled in a way he'd never seen before. Tag supposed Sam was simply tired and stressed. But it also confirmed to him that Sam's interest in Malorie was far more than casual.

Betsy sat in an empty chair across from Tag. "The two of you might just as well go back to Sweetbranch. The girls and I can manage fine from here."

Tag decided that any answer he gave would end up sounding antagonistic. He wasn't in the mood for Betsy. He wasn't in a mood to tolerate much of anything, truth be told. What in blue blazes had happened last night? he kept asking himself. How had things gone so quickly from feeling right to feeling uncertain?

"What exactly do you hope to accomplish with my daughter, Eugene?"

For spite, Tag wanted to snarl that he was going to marry her daughter. But the words stuck in his throat, jammed up by his memory of the awkwardness that had surfaced once that engagement ring lay in the palm of Susan's hand.

"That's between Susan and me, Betsy." He told himself to keep calm, but he doubted he'd been able to keep the resentment out of his voice.

"You do realize, of course, that Susan is not quite... right. And she may never be."

"She has a lot to relearn," he said. "And she's doing fine. No thanks to you."

Betsy set her coffee cup down on a plastic table littered with six-month-old magazines. "You're living in a dream world, Eugene. And I'll thank you not to hurt my daughter through your own selfishness."

"What the hell is that supposed to mean?"

"As bad-tempered as your father, I see," she said, smug satisfaction written all over her face.

Tag wanted to deny that he was anything like his old man, but those words stayed balled up in his chest, too.

"Eugene, let me ask you one thing. What kind of life do you plan for yourself?"

"Your interest is touching, Betsy."

"Does that mean you have no plans? Or do you plan for more of the same?"

"I have the store now."

"Mmm-hmm. And I suppose you plan to settle down in Sweetbranch?"

Tag wasn't sure which made him feel more like squirming, Betsy's interrogation or the idea of settling down in Sweetbranch. As often as he'd longed for a family, for normalcy, he'd never quite imagined finding it in Sweetbranch.

"I wonder how long that would make you happy, Eugene. How long it would be before you wanted to get back into that tacky little trailer of yours and go off on some more little adventures."

"Listen, Betsy—"

"No, you listen, young man. I know the way you've lived. I know what it did to your mother, too. Her only living son tramping around the country like some no-account, never doing a useful day's work in his life. Why, if it weren't for my granddaughter, you would have run that store into the ground by now."

True, true, all of it true. Tag had no defense.

"Can you honestly tell me you want to spend the rest of your life living in a backwater town like Sweetbranch, renting out backhoes, selling fertilizer and taking care of a crippled woman?"

The images bore down on Tag relentlessly. He told himself the picture she painted wasn't accurate, but Betsy's vision of the future—and her assessment of him—filled his mind, nonetheless.

"How soon before you start hankering after a little excitement, Eugene? Before you get tired of the burdens on your shoulders? How long before you run out on my daughter?"

"It won't be like that," he said, but he knew his protest was weak.

When he looked up and saw Susan sitting in the doorway of the waiting room, he knew she could see the uncertainty on his face, had no doubt heard his hesitation in the face of Betsy's questions.

He wanted to hate Betsy for the hurt he saw in Susan's face. But he knew that this time Betsy didn't bear the blame. This time, *he* had caused the pain.

AS CODY SLEPT STRAPPED into his carrier on the van's back seat and Malorie sat huddled against the passenger door, Sam wondered how he could convince Malorie the three of them belonged together. He only knew he had to try. That's why he had insisted on driving them home from the hospital, although Malorie had seemed reluctant to be alone with him.

He decided to plunge right in. "I love you, Malorie."

His heart began to pound faster as he realized she had no intention of replying.

"No matter what," he added.

"I was nineteen," she said. "I thought I was pretty grown-up, but I guess I wasn't."

"Mal, you don't have to—"

"Yes, I do," she said with a determination he knew better than to question. "It was just dumb, that's all. I'd gone away for college. My first time away from home. And I wanted to be so sophisticated and so mature. So when one of the graduate assistant instructors started paying attention to me, I knew exactly why— because I was so sophisticated and so mature."

Sam wanted to pull over to the side of the road, wanted to take her in his arms and comfort her. He wanted not to hear this story, but he knew she needed to tell it. And that need far outweighed his need to pretend it hadn't happened.

"He was furious when he found out I wasn't doing anything about birth control." She laughed softly. "But not nearly as furious as I was when I found out he was engaged to some law student in Boston.

"Anyway, I found out I wasn't sophisticated and I certainly wasn't mature. I was just plain scared. And when Grandmother suggested that Mother and Daddy take my baby... Well, it made sense at the time. Better for the baby, everybody said. Better for me."

"But it wasn't better for you?"

Again, she was silent. Then, "I've made a mess of everything."

"Every life is difficult," he said softly. "We all screw stuff up. I like to think we aren't measured by how many things we manage to get right, but by how we handle our problems."

"If that's the measure," she said, "I come up pretty short."

"You were young."

"That's a cop-out."

"So maybe it's time to be measured again." From the corner of his eye, he could see that she had turned to look at him. "I love you, Malorie. No matter what," he repeated.

"But you're so... admirable," she whispered so softly he could barely hear her. "You wanted to wait. And here I'm..."

"Not perfect?"

"Far from it."

"Good. Look what being perfect has done to your grandmother."

She groaned in response, but paused to think it over. "But how could you ever forgive me?"

"It isn't my place to forgive you. You did the best you could. The only person you need forgiveness from is yourself."

He glanced at her in time to see her skeptical look. She looked into the back seat and said, "And from Cody."

SAM CARRIED CODY up the stairs when they reached the house. By the time they got him ready for bed, the little boy was awake. Mustering her courage, Malorie asked Sam to leave them alone for a few minutes. He nodded and closed the door behind him. But she didn't hear his footsteps on the stairs and knew he was waiting for her.

She almost wished he would leave.

"Arm hurts," Cody said, snuggling his stuffed bear against his cheek as Malorie tucked the covers around him.

"Want me to kiss it and make it well?"

He nodded and offered her the arm that was bruised from the IV needle and scraped from his fall. She kissed it thoroughly.

"Cody, you're a pretty big boy now, and I have a very important question for you." Her mouth was dry and she wasn't sure she could continue. "I want to be your mommy from now on. Would that be all right with you?"

He frowned. "Aweady have a mommy."

"She'll be your grandmommy. And that means you'll have something you never had before. A great-grandmommy."

"Who'll be my sissy?"

"Someday, we'll get you a new sister. Or even a brother." Surely, she told herself, it would happen sometime. Surely, now, thanks to Sam and a strange quirk of fate, she could get on with her life. "How would you like that?"

Cody seemed to consider the possibilities, then his eyes began to drift shut. "And a new kitty, too? For Butch to play with? Jake has a kitty."

Malorie chuckled. "We'll see."

"Okay, Mommy," he murmured, and then he was asleep.

Telling herself the worst was over, Malorie watched her son sleep for a few more minutes. She knew the adjustment might take some time; she knew there might be repercussions from Betsy. But at least she had started down the right path. And if Sam was right, she might measure up a little better once she reached the end of this particular branch in the road.

Sam. She still had to face him, tell him what she'd done.

She waited for a moment, hoping her heartbeat would slow. But it didn't. Maybe the worst wasn't over, after all.

CHAPTER TWENTY

SAM LEANED AGAINST the wall, wondering what was happening now. He wanted answers, but he didn't know what questions to ask.

From behind Cody's bedroom door, he heard the soft murmur of voices. He wanted to be in that room with Malorie, that was the only thing he knew for certain. He loved her—maybe even more so now that he understood what she had been through.

But did *she* love *him* enough to accept his support?

When the bedroom door opened, he stood upright and faced her. She looked into his eyes, and he saw that all her fear was gone. In its place was a new determination, and a certain serenity that lifted his own heart.

"Marry me," he said.

"Don't. Not yet."

"Why not?"

She raised her chin in that defiant way she had learned from her mother and looked him squarely in the eyes. He knew that, whatever she said, it couldn't possibly make a difference.

"I've decided to raise him myself. I already asked him if I could be his new mommy."

Joy wasn't something Sam had much experience with; but if he'd had to put a name to what he felt fluttering to life within him, that's the word he would have chosen. What a joy to see the woman he loved growing in courage and strength. "Will this confuse him?"

"He's young. We'll go slow." She sounded so calm, so sure, that Sam didn't have a moment of doubt she was doing the right thing. "All I know is, what we've been doing will never work. Someday he would've learned the truth. And by then it might've been too late to make things right."

He could have kissed her for her wisdom. "How will Susan feel about it?"

"She understands. I think she agrees it's the right thing to do."

"So do I."

She smiled softly. "Do you?"

"Absolutely." Now, he thought. If I sound as rational as she sounds, maybe this won't strike her as crazy. "Do you think it would be too much all at once if Cody suddenly had a new father, too?"

Malorie shook her head. "No, Sam. That's not necessary. And it's not the right reason. I'll be okay, you know."

He took her hands in his. "There's only one reason I want to marry you. I love you. I want you to be my wife."

"But now—"

"Now I'll be doubly blessed. I'll have a wife *and* a son."

She hesitated, searched his face. He saw the moment when her decision came, saw the impish gleam that suddenly came into her blue-gray eyes. "He wants a kitten, too. For his puppy to play with."

Sam laughed. "Whatever he wants." He pulled her into his arms. She felt soft and giving in a way she never had before, when there were secrets between them. "Whatever *you* want."

"You wouldn't feel . . . cheated?"

"No, Malorie, I won't feel cheated. But I don't feel especially patient, either. How would you feel about a Christmas wedding?"

THE ANNOUNCEMENT of the wedding was the only bright spot in Susan's day. And she was grateful when Malorie and Sam left, hand-in-hand and chattering enthusiastically, to talk to the minister about a Christmas wedding. Their departure made it easier for Susan to sneak off into her room. She wanted to be alone.

She should have known better.

Tag came in without knocking. Susan's chair faced the side porch, and she pretended to watch the rain trickling down the screen.

"I'm tired." She didn't turn around. "You should go home."

He put something on her bed. Her bag, she supposed. Her bag with the engagement ring tucked inside.

"We should offer Sam the ring," she said. "That would be a nice touch, don't you think? Sort of a family heirloom."

He came and knelt beside her. She tried not to register his presence.

"Don't do this, Susan."

"It's best."

"How can it be best?"

His voice commanded her attention, and she looked at him. Twenty-five years of emptiness and betrayal and broken dreams shone in his eyes, and she looked away quickly.

"Susan, when I was talking to Betsy, I—"

"I heard it. She's right."

"No, she's not. I—"

"She *is*. Who are we fooling?"

"Didn't we just have a wonderful day in the mountains together? Didn't we?"

"I'm tired." She rubbed her forehead, felt the scar beneath her fingertips. Whenever it started to hurt there, she knew she would soon be reacting irrationally, behaving childishly. She didn't want Tag to see her that way. Not now. Not ever.

"Go away, Tag. Go away and leave me alone."

SUSAN LOST HERSELF in frenetic wedding plans over the week and a half that remained before Christmas. She hadn't the heart for much physical therapy, and completely avoided work on her reading and writing. It reminded her too much of Tag.

"Mother, you can't put everything on hold," Malorie said one day after a discussion of using the traditional wedding vows versus writing her own. She had come home at lunchtime to discover that Susan and Addy Mayfield had spent the time they normally spent quilting planning a reception menu. "Your progress is a lot more important than this wedding."

"Don't be silly," Susan said briskly. "There'll be plenty of time to worry about reading and writing after your wedding. But my only daughter just gets married once."

Malorie dropped to her knees beside her mother's chair. "Oh, Mother, sometimes I get scared. It's all worked out too perfectly."

Susan brushed her daughter's cheek with the back of her hand. Soft, almost as soft as Cody's cheek.

"Sometimes life treats us that way. Makes up for all the times it shoves us around, wouldn't you say?"

"Yeah. I guess so."

"First love is a treasure," Susan said. "Always remember that."

Despite the misery dwelling in the center of her being, she did find happiness in watching Malorie blossom. She also found a certain peace in having recovered the treasured memory of her own first love. Over and over, she allowed herself to revisit those memories and tried to accept the fact that was all she would ever have.

But it's enough, she told herself. She almost believed it.

Susan also watched with satisfaction as Malorie stepped into the role of Cody's mother. Although she hated admitting it, even to herself, at least part of her satisfaction came from Betsy's grim-lipped disapproval of this change in their lives.

"Guess what, Mommy!" Cody had flung himself into Susan's lap the morning after he came home from the hospital, once again apple-cheeked, despite the ugly scrapes on his face, arm and leg. "You're my gramma now! I love you, Gramma!"

She hugged him back and, for the first time since her accident, felt the fullness of her love for this little boy. "That's wonderful, Cody!"

"And I have a new mommy and soon I can have a new sister and a new brother and a new kitty like Jake and—" he paused for dramatic effect "—best of all, a new daddy!"

Susan gave him another hug before he toddled off to be lifted into his high chair. Betsy plopped him into place without a word. But later she leaned over Susan and hissed, "What kind of insanity has taken hold of you and that daughter of yours?"

"Malorie has decided to—"

"Malorie. How very unlikely. More likely Eugene has talked you into abandoning the boy because he'd be a hindrance."

"Mother, I won't discuss Tag with you. And I suggest you get used to the idea that Malorie and I are no longer going to live our lives under your thumb. We're both grown now. It just took me a little longer than it took my daughter."

Susan calmed her seething temper by reminding herself that she, at least, would count the blessings in being a mother and grandmother. Anyone lucky enough to be in her place, she told herself, shouldn't spend her time pining for the loss of her childhood sweetheart. And that's all Tag Hutchins was. A part of her lost youth.

RUMMAGING THROUGH the toolbox on the ground, Tag sensed a presence and peered over the seat of his motorcycle. He gasped. Sixteen-year-old Susan, dressed in a flowing skirt and a tie-dyed peasant blouse, walked toward him.

"Hi, Mr. Hutchins."

Tag braced his bad knee and stood. "Afternoon, Mal."

She looked shy, but not as uncertain of herself as she had six weeks ago when she first walked into his store. She'd taken on a certain mature dignity since claiming her son. That made her look even more like Susan, he realized, because his young Susan had never been plagued with uncertainty.

Damn it all, he thought. *Forget her.*

Oh, yeah, his ill-temper snapped back. *And while you're at it, why don't you stop breathing for the next few hours. That'd be a helluva lot easier.*

Malorie stared at the ground, where he'd scattered his bike-maintenance tools. "I wondered why you hadn't come into the store today. Getting ready for a race?"

Tag wasn't sure what he was getting ready for. He only knew that it had seemed like the right time to get his bike tuned up again. Maybe even time to check on his trailer, which he'd left in the two-bit town where Sam found him after his mother's stroke. The road kept calling; the familiar pull was the only thing that counteracted the powerful lure of the woman in the house across the street.

"Something like that," he said.

She nodded, leaned over and picked up one of the tools. "What's this for?"

"Whatever's on your mind, spit it out," he said as softly as he could manage. Visions of Susan began to crowd into the parts of his mind he was trying to fill with that map he kept in his head, the map of all the side roads and off-the-beaten-path routes to nowhere he'd traveled over the years.

Malorie took a long, deep breath, but she was smiling. "I'm glad Sam didn't get the Hutchins temper."

"You should be."

"I wish you'd come see Mother."

Tag leaned over and snatched a greasy rag off the nearly bare ground behind his mama's house. He wiped his hands, paying careful attention to the grease accumulating beneath his nails. They'd been damn near grease-free these past few months. Old habits died hard, he supposed.

"She doesn't want to see me," he said when he was satisfied that the greasy rag wasn't doing a thing to clean him up.

"Yes, she does. She just...maybe she's just scared."

"Maybe." He took in her earnest expression and felt a softening. "Maybe we all get scared."

"Think about it. Okay?"

"Sure." He wasn't soft enough yet to tell her that was *all* he thought about.

She made no move to leave. "The new part-timer, she's doing pretty well. I was thinking, maybe she could take over a few days after Christmas. So Sam and I can get away. Just a few days, and you'll be there to keep an eye on her. Not a whole week or anything."

Tag didn't see any point in mentioning that he might not be around to keep an eye on the new clerk or the store or anything else in Sweetbranch. "Take all the time you want."

"Thanks, Mr. Hutchins. Is there something you'd rather I call you—instead of Mr. Hutchins, I mean?"

At this late date, he saw no point in telling her that every time she said it, he felt like a broken-down version of his old man. "Doesn't matter to me, Mal."

"Oh. Well, there was one other thing."

Now she looked uncertain. Tag fingered the key ring in his pocket and wished she would go away.

"At the wedding...well, I wondered if you'd, you know, walk down the aisle with me?"

Tag flung his rag to the ground. The request slammed him in the gut, took the wind right out of him. He wanted to knock the tires out from under his bike with one vicious kick. Violence seemed a better alternative than crying.

"Sorry," he said. "I'm...not sure I can make it."

He didn't look at her, but he heard the little-girl disappointment in her voice. He called himself a lot of names he wouldn't have repeated aloud in front of her.

"Oh," she said. "Well, if you change your mind—"

"Sure. I'll let you know," he said.

She sighed. "Well, I guess I ought to let you get back to your work."

He watched her walk away. Her skirt swished around her calves. The little bit of late-afternoon sunlight glinting through the bare trees caught on her hair. Tag opened his mouth to call her name, tell her he would be there for her. But he told himself the only thing he could accomplish would be to hurt a lot of people.

Better if he stayed out of it.

He looked back at his bike. Afraid he still might give his tires a good, hard swipe with his boot, he turned and walked into the house. Just so he finished by Christmas Eve.

SUSAN HAD FORGOTTEN many things, but she still remembered that Santa Claus existed only for the very young.

As Christmas Eve wound to a close, she nevertheless harbored a secret hope that the old elf would put something in her stocking to ease the hurt.

More than a mouse still stirred in the house when she wheeled herself into her room with the excuse that she was tired. She sat in her chair in the darkness, listening to the sounds of her brother, his wife and their grown children, laughing with Malorie and Sam as they experienced the joys of Some Assembly Required.

What had she done? How had she been so cowardly? And could she ever find the courage to do anything about it?

Sam had gone out the front door, the lights downstairs had just gone out, and she heard five giggling adults creeping up the stairs when another sound split the night.

Tag's motorcycle roared down Mimosa Lane. Heading out, away.

Susan didn't need Santa Claus to tell her he wouldn't be back.

CHAPTER TWENTY-ONE

SUSAN GAVE HERSELF to the spirit of Christmas the next morning, vowing she wouldn't dwell on the way her heart had broken when she heard Tag leaving in the middle of the night. Until that moment, she hadn't realized that a part of her had clung to the hope that when he showed up for the wedding this afternoon, she could set things right.

That was not to be her Christmas gift, it seemed. But she made up her mind not to brood over it. Today would be joyous, regardless.

She smiled through the delighted squeals of Cody and her brother Steve's young grandchildren. She focused on the rich sound of foil paper crumpling in the center of the room and the smell of cinnamon-spiced cider. She gave and received hugs and tried to remember that love was the best gift of all, even if it didn't come from the person at the top of the list you'd sent to the North Pole.

At last the gift-giving was over and the holiday brunch devoured, and everyone dashed off to dress for the wedding. Susan relaxed, let go of her smile.

Betsy's sharp voice cut into the quiet. "There isn't time to sit around and daydream."

"I know."

As she watched her mother scoot around the room filling a garbage bag with torn paper and curling ribbon and smashed bows, she tried to understand what Betsy had done to the lives of everyone around her. She doubted she would, because she doubted Betsy knew herself.

"You know you're going to be slow, Susan," her mother prodded one more time.

The one thing Susan did understand, though, was that she had two choices when it came to her mother. She could either forgive her, or she could let resentment poison the rest of her life. And she'd wasted too much time already to be wasting any more.

"I'm going back to Atlanta, Mother. As soon as the holidays are over."

Betsy straightened, a trail of red-and-green ribbon in her fist. "Don't be ridiculous. You're in no condition to take care of yourself and you know it."

"Yes, I am," Susan said. "Plenty do, and so can I."

"I won't allow it."

Susan rolled toward her mother. "It isn't your choice, Mother."

Then she reached for the hand that had slowly dropped the ribbon as Susan's announcement sank in. Susan took it between her own and squeezed. The first step toward healing, she hoped.

"I'll be fine," she said. "It isn't that I don't love you. It's just time, that's all. Time I got on with my life."

THE STRANGER IN TOWN sat a block from the church in a car with North Carolina plates, watching intently as the wedding guests trooped in.

She grew impatient. She saw the slight strawberry blonde and the handsome dark-haired man, with a brood of a half-dozen children, none of whom looked alike. She saw the strikingly lovely woman with gleaming mahogany skin, accompanied by a lanky fair-haired man and two beautiful children, but where was the family she was waiting for?

She began to fidget, first with the mother-of-pearl buttons on her crimson silk blouse. She patted her platinum hair and checked her makeup in the rearview mirror. She looked perfect, except for the red tracks through the whites of her eyes.

She needed more sleep. She'd had too much to think about to rest easy lately. But that would change. Soon.

They came on foot and she felt certain her heart had stopped.

A wiry old man with flyaway white hair led the way, holding a little boy by the hand. Then Ben, who looked more distinguished and more attractive with every year that passed, damn him. Then the auburn-haired woman he had married. She barely noticed Rose because walking beside Ben's new wife was the reason Cybil Richert McKenzie had come to town in the first place.

Krissy.

"Baby," Cybil whispered as the little dark-haired girl skipped along beside the woman. She hadn't seen Krissy since summer and already the girl had grown. Long-legged and lean-limbed, her shining hair touching her shoulders, Krissy was her father's daughter in every way.

Pain twisted at Cybil's stomach as she watched the little girl who had told her last summer she didn't want to stay in North Carolina.

"I want to go home," Krissy had said, and Cybil had been unable to persuade the six-year-old that North Carolina *was* home.

Once again pain clutched Cybil's heart as Krissy tugged on her stepmother's sleeve, then stood on her tiptoes to give the woman a kiss. Cybil told herself there was no need to hate Rose Finley McKenzie, but that line of persuasion was wearing thin.

If not for Rose, her ex-husband would never have stayed here, would never have dragged her daughter hundreds of miles from home.

But Cybil knew she could set things right. She had thought about it long and hard while nursing bottle after bottle of gin. Soon, Krissy would be hers again.

"DEARLY BELOVED..."

Susan couldn't be sure what other mothers thought about when they watched their daughters walk down the aisle and take the hand of the man who vowed to love them forever. She only knew she was having trouble keeping her mind on the words of the ceremony.

She kept remembering all the ways in which Malorie had brightened her own life with her unique outlook, her impish humor, her warm heart.

"I promise to do my best to be a good partner," Malorie was saying now, the first line in the vows she and Sam had written together, "supporting you in all you try to accomplish in life."

Susan remembered seeing her daughter through periods of overalls hand-painted with life-size sunflowers; hiking boots with flirty little miniskirts; a fringed cowgirl skirt in elementary school when everyone else was wearing the uniform of jeans and T-shirts. Today, Malorie had walked down the aisle on Bump Finley's arm wearing a crocheted lace dress with drop waist and uneven hem, something a very elegant flapper might have worn in 1926. Susan smiled.

"I will do my best to make the hard times we will encounter easier, using the understanding and patience I've learned from you," Malorie continued.

"I promise to keep learning all the goodness you have to share with me," Malorie said, "and to share with you what goodness I have to give."

Susan remembered the gap-toothed smile Malorie had hated so much when class-picture time rolled around in the second grade. She remembered the adolescent agonies of prom night and the very real grown-up agonies of unexpected pregnancy.

And she remembered the courage with which Malorie had faced the small congregation of friends and family as she told them the truth about Cody right before the ceremony began. The secret had drawn a few muffled gasps, but Malorie had held her head high.

"And I promise you a love that grows stronger through the years," Malorie said, slipping a ring onto Sam's finger.

Susan didn't cry, but tears were close to the surface. Tears of joy as well as her own tears of loss. When she had already lost so much, how could she have been foolish enough to throw away so much promise?

"Ladies and gentlemen," intoned the minister, "I give you Mr. and Mrs. Sam Roberts."

Malorie and Sam faced the small group of assembled guests, Malorie's face aglow, Sam's serene as usual.

From Susan's lap, Cody clapped his hands and said, loud enough for everyone to hear, "New mommy *and* new daddy!"

Everyone laughed, except Betsy, and Susan felt her heart go out to the woman who had visited so much misery on others. That misery had finally come home to nest, it seemed to Susan.

Because of the holiday, Malorie and Sam had planned a brief ceremony and even briefer reception so the small circle of invited guests could get back to their family celebrations. They had decided to dispense with many of the traditions, but Malorie had refused to forgo the tossing of the bouquet. She had arranged to throw it immediately after the vows.

So while Sam and Malorie stood at the altar, Rose McKenzie, by prior arrangement, stood and said, "Okay, all you unmarried women out there, step up and take your chances."

Most of the females who rushed to the front were teens; there were even a couple of preadolescent girls. It was all in fun, of course, but as Susan watched them head for the front, she was suddenly filled with longing.

She wanted that bouquet. She felt it would be symbolic of the fact that she had decided she wouldn't be cheated out of life a second time. She rolled forward, vowing to herself that whatever it took, she would find Tag. She would track him down in whatever one-horse town had a Saturday-afternoon motorcycle race. She would make it up to him.

She caught her daughter's eye and knew from the twinkle there that this was exactly what Malorie had in mind. Susan watched the bouquet leave her daughter's hand, saw it arcing in her direction. As it came toward her, one of the giggling preteens stepped in front of Susan's chair to grab the prize.

Swallowing a gasp of disappointment, Susan watched the moment being snatched away. Then, at the last moment, another hand reached out from behind

Susan, over the head of the young girl. Susan looked over her shoulder.

Betsy stood there with the bouquet of white rosebuds in her hand, holding it out to her daughter.

With tears in her eyes, Susan accepted the beautiful peace offering. She barely noted the teasing crowd that gathered around Betsy, or the way Bump Finley conspicuously backed away from his one-time sweetheart. Susan's attention was on the bouquet in her lap and the promise it seemed to express.

She had been given a second chance.

As the crowd began to drift toward the Fellowship Hall, Susan looked up and saw Tag sitting in the back row. He looked out of place and uncomfortable in a gray pinstripe suit, his hair trimmed and combed.

One thing hadn't changed. The look he leveled at Susan—a look of love and longing that fed the emptiness in her heart.

Her legs trembling with the effort, Susan put her bouquet on the nearby pew and pulled herself out of her chair. She took one step toward Tag, then another before Tag was down the aisle, sweeping her into his arms.

"I'm sorry," she whispered, although the sanctuary was empty now, except for the two of them.

"Me, too. I was stubborn. As usual."

"If you don't mind that I'm not perfect, I don't know why I should mind."

"You are perfect. For me."

"I don't want to slow you down," she said.

"I want to slow down," he said. "I sold the bike this morning. I don't ever want to break a bone or throw out a shoulder in another race or stunt as long as I live."

"You don't?"

"No. I want to live a nice, quiet life right here in Sweetbranch, in a little brick house on Mimosa Lane."

"It might get dull."

"Haven't you heard? I'll be a ready-made grandfather. And I'll live across the street from a meddling mother-in-law. How dull could it get?"

"Dull enough to send you looking for something better."

He laughed softly. "I've been looking for something half my life. How could I be fool enough to go looking for something better now that I've got what I wanted all along? Oh, no, Susie. This is as good as it gets."

He set her down in the chair and put the bouquet back in her lap. "Now, let's go. I think I need a little practice eating wedding cake."

And Susan knew that the treasure of first love was hers—again—to keep.

BRIDE'S BAY RESORT

UNLOCK THE DOOR TO GREAT ROMANCE AT BRIDE'S BAY RESORT

Join Harlequin's new across-the-lines series, set in an exclusive hotel on an island off the coast of South Carolina.

Seven of your favorite authors will bring you exciting stories about fascinating heroes and heroines discovering love at Bride's Bay Resort.

Look for these fabulous stories coming to a store near you beginning in January 1996.

Harlequin American Romance #613 in January
Matchmaking Baby by Cathy Gillen Thacker

Harlequin Presents #1794 in February
Indiscretions by Robyn Donald

Harlequin Intrigue #362 in March
Love and Lies by Dawn Stewardson

Harlequin Romance #3404 in April
Make Believe Engagement by Day Leclaire

Harlequin Temptation #588 in May
Stranger in the Night by Roseanne Williams

Harlequin Superromance #695 in June
Married to a Stranger by Connie Bennett

Harlequin Historicals #324 in July
Dulcie's Gift by Ruth Langan

Visit Bride's Bay Resort each month wherever Harlequin books are sold.

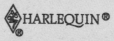

HARLEQUIN®

BBAYG

HARLEQUIN SUPERROMANCE®

A Superromance *Showcase* book.

His Friend's Wife
by
Janice Kay Johnson

Obsessed with another man's wife!

Jake Radovich had tried to be a good friend during Don Talbot's illness. He'd provided a shoulder for Clare, Don's beautiful new wife, to cry on; he'd been a surrogate uncle to Don's young son. Still, Jake wasn't fooling himself about his motives—Don was his friend, but Jake was in love with Don's wife. And Don knew it. Did Clare?

Now Don is dead—but the passions and resentments friendship once held in check are alive. And about to flare out of control....

Watch for *His Friend's Wife* by Janice Kay Johnson
Available in January 1996
wherever Harlequin books are sold.

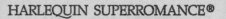

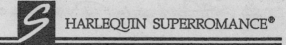

HARLEQUIN SUPERROMANCE®

CAN'T FORGET HIM
by Cara West

Nate Kittridge could kick himself.

While he was sowing his wild oats, his best friend's youngest sister, Megan Grant, had grown up.

She was no longer the little tomboy, content to hang around and hero-worship her big brother and his friend. Megan had become a beautiful and interesting woman. A woman who'd seen too much of Nate's love-'em-and-leave-'em attitude in the past to trust him now. And the entire Grant family—who'd always treated him as a son—wanted no part of him as a son-in-law.

Determined to prove himself worthy of Megan, Nate uncovers a secret that will change his life.

First Love, Last Love

**Available in January, wherever
Harlequin books are sold.**

REUNIT8

Harlequin Romance ®
brings you

How the West Was Wooed!

Harlequin Romance would like to welcome you
Back to the Ranch again in 1996 with our new
miniseries, Hitched! We've rounded up twelve of our
most popular authors, and the result is a whole year
of romance, Western-style. Every month we'll be
bringing you a spirited, independent woman whose
heart is about to be lassoed by a rugged, handsome,
one-hundred-percent cowboy!

Watch for books branded Hitched! in the coming
months. We'll be featuring all your favorite
writers including, **Patricia Knoll, Ruth Jean Dale,
Rebecca Winters** and **Patricia Wilson**, to mention
a few!